DOLLHOUSE

ANYA ALLYN

DOLLHOUSE
ANYA ALLYN

First print edition: January 2017

Cover design: Clarissa Yeo
Formatting: Polgarus Studio

ISBN-13: 978-1541139466
ISBN-10: 1541139461

"Something happens when you read this.
You will be changed . . . It's. Just. That. Amazing."
Nancy Holder NYTimes best –selling author of the
Buffy, The Vampire Slayer books.

1. UNDERGROUND

A penny for a spool of thread
A penny for a needle
A penny for the blood so red
That trickles down like treacle

—P

Heart pounding.
Blood pumping. Shivering.
So cold in here.

Frigid air, black like oil.

My chest hurts. I'm breathing too fast.

I need to hurry.

I clutch the hem of my dress so the stiff fabric doesn't brush against the wet cave walls. The clothes I'm forced to wear each day are these brittle, starched vintage dresses.

With my free hand, I feel my way along the rough stone of the wall. Icy water drips on my fingers. The wet, dank odor envelopes me as I venture in further.

I *will* find the way out. I have no choice.

Stop.

Wait.

They're coming.

Beings that shouldn't exist. Beings from nightmares. Beings that will -

Don't panic.

Be still.

Listen.

Did they hear me?

I hold my breath. Slow my heart rate.

There. Calm.

Better. Much better.

It's too dark to see, but I know they're coming closer.

Scrape. Plod. Scrape.

The sound on the stone floor sends a rush of shivers along the small of my back.

Have they passed me?

I can't waste time but I need to be sure.

Time . . . .

I'm losing track of time, losing track of the days. I don't know how long I've been here . . . down, down in the underground dollhouse.

A life-size dollhouse filled with horrors.

I have to be brave.

But in here, brave is bad.

Bad.

If we're bad, we're made to sit on the Toy Shelf. And if we're very, very bad, we're locked away in the Toy Box. The Toy Box is the darkest place I've ever known. And the Toys . . . the Toys terrify me.

Beyond the Toy Box are realms that almost made me lose my mind. Realms worse than death.

Even if we're good, we're made to dance until our feet blister, until we can barely stay upright.

I'm beginning to forget who I was.

Remember. Remembering is the only thing that will keep you whole.

You are Cassandra Claiborne. You have a life outside of here. You're fifteen. You came here with Ethan and Lacey desperately seeking your friend, Aisha, who vanished in the forest near your school. Not knowing you'd be trapped, too.

Remember Ethan.

Ethan has been made to sit on the Toy Shelf, because he tried to fight back. He was bad. I can't find Lacey. I don't know what they did to her. The last I saw of her, she was sitting, trembling, on a chair—her face deathly white—and when I came back to get her, there was nothing but a shadow slithering across the ceiling.

None of us will get out of here alive.

No, stop thinking that.

All is still silent.

Are they gone? Yes. Gone.

Go now.

I take a step.

There's a sudden, sharp tug on my dress . . . .

2. DEVILS HOLE

Out of this wood do not desire to go:
Thou shalt remain here, whether thou wilt or no.
—Shakespeare, *A Midsummer Night's Dream*

TWO WEEKS EARLIER

When we first caught sight of the dolls—hanging by strings in the trees—we should have guessed that something was very, very wrong in this forest. The strings were stretched far across the branches, in patterns like that old cat's cradle game grandma used to play with me. The vintage dolls were slightly swaying on long, noose-like strings, with cracked ceramic faces and missing eyes.

But we didn't know and we didn't guess.

It seemed like a stupid gag to scare people. Something made by teenagers, though they would have had to climb terrifyingly high in the trees and they would have had to have spent painstaking hours to make patterns like that with the strings.

I know now how wrong we were.

But back then, my thoughts were on a boy and on getting a school assignment done and dusted. Ethan, Aisha, Lacey and I had been hiking through the forest to collect information about the flora and fauna for the assignment. At the back of my mind had been a nagging sense of despair—just a few months earlier, my mother had dragged me all the way across the world, from our home in Miami, Florida to this tiny, mountainous town in Australia. This place was never going to feel like home.

Maybe if I'd been listening at the moment that I first entered the forest that day I would have heard a sound above the whispering and the calls of the breeze and birds in the canopy.

Yes, if I'd been listening, I might have heard a clock whirr to life and start ticking.

The calves of my legs ached and burned. Ethan, Aisha, Lacey, and I had been trekking uphill at Barrington Tops for hours—Ethan said these mountains were extinct volcanoes. Just beneath my feet were the tunnels that red-hot lava had once burst through. Now these caverns lay dark and empty. Were there places here you could just fall through the earth and no one would ever know? An unease settled on me.

But my fears eroded as I eyed the steep path in front of me. Ethan walked ahead of everyone—the sun touching his shoulders. He'd known these mountains most of his life, and he'd know if any parts weren't safe.

The misting rain from earlier had moistened the hair on the back of his neck into tiny curls. Everything about him was off-kilter, from the wiry slant of his back—where his backpack swung from one shoulder—to the carelessness of his voice.

5

He was the most real person I'd ever known.

But he wasn't mine. He was Aisha's.

Aisha and Lacey strode ahead of Ethan and me in their cropped shorts—Lacey with her matchsticks for legs and Aisha with curves that hugged every inch of the fabric. Back in Miami, I was used to seeing girls in bikinis that revealed nearly everything, and it had never bothered me, until now. I looked down at my long shorts and paused to cuff them up a bit.

Aisha took a step back to let Ethan catch up to her. His mouth flicked upward in that familiar grin—holding the expression in a way that made her cheeks flush. My mom always said we shouldn't compare ourselves to others, but I couldn't help it. Aisha was tall while I was on the short side. Her hair was thick while mine was fine like a little kid's. I was sure I'd seen the exact pinkish-olive shade of her skin on the inside of a conch shell. Even her eyes matched the aqua of a tropical ocean. My eyes were deep brown like my Mexican mother's—my dad's eyes were blue, but the only things I seemed to have inherited from him were a high, round brow and skin that burned and peeled in the summer.

I wasn't pretty in the way that Aisha was.

That wasn't the only thing that was making me desperately try to forget what I felt for Ethan. Aisha was my friend. When your friend has a boyfriend, the boy is off-limits. I knew the rule because of my friends from back home in Miami. Christina and Evie seemed to have a new boy every couple of months. To them, it was an unwritten code that you kept your hands off another girl's guy. At least, until he was up-for-grabs again. I hadn't had a boyfriend yet—not even close. I wasn't sure why. Evie said it was because I always looked so intense.

I'd started hanging out with Christina and Evie a year ago. They were rebels—always where they weren't supposed to be, and I liked that. I guess the biggest part of me didn't want to grow up. I looked at Mom's life, and it scared me stupid. *Study your eyeballs out, get a high-stress job, get married, spit out a kid, get divorced, stress about everything, live out your life on antidepressants and too much coffee.*

I hadn't told Christina and Evie about Ethan. I knew they'd laugh. But I was terrified by what I felt for him. Thoughts of him kept me awake at night, made my skin feel on fire, made my heart bunch up like paper.

Aisha and Ethan had hooked up for the first time two months ago, at Lacey's fifteenth birthday party. Maybe they'd be together forever and have babies and two SUVs and live in a big old house in the country. Whatever. I just had to accept it.

Breathing deeply, I stretched my arms, studying the change in the forest as we made our way higher on the mountain. Bird and animal noises followed us, echoing and bouncing through the branches overhead. Earthy, spice-laden scents rose like secrets from the ground. My mood shifted and calmed.

Lacey tied her long, pale blonde hair up into a knot, glancing from side to side into the forest. She looked as anxious as I'd felt a few minutes ago.

"You okay, Lace?" I asked her.

She gave me a smile that vanished quickly. "Yeah. I'm just not much of a hiker. Freaks me out being on the mountains."

"I guess it's pretty isolated."

Drawing her lips into a tight circle, she exhaled. "Yep. You feel like you're in another world."

Ethan twisted to look back over his shoulder. "You've just never forgotten that school camping trip, have you Lacey?"

"Hey," I said. "What happened?"

Ethan stopped to let us catch up to him. "It was back when we were all about nine. The school took us on a camping trip to Devils

Hole, where we're headed now. My best friend—Ben Paisley—woke us all in the middle of the night, saying he'd seen big shadowy creatures. I didn't hear or see anything, but I believe Ben saw *something*. I just don't know what. Probably the shadows of large kangaroos. Nothing to get worried about."

"Still, it was scary." Lacey chewed her lip. "Anyway, it was a long time ago. I'm being silly."

A frown wrinkled Aisha's forehead. "Poor Ben. The others never let him forget it. They called him *monster boy* for years after. It *is* freaky that girls started disappearing in the forest after that night."

Ethan half-shrugged a shoulder, and he shook his head slightly. "It was a little three-year-old who wandered away from her family and a teenage runaway. It's terrible, but it's not a lot of people over the years. They must have fallen down some deep hole, into an underground river maybe." He turned to eye the path ahead. "We should go."

As we moved off, I recalled my thoughts from earlier, when I was worried about people falling through the mountain. Maybe I was right to worry.

We reached Devils Hole Lookout half an hour later. We had the bulk of the assignment done already—cataloguing the plants and animals found here in Barrington Tops. The 'Tops had the distinction of being one of the few places in the world where you could walk through such a range of forest types in a single day—everything from sub-alpine to sub-tropical.

I traced my finger along a dirt-encrusted metal plaque:

DEVILS HOLE LOOKOUT

1,450 METERS ABOVE SEA LEVEL

"That's about one thousand miles for you Yankee folk," Ethan's voice boomed directly behind me.

I elbowed him without looking around, then turned to give him a cheesy smile.

"Ouch!" Ethan rubbed his ribcage. His forehead creased upward, his mouth sliding into a grin that made my blood caramelize. I was about to push him away, when the look in his eyes switched—he still held the smile but there was something almost sad and wistful in his gaze now.

Aisha motioned us over to the viewing platform, where she and Lacey were headed. "Whenever you two are ready?" she said pointedly.

He hesitated, staring skyward for a moment before turning to go and join her. I followed, but kept my distance, moving to the other side of Lacey. Did I imagine the way he looked at me? The crazy feelings inside me were starting to make me see things that weren't there.

The forests below the lookout stretched in almost unimaginable distances, undulating and falling away into deep gorges and wild rivers. Wafts of mist still drifted above the tree line, even though it was past noon.

Aisha set up her tripod and camera. She was soon lost in her own sphere—so wrapped up in herself that it was half an hour later before Ethan could talk her into stopping to go and eat.

We moved to the picnic tables to have a late lunch. I devoured my squashed sandwiches and waterlogged grapes, and wished I'd brought more food. Lacey nibbled a meager portion of crackers. Aisha remained uncharacteristically quiet, pulling out her sketchpad and drawing a bird perched on the picnic tables next to us—every feather in painstaking detail.

"That's amazing," I told her.

She didn't answer me.

Shrugging, I reached for my backpack and took out a map of Barrington Tops. With an orange marker, I circled the forests we'd walked through, and made quick notes of the flora and fauna we'd found in each.

Ethan leaned over and jabbed a finger at an area named Captain Thunderbolt's Lookout.

"That's named after a relative of mine."

"Yeah, Ethan," I mocked. "I believe there was actually a person named 'Captain Thunderbolt.' Did he carry bolts of lightning in his holsters?"

"Nah. He basically just stole stuff."

"He did what?"

Ethan shrugged. "He was a bushranger—back in the 1800s. He used to hide out in caves and steal from the rich. His woman was Aboriginal and a bushranger, too—and so beautiful she used to get away with doing raids and stuff."

I laughed, shaking my head. Ethan always had a story. Half the time you didn't know if he was making it all up.

He took my marker and drew a lightning bolt on a couple of spots where he said the Captain had hidden out at. Still laughing, I closed my fingers around his, trying to grab the marker back.

Aisha began packing her camera into her backpack with more force than necessary. I realized I'd had my eyes—and hand—on Ethan a fraction too long. I snatched my fingers away.

A busload of tourists pulled into the parking lot.

Ethan was first to rise from the table. "Well kiddies, I reckon we've just about got it in the bag. We can take it easy down the mountains."

Lacey eyed the forest. "Aish, did you get enough shots? I mean, I barely took any. The animals kept running away from me."

A frown wrinkled Aisha's forehead as she gazed back at Lacey. "I really want us to get good marks for this project."

"I know. That's why I asked." Lacey shrugged her thin shoulder, her eyes widening in that typical blank stare.

Talking about marks was sure to make Aisha's hackles rise. I didn't understand why, but she was really sensitive about getting good marks when it came to art and photography.

Puffing up her cheeks, Aisha nodded. "We need to do a bit more exploring and grab some extra photos of the animals."

Ethan flicked crumbs from the side of his face. "They're not expecting David Attenborough. What we've got is good enough."

"Eeth, I wanted to do a bit better than good enough," Aisha pleaded.

Ethan exhaled slowly. "Yeah, okay, no problem. We can head off the track and see what we can find down near the river."

"How far?" Something about the dark spaces between the trees was urging me to leave. I didn't want to go into the forest again.

"Depends on Aisha and Lacey and what they need to finish the project." Ethan was in an unusually serious mood.

"Okay," I said. "But we can't be too long. Our parents will be expecting us at the pickup point soon." I tried to keep the nervous tone from my voice.

Aisha turned on her heel, strapping her backpack on.

We headed back up the path, following Ethan. Ethan stopped still, and then wandered up and down for a few minutes, trying to determine the best way off the trail and into the thickly wooded forest.

"Okay, here," he said finally. "I think this will be a shortcut to the nearest river. There might be some animals hanging around there. I haven't been this way before, so I don't want to go too far in."

I nodded. *Yes, not too far in.*

The trees seem to crowd in as we stepped in further. Growing denser. Almost making me feel claustrophobic.

What was wrong with me?

I forced myself to think about something else. I tried to picture what Christina and Evie would be doing this June. It was almost time for summer break back home. Christina would probably be dying her hair yet another weird shade of orange and she'd be checking out all the shirtless guys on their skateboards. Evie would be sneaking out of her parents' house with denim shorts so small that the pockets hung twice as low, and spending all her babysitting cash at the mall. Last summer, we ran along the boardwalk on Friday nights—stealing vintage hats off hipsters' heads and inviting ourselves to posh parties in the hotels. The last thing my friends would imagine me doing now was going hiking for a school project, *God forbid*.

I caught up with Aisha. "Hey, I bet none of the other groups went to as much trouble as us. We're going to smash this." I didn't want Aisha and me drifting apart. I needed to make sure we were okay.

She eyed me warily for a moment but then a smile cracked across her face. "Do you think?"

"Yeah. No contest."

She smiled again, glancing upward at the tree canopy. "I guess this must seem a world away from your home."

"We had some forest stuff back in Miami, too—well, really it was, like, swampy, jungle-y kind of stuff. With alligators, raccoons, and wild pigs. The Everglades."

"I'd love to see it. I want to travel everywhere."

"I'd really like to—"My reply caught in my throat when I noticed small shadows swinging to and fro on the forest floor. My gaze darted upward.

Eyeless dolls on long strings.

Strings threaded between branches of trees, in some kind of crazy patterns. They reminded me of a game my grandmother used to play with me—she'd deftly twist a loop of string between her fingers, making all kinds of shapes that I was meant to copy. These patterns looked like that, only on an enormous scale, the trees' branches acting as gnarled, bony fingers.

"Freaky . . . ." Aisha squinted into the trees.

Ethan jumped up and grabbed a doll from a string. It shattered in his fist.

"The dolls are old," I said, "really old. Someone must have thought this was funny. Trying to creep people out."

The truth was, they *were* creeping me out. I just didn't want to admit that in front of the others.

Lacey was shaking her head, closing her eyes and refusing to look. "Let's go back."

"Yeah, good idea." Ethan dusted the crumbled bits of ceramic from his hands.

"Wait," said Aisha. "We didn't find the river you said was here." Taking out her camera, she snapped a picture of the dolls.

He shrugged. "I must have got it wrong."

Aisha shot him an exasperated look from over her shoulder.

"I think I can hear it," Lacey said softly, twisting the bracelet on her arm. Her eyes were still jammed shut.

Ethan frowned, listening. "Yeah, me too. Don't know if it's worth it to keep going though. The river could be—"

Without waiting for Ethan to finish, Aisha whirled around and continued on the track, almost running. Lacey followed close behind, giving a quick, shuddering glance to the dolls as she ran past them.

Ethan and I glanced quickly at each other before we began jogging through the woods after the girls.

Another five minutes and we heard the river gurgling. It was close.

I caught sight of Aisha's pink Marilyn Monroe T-shirt up ahead.

She tripped and fell, water splashing high around her. She'd found the river.

Picking herself up, Aisha stopped dead still, staring upward. I followed her gaze to a bulky, dark form that loomed through the trees.

A house. Mansion-sized.

Ethan and I ran up to Aisha and Lacey.

"A house? Here?" Lacey stood delicately on the rocks that edged the river. "Let's go. It's private property."

Ethan shrugged off his backpack, letting it fall to the ground. "No, I want to see it."

After being in the forest for hours, it was weird to see some remnant of civilization—especially something this big. Curious, Aisha and I dumped our backpacks next to Ethan's and stepped after him.

"You guys can go. I'll watch our bags." Lacey plunked herself heavily down at the water's edge, fixing her ponytail.

The features of an ornate house filtered through the trees. Built of stone and wood, the mansion looked large enough to accommodate fifty people or more. Peeling metal grills barred the narrow sash windows. A massive chimney dominated one wing, mock triangular turrets like teeth along its rooflines.

"Why would anyone even build a house all the way out here?" I asked Ethan.

Ethan thumbed his chin absentmindedly. "Don't know. Granddad did tell me a lot of this land was cleared back when it was first settled. Mostly for logging. There might have been a clear road up here once."

"But there's just one house," I said. "One big mother of a house. Doesn't look like something you'd build for logging either. Unless you're a very rich logger."

"It's beautiful. I love old houses." Aisha raised her camera to one eye and started taking photographs. "This would look amazing in a frame. But I need a clear view. I'm going around to the front."

The house was definitely old—and not in a quaint way. Patches of black moss ate into the house like disease, like something sinister. I hated the house on sight. But I stood staring at it, unable to tear my gaze away. It was as if the black moss was burrowing into my head. There was something very wrong about this house, just like the hanging dolls. My boots crunched on the bark and twigs as I stepped toward Aisha. The dark, narrow windows of the mansion were piercing eyes, watching us. Revulsion crawled over me. I'd seen this place before—I was sure of it. But I didn't know where. All I knew was that I wanted to scream at Aisha and Ethan to get away from it. Suddenly, I wanted to be as far away as we could get.

The sound of frenzied barking ricocheted through the trees. Aisha froze with the camera at her face.

"Let's go!" Ethan whipped around.

We bolted toward the river.

The noise of the dogs died away.

"The dogs must be locked up. They're not chasing us." Aisha was almost out of breath.

Lacey ran toward us.

"Are you guys okay? I heard barking."

"Just a pack of dogs trying to kill us," I said, going to grab my backpack. I was done with this place.

"Yeah, time to head out of here." Ethan collected his own bag.

"Aish still hasn't gotten the photos we need," Lacey told us hesitantly, her voice rising in pitch. "We haven't looked for any animals along the river yet."

I was starting to think Lacey idolized Aisha. I guessed all three of us idolized Aisha, in our own ways.

Aisha nodded insistently. "Yeah. The teacher isn't going to want to see images of dolls and old houses."

Ethan glanced at Aisha as he slung his bag over his shoulder. "I know your pictures are important to you. But I don't even know this part of the mountains and we could get lost out here—we should go."

Six different emotions seemed to cross Aisha's face. "Pictures?"

Ethan stared back, confused.

"They are not just *pictures*." Her voice was pained. "You sound just like my parents. They don't understand either. This is what I want to do with my life. But they talk like my photography is a hobby. Like I should go study law or something. Photography and art are everything to me. You don't get it at all. And you don't get *me* . . . ." She fired the words at him like bullets.

I finally understood why Aisha was such a perfectionist when it came to those things. She had something to prove to her parents. Another part of me wondered if the sharp change in her was something to do with the house. Maybe it wasn't just me—maybe we could all feel its presence, making us anxious and on-edge.

He opened his mouth to speak, but jammed it shut again. Holding up a hand, he seemed to be trying to use some other sense to figure out the new strangeness in her. "I didn't mean to say anything bad. Honest."

"Ethan was just trying to agree with you, Aisha," I told her. "He's bending over backward for you."

Aisha's mouth set into a tight, small line. "*You*—and *Ethan*—are forever sticking up for each other. I'm a bit outnumbered with you two around, aren't I?" She shot me an odd, questioning look. "Don't think I haven't noticed you and my boyfriend staring at each other. What are you trying to do, snatch him away when you think I'm not looking?"

"Now you're getting hysterical." I regretted the word as soon as I'd said it. I wasn't thinking straight. All I wanted was for us to get off the mountain—as soon as possible and now I'd said the worst thing possible.

"Don't you call me *hysterical*. Don't even try it. Ethan—are you okay with her calling me that?"

"Aish, you're over-tired, or something," said Ethan. "Let's just go."

She blinked in reply, her eyes large.

Turning to Lacey, she demanded to know whose side she was on.

"I'm on the side of getting off these mountains before dark. We all need to stop arguing with each other." Lacey kept her head down.

Aisha stared at Lacey as though she'd just betrayed her. She was used to little-mouse Lacey agreeing with her on everything. Snatching up her backpack, she walked away stiffly, crossing the river and breaking into a run at the tree line.

"I'll go after her," Lacey offered.

"Seems to be me who's upsetting her. I should go." Ethan's shoulders hunched as he trailed the direction Aisha had run.

Lacey and I watched the woods anxiously, waiting for their return. Lacey fiddled idly with her bracelet—a darkened silver piece with a tiny filigree tree set into it. I tried to make conversation, telling her it was pretty and unusual. Lacey flinched, hiding her wrists as she folded her arms around herself. She said she hated the bracelet but she was forced to wear it because her grandmother had given it to her.

Lacey, I thought, was impossible to get to know. If Lacey were a place, there'd be no signposts.

Ethan crashed back through the bushes, his face coated with sweat. "She come back this way?"

Lacey stared. "You didn't find her?"

"No—she's out there hiding from me."

"Maybe she's embarrassed." Lacey always tried to find the most flattering solution to a person's crappy behavior.

We called and searched for the next hour, but no Aisha. The sun was setting and the light slanted through the trees, making every shadow seem alive. I tried to shake the thought that the mansion we'd found was the one place we should have checked. But that was crazy. She hadn't run toward the house. She'd gone in the opposite direction.

"What if she's trying to get back to the pick-up point all on her own?" I ventured.

Ethan stared at me thoughtfully. "Yeah, she might have tried that. If she did, she could be a long way from here by now. And well and truly lost." He cupped his hands over his mouth and bellowed Aisha's name twice, his voice rising in desperation.

"Look," he told us. "I'm going to walk you girls back to the path. You just need to follow it down to the pick-up point. As soon as you get phone reception, call your parents and the police. I'll stay here and look."

3. FUGITIVE

Shadows coil
And wait to strike
Do not linger
In the night.

—P.

Two weeks after Aisha vanished

Before, I didn't understand that someone could just disappear. Now, I do.

We didn't find Aisha.

Ethan couldn't find her.

The police and thousands of rescue crew members and searchers couldn't find her.

It was like she'd been devoured by the forest.

It seemed impossible that days could flip past without Aisha being found. But they could and they did.

I rolled on my side in bed, staring at the moon, willing myself to go to sleep. I'd spent every night like this for the past fortnight, unable to fall asleep until the small hours.

Finally, I felt myself drift in an exhausted haze.

I woke before I'd fully fallen asleep, confused and startled, with a hand clamped over my mouth and a voice whispering, "Cassie, it's me."

Gasping, my eyes flew open.

Ethan crouched on the floorboards like a fugitive, gently taking his hand from my mouth. "I need to stay here tonight. I'll be gone before daybreak."

I nodded, not understanding, struck by the strangeness of Ethan McAllister here in my room. I breathed in that warm scent of earth and trees and the faint tang of wood fires that was Ethan. He always smelled of the forest. He lived with his grandfather in a ramshackle cottage right at the base of the mountains.

"They're coming for me," he said.

"Who . . . ?" I sat up rod-straight in the bed.

He cast his eyes downward. "The police are saying Aish was murdered."

"Murder?" I shivered in my thin pajama pants and tank top. "Why are they after *you*?"

He shook his head close to my mine, dark hair brushing my shoulder—woodland scents thickening in the air until I could barely breathe. "Something happened tonight."

I waited for more.

His eyes grew distant. "I was outside—getting wood for the fire— when the police came. I stayed outside, listening. I wanted to know what they were saying to Granddad. They had a search warrant. Didn't take long to search our house—you know how small it is." He paused. "They found Aisha's camera underneath the floorboards."

All air sucked from my lungs, words choking in my throat. How could Aisha's camera be *there*?

He swallowed, his mouth pressing into a grim line. "You think I'm guilty, too, don't you?"

"No . . . ."

"Yeah, you do. The cops are trying to pin it on either me or Granddad—or both of us. Everyone's going to think the same."

Thoughts raced through my mind. I'd only been to Ethan's house once, but I remembered a scrapbook of yellowed newspaper clippings that his grandfather had kept—articles about girls who had gone missing in the forest over the past few years. But Ethan's grandfather was a frail old man in his nineties—he wasn't capable of doing anything to anyone.

If someone put Aisha's camera in Ethan's house, then that someone had to have been following us out there on the mountains that day—someone who had abducted Aish, and then tried to put the blame on Ethan.

A cold shiver sped down the length of my spine. "Of course I don't think anything bad about you or your grandfather. *God,* Ethan, how could you even say that?"

Breathing a low sigh of relief, he turned his face slightly. A dark bruise curved from his temple to his cheek.

"Who did that?" I gasped.

"Doesn't matter."

"Raif . . . right?"

Aisha's brother had been pushing Ethan around ever since Aisha disappeared, demanding to know *what he did to her.*

"Forget it."

The smell of cold sweat hung in the air as Ethan shrugged a backpack from his shoulders. I realized he must have run here all the way from his grandfather's house. The chill of the night crept across me. It was July in Australia, and the temperatures had plunged so low, there was ice on the ground in the mornings. Back home in Miami, the weather would be heading into the hottest time of the year.

I eyed the heavily laden backpack. "Where are you going?"

He stared at me. "I'm going to go find her. I need to clear my name—and Granddad's."

"You can't go back to the mountains. If the police are looking for you, their dogs will track you no matter where you go. And you'll be automatically guilty."

He shrugged uneasily. "I know how to dodge being tracked."

"How long can you stay out there? It's crazy."

"What choice do I have? I've got no other way of proving I didn't do anything wrong."

"But there've been search and rescue parties all over the mountains. And you and me and Lacey. We all looked. But the only thing that was found of her was her backpack—and that was found miles and miles from where we last saw her. How are *you* going to find anything?"

His jaw clenched. "Because I'm not coming back until I do. Until I find her. And I don't care where they found the backpack. We know where she went missing—near that old mansion. Someone must have been there. Someone must have *seen* her."

I shook my head. "The guy who owns it was away when Aish disappeared. The police checked. Besides, they searched it anyway."

"I know. But I can't get that house out of my head. There's something about it . . . ."

It was going to sound weird if I said it out loud, but it was the same for me. That mansion was in my dreams every night. I'd wake up in a sweat, seeing strange reflections in its dark windows. When

I'd told Mom—a child psych—about my dreams, she'd said I might be focusing on the house because it was close to the last place we'd seen Aisha.

But even weirder: I was sure I'd seen it before the day of the hike. Somewhere in the maelstrom of nightmares that had always churned through my nights stood that house. But I couldn't confess that. Mom was already dealing with the man she'd moved out to Australia with—Lance—taking off and leaving us. And besides, my dreams were too weird, too morbid to even put into coherent words.

I toyed numbly with the ties of my pajama pants. "Who's going to look after your grandfather? He's been sick a lot lately, yeah?"

"Yeah, he has. But if I don't fix this, maybe both me and Granddad will end up in jail. He'll die in there. I can't let that happen." He exhaled a short, sharp breath. "Cassie, I need to trust you. You can't tell anyone I was here. And you can't tell anyone where I'm going." He glanced at his backpack. "I went to Ben's first and got a tent and food. I couldn't stay there—the cops know he's my best friend. I just need to stay here for the next few hours, if that's okay with you? I'll be gone before daylight."

His eyes were fathomless as he held my gaze. I'd do whatever he asked, even if I ended up wading in so deep I drowned myself. And I knew with all certainty that something had begun, like an invisible stream pulling me adrift.

As a reply, I took a scatter cushion from my rug and threw it to him. Nodding gratefully, he gathered up the other cushions and stretched out on them on the floor. I pulled a spare blanket from the end of my bed and gave it to him. Sitting cross-legged beside him, I watched as he fell into a troubled sleep. My bedroom suddenly felt too small to have the long, wiry frame of Ethan lying there. He was wild like the forest, and nothing could hold him back or contain him. Dark moonlight washed across features that were beautiful, almost dangerous.

Outside my window, the mountains of Barrington Tops were far away, black teeth edging toward the moon.

His face fell into shadows beneath the faint yellow of my desk lamp. Stupidly, I wondered if he guessed I slept with the nightlight on all night, too afraid to sleep in complete darkness. He'd climbed through my bedroom window at the worst possible time. Night.

I hated *night*. I'd had night terrors since I was a little kid—I was supposed to outgrow them, yet they were only getting worse.

A ball of pain sat low in my stomach and I knew I wasn't going to sleep. The thought of Ethan going away tore at me like nothing else ever had.

Seven months ago, the worst thing in my life had been my mother and her new boyfriend dragging me to the other side of the world. After the nonstop parties and crowded beaches back home in Miami, this tiny inland Australian town had seemed the end of the world. I'd arrived just before the start of the school year in Australia, angry out of my skull that I'd have to redo a whole year of tenth grade—from February to December—even though I'd already passed two terms of tenth grade in Miami.

On the first day at my new school, I'd laid eyes on him, and I'd glimpsed a piece of home—not any home I'd ever known before, but just *home*. Meeting Ethan had changed my world.

I'd felt broken in two when he and Aisha got together. I'd had to force myself to see him just as a friend. And now he was here with me, in my room.

I'd never wanted any boy before him.

And now, I might never see him again.

Every hour of every day, Aisha's disappearance haunted me. The *what ifs* rioted in my head. If she hadn't run off like she did, she'd still be here. And right now, Ethan wouldn't be running off to find her.

If I could go back to the day of the hike, I wouldn't let myself notice the exact hue of Ethan's sepia eyes, and I wouldn't allow myself to stand so close to him that we breathed the same square inches of air.

Because Aisha noticed everything. Every detail. Every moment.

I'm the reason she ran off that day.

And now I have to live with that.

4. QUESTIONS AND LIES

Fix your ribbons
Tie your bows
Curtsey in the mirror
Strike a pose
Paint your cheeks red
Lips red too
But nothing can hide
your dead doll eyes.

—P.

Lacey met me at the school gate, her arms rigid at her sides. "Did you hear?"

I ran my hands through my hair, ruffling it—I'd barely bothered to brush it this morning. "Hear what?"

"On the news. Police found Aish's camera hidden at Ethan's house." She watched my face carefully, chewing her bottom lip.

The dead of winter had blown in as though straight from the

26

mountains—cold and dark, leaves eddying across the playground. The air was heavy with the threat of rain. Kids streamed past us, lots of them turning to gawk at Lacey and me. Ever since Aisha went missing two weeks before, it was like people were always observing us—not just at school, but everywhere—in town or at church. We were the ones who came back alive from the mountains and that meant *we surely must know something we weren't telling*.

I pulled my jumper up around my neck. "Yeah, Lacey, I heard. That's insane. I mean, who did this?"

A flicker of suspicion in her eyes was quickly replaced by a wide-eyed expression. "I just . . . don't know what to think."

She turned on her heel as two small girls jostled and elbowed each other behind her. Lacey's sisters—Jacinta and Amy—looked like little identikit Laceys, their white hair held back in ponytails. Nine-year-old Jacinta snatched a baby doll from kindergarten-aged Amy's hands. "If you call me fat again, I'm throwing Mitzy in the garbage bin." She thrust the doll at Lacey. "You keep her, 'cos Amy's being mean again."

Lacey paled. "Get that thing away from me!"

Lacey freaked at the sight of dolls. The one time she'd stayed over at my house, I'd had to stuff my old childhood bear in my wardrobe, because Lacey couldn't sleep with it *staring* at her. When we'd seen the dolls in the forest, Lacey had almost lost her mind.

Giving her sister a sweetly mocking grin, Amy grabbed the doll back and tucked it into her backpack. Jacinta reached out and tugged her sister's ponytail.

Sighing, Lacey tidied Amy's hair. "You two should get to school now. And Jaz, you're not fat, okay?"

Jacinta pointed toward the gate. "Why's Dad here?"

Two police officers stepped together along the sidewalk. Lacey's dad was the one in uniform and the other one, in the dark suit, was

Detective Martin Kalassi—the guy who'd questioned us in the days after Aisha's disappearance.

I tensed, waiting, knowing why they'd come.

My throat dried. *Cassie, you know nothing. You never saw Ethan.*

"Get off to school," Lacey ordered her sisters. "Dad will get cranky if he sees you here after the bell."

The girls' expressions grew serious as they glanced at each other, and they raced off together. Lacey had told me before how strict her father was.

Sergeant Dougherty nodded a curt acknowledgment at Lacey as she moved toward him and spoke a quick hello, blocking his view of his two retreating daughters.

He centered cold, steel-blue eyes on me. "We're here to ask the kids in Ethan's year a couple of questions."

Pinpricks of sweat dampened the back of my neck.

Detective Kalassi shot us a quick smile. "We've got permission from the principal. Won't take long." He was a big man, with a generous sort of face. When he'd taken statements from me about the day of the hike, he'd seemed like the kind of person you'd trust.

But he was a cop, and the *last* person I could trust.

Kids were milling around, doing a bad job of pretending not to be eavesdropping. If anything was going to be revealed, everyone wanted to be the first to hear it. Then Raif Dumaj shoved his way through the crowd, the muscles in his neck and jaw taut. "This about my sister?"

Sergeant Dougherty nodded. "Yes, it's concerning Aisha." He raised his voice slightly to be heard above the murmuring of the assembled crowd. "We're looking for Ethan McAllister—we just need to talk to him. Can any of you tell us where he is?"

"You going to arrest him, right?" Raif's aqua-blue eyes darkened under the morning sun. "You guys found him with Aish's camera—what other evidence do you need?"

"That's police business," said the sergeant sharply.

"You know he did something to my sister," Raif insisted. "Everyone already knows he's a criminal. Why didn't he get locked up when he stole a car back in December?"

My stomach turned. I hadn't heard about the car. I'd started school here in February and had totally missed that. If Ethan had stolen a car . . . what *was* he capable of? When he'd gone to look for Aisha . . . what if he'd actually found her? I pushed the thought out of my mind.

"That's enough, Dumaj," Sergeant Dougherty barked. He looked around the group. "It's vital that we find Ethan. Has anyone seen him at any point after five in the afternoon yesterday, or this morning?"

No one said anything.

Detective Kalassi rubbed his temple with the heel of his hand, turning to Lacey and me. "What about you two?"

Lacey told him she hadn't seen or spoken to Ethan since the day of the hike.

"I haven't seen him for days." My voice sounded tight and wrong. I was sure that his eyes were burning a path inside my skull, probing for answers.

Lacey shot me a questioning look.

Raif jabbed a finger at a tall, lanky boy who walked in hesitantly through the gates. "Why dontcha ask Paisley? If anyone's seen him, he has."

My spine went rigid. Ben Paisley had given Ethan supplies to take up to the mountain.

Ben stopped on the spot, stiffening as though a current had gone through him. "What's going on?"

Sergeant Dougherty fixed his gaze on Ben. "Ben Paisley. You're a good mate of Ethan McAllister's—you must know where he is right now?"

Ben drew his mouth down, shrugging. "No idea. I thought he'd be here?"

Raif's best friend, Dominic, flicked his streaked-blond surfer hair back from his eyes. "I bet Ben could give us some clues about the mountains though." He smirked at Ben. "Been seeing any more giant people out in the forests, Paisley?"

Ben seemed to shrink a little. "Get lost."

"I'm afraid to get lost," said Dominic in a taunting little-boy voice. "The giant boogie men might get me."

"Leave him alone." Lacey bit down on her lip, recoiling as everyone turned her way, as though she hadn't meant to say that out loud.

Dominic guffawed. "Look at that, Paisley, the girl you've had the hots for forever just stuck up for you. Better make your move now while she's warmed up."

Sergeant Dougherty stared poison daggers at Ben and Dominic. "That's enough. Speak again and I'll have you arrested for harassment." He jerked his head around, casting a strange look at his daughter. Lacey looked like she was ready to crumble and fall to pieces on the ground.

Ben's face flushed and then paled beneath his freckles. "Whatever. There's something out there, in those mountains. I saw what I saw," he muttered under his breath.

He said it like someone who'd spoken those words a thousand times, with no one ever believing him. I'd heard the story only two weeks back, when Ethan told me. When Ben was nine, he went on a school camping trip to Devils Hole. He'd woken everyone up in the middle of the night, screaming he'd seen strange, giant shadows.

Detective Kalassi pulled out a set of large photographs from a black leather folder. "We need to make something very clear—no one is to head anywhere near the mountains. It's a restricted area until further notice. The only people allowed in there are those searching for Aisha Dumaj. This is the third disappearance in five years, and although we're not making a definite connection, we're not ruling out the possibility either."

The detective glanced at the pictures. "These are the girls who disappeared." He held up a photo of a young girl. Her defiant blue eyes stared out from beneath a crop of purple-streaked red hair. She had multiple piercings in her ears, and one on the side of her nose. "This is Molly Parkes. Vanished at Devils Hole five years ago at age thirteen. She'd run away from home."

Next, he showed us a photograph of a little girl of about three. She stood beside her parents and an older sister in a Christmas photo, her mother holding a chubby baby boy. Honey-brown hair fell about a pouting *I-don't-want-to-be-here* face. "This is Frances Allanzi. Age three. She went missing on a family picnic at Devils Hole."

The last picture he showed was of Aisha—chocolate-brown hair framing her startling aqua eyes.

"Remember," he said, "If anyone has any information at all, about Ethan McAllister's whereabouts or anything else, then you're helping no one by keeping it to yourself." He hesitated for a moment, tucking the photographs away. "The families of these girls deserve to know what happened to their daughters," he finished softy. Then they moved off, leaving everyone standing, mute and still, like statues.

Grabbing my elbow, Lacey moved me across the school quadrangle and into the hall. It felt weird, to be herded off by Lacey—as far as I could remember, she'd never actually *touched* me before. I still felt like I barely knew her.

She pulled me into a recess on the other side of the lockers, eyeing me with a grave expression. "I heard my dad on the phone this morning. If the police can't find Ethan, they're getting tracker dogs." Her eyelashes settled downward. "Cassie, this is serious. If they see him and he tries to run, they'll shoot."

A thread of fear pulled my spine tight. "He's a fifteen-year-old kid!"

"This is a *murder* investigation now. The whole town wants answers and there's a lot of pressure on the police."

The wood-paneled corridor seemed to close in around me, the ceiling and walls winding down until the end of the hallway was just a hazy pinprick. The smell of cleaning wax caught in my nostrils, making my mind spin. Thoughts unspooled themselves crazily in my head. Aisha had run off in the first place because of me. And now Ethan might die because of me, too.

I had to do something.

A group of eighth-graders moved noisily past, in a clatter of shoes and books. Only a couple of them looked our way. I waited until they were gone. "I need your help," I told Lacey.

"What with?"

"I have to go somewhere tomorrow. And I need to tell my mom I'm at your house."

She inhaled a sharp breath, her eyes growing large. "You know where he is, don't you? That's where you're going."

I hesitated before giving a brief nod. "But you have to promise you won't tell anyone. Especially not your father." I squeezed my eyes shut "I . . . saw him. Last night. Briefly." I didn't want to add that he'd slept in my room last night. It would sound wrong somehow. I avoided her gaze as I opened my eyes again. "He's gone to the mountains. To look for Aish."

"You can't go after him," Lacey hissed. "It's too dangerous. You heard what the detective just said."

"Lacey, I have to."

She stared, her pink lips parting in surprise. "You . . . like him, *don't you?*"

"No. Of course not." Wrapping my arms around myself, I felt raw and exposed. "I just . . . care about him as a friend."

She was quiet for a moment—it was impossible to tell whether she believed me or not. In usual Lacey style, she never gave anything away. "What if you can't find him? It could take days—or weeks. It's moving toward the dead of winter now, and it snows on the mountains some years. And what if . . . what if whoever took Aisha is still out there?"

Warning signs flashed with red neon lights in my head—but thoughts of Ethan crowded them out. "I know where he'll be because he told me. He's going to search the old mansion." Cold shivers needled my spine. "And I'm going to help him."

Her cheeks drained of color. "I'm sorry, but that's just stupid. The police have already searched it top to bottom. And the guy who lives there was in *Europe* when Aish disappeared."

I shook my head. "The police might have missed something. The search parties are all looking on the wrong side of the mountain—where her backpack was found."

The school bell made me flinch as it rang out and echoed along the hall.

Lacey bit her lip—super hard—as though to hurt herself. "I'm going to come with you."

"What?" I blurted.

She nodded, tugging her ponytail over her shoulder and tangling her fingers in her hair.

"Are you sure?" I hadn't even considered the possibility she might want to come along. "Like you said, it'll be dangerous. And how will you cover for me if we're both going?"

"I'll figure it out. My mother doesn't check where I go—as long as I'm out of her hair and she can spend time with her friends. And Dad is never home."

We stepped quickly away into the throng of kids, not looking at each other again—as though to do so would clearly signal to anyone watching the thing we were about to do.

5. BLACK WINDS

For the wind gives Aeolian harps their sound
But no wind blows deep underground
Harps wait and wish for bluest skies
Whilst in their hearts all dreams must die.

—P.

Less than a day later, Lacey and I were trekking the same path that we'd traveled with Ethan and Aisha. It was almost as if it were just another bushwalk, except this time our backs were heavily laden and the early morning wind was icy.

The air hurt the insides of my nostrils and made my eyes sting. I wound the scarf higher around my face. We'd told both our moms that we were going to the movies and that I would be sleeping over at Lacey's, and come home the next day—Sunday. We were covered.

In my mind's eye, I saw Aisha stopping to carefully frame a photo, wisps of dark hair blowing around her face. It was the spot where she'd photographed a group of spindly orange mushrooms growing on a mossy log. But there was no photographing and recording on this trip—just a relentless walking pace.

At Devils Hole, I gazed into the woods, jumping from foot to foot, trying to warm myself. We'd found the general location where Ethan had taken us off the trail last time, but not the exact spot. And if we didn't find the exact spot, then we could easily end up hours away from where we needed to be.

Lacey pointed to a small, ripped piece of police barrier tape still attached to a tree. We stepped over to the tape. When I looked closely, I saw snapped twigs on the trees—a sign that many people had recently passed through. There had been many dozens of search and rescue teams looking for Aisha—many of them volunteer. On the other side of the mountain, there were a few teams still searching.

"This has to be it," Lacey said.

I followed her into the bush.

It seemed even colder in the middle of the trees, with barely any sunlight touching us. At least the creepy hanging dolls were gone now, stripped from the trees by souvenir-hunters who'd seen images of them in the news. The empty strings flapped in the wind.

I exhaled slowly when the sound of running water announced itself below the birdcalls. Lacey and I practically ran toward it. She jumped nimbly onto the rocks that edged the riverbank. I balanced carefully, trying to avoid wetting my socks and shoes.

Aisha had fallen in that river, not long before she disappeared. As night fell, she would have been wet and freezing. That's if she'd even made it through the night alive.

I shivered. Tiny kangaroos—wallabies—were drinking at the water's edge ahead. A miniature joey leapt into its mother's pouch, bundling itself in against the cold.

A shadow that could have been a human shape flitted between two trees ahead. I reached to grab Lacey's arm. "Did you see that?"

"What?"

"Someone. Up farther."

"Okay, maybe we found Ethan."

"No, smaller than Ethan I think."

We stared at each other.

Aisha?

"Could have been a wallaby up on his hind legs," she said quickly, but then stepped behind a tree and gestured for me to do the same.

We crept from tree to tree, until we didn't dare to go closer. First came a sound of something heavy dragging across the ground, and then a voice, a deep voice—whistling.

Not Aisha.

Not Ethan.

We pressed our backs into the tree. The voice came closer, clearer.

"What the . . . ?" Lacey whispered.

I twisted myself around. There was the tiniest space between two branches, no bigger than my little finger. On the tips of my toes, I rose to take a look. Lacey looked up at me, her expression warning me not to make myself seen.

A scrawny man in his early twenties set down a large canvas sack. He bent to take a shovel from the ground. With more force than I imagined a man his size could muster, he struck the ground with the shovel. He dug deep into the earth, sweat running from his temples.

I slid down the tree trunk to stand shoulder-to-shoulder with Lacey. "He's burying a sack."

"A sack? How big?"

"Big enough." I knew Lacey would know what I meant.

Heart hammering in my chest, I stole upward to take another look.

The man crouched to heave the sack into the hole he'd dug, and then he shoveled dirt on top of it. Kicking leaves on top of the dirt, he seemed satisfied with his work.

Then, suddenly, he jerked his head up and stared straight at the tree where I stood. I closed my eyes, praying he couldn't see me. Dry leaves on the forest floor rustled.

Go away, I thought. *Go away, go away.*

I opened my eyes again and exhaled. The prayer had worked. He was gone.

Then hard taps hit Lacey and me in the middle of our backs. I whipped around, suppressing a scream, ready to fight or run.

Ethan's face was in front of mine, hard and incensed. "What are you doing here?"

Ethan's here and he's okay. And he's angry with me. The bruise on the side of his face had begun to fade. I tried to speak but nothing came.

"A man just buried a sack," Lacey said, her eyes wild. "A big one."

His eyes widened. "A man just . . . *what?*"

"We've got to dig it up," I told him in a rush.

Ethan pushed through the trees to the freshly turned dirt and mud. Throwing himself to his knees, he began digging with his hands—wet earth flying in the air. Lacey and I followed and began digging from the other end. I felt vaguely nauseous. I didn't know if I was ready to uncover what was inside.

My fingers touched the rough canvas. Whatever was beneath the sack felt both hard and soft in different places.

Ethan hauled the sack up by himself, grunting with the effort.

Lacey tried to undo the ties, but they held fast. Ethan reached into his back pocket and produced a Swiss Army knife. Pulling the canvas up, he cut into the fabric.

The smell was the first thing that hit me. I didn't know what a dead body should smell like, but that wasn't it. The insides of the sack smelled more like rotting food.

Ethan let out a sound that sounded both of anger and anguish. Tin cans, empty packets of oatmeal, and moldy bread spilled from the sack. All of it was compressed tightly and the cans had been flattened.

I wiped a streak of mud from my forehead. "So . . . he was just burying his trash." I felt both disappointed and relieved.

Lacey rocked back on her heels. "That must have been Donovan Fiveash—the guy who owns the house up here. I saw him on news reports a couple of times."

Ethan was already walking away, cursing to himself. Lacey and I did our best to cover the canvas sack over again, and then we trailed after Ethan. He didn't speak or turn around during the twenty minutes it took to return to his campsite. How Ethan was able to remember the way on this winding, unmarked track was beyond me. He'd positioned the camp in a clearing between high crops of rocks—a good place for hiding out—beside a narrow fork in the river.

He seated himself on a log next to his tent. "You shouldn't be here."

I shrugged the cumbersome backpack from my shoulders. "We came to help you search Donovan's house."

"You what?" He stared at me. "Any minute now, Lacey's dad, and the whole frigging police force will be charging up the mountains—coming after you two."

"No one knows we're here." Lacey folded her arms around

herself defensively. "And the police are coming anyway. My dad told me they're organizing a task force and sniffer dogs. They were at school yesterday looking for you."

He bent his head, exhaling hard. "Then you both need to get off this mountain—now."

I dropped my backpack onto the leaf-littered ground. "We're staying."

"We're trying to help, okay?" Lacey gave an exasperated shake of her head.

"Help how? By digging up more buried garbage?"

"C'mon," I said. "You have to admit, it looked suspicious."

"Whatever," he said. "Stay. But you have to do exactly as I tell you to do, and stick with me every step of the way."

I steeled my resolve. "Fine. We'll do that. But you have to do something, too—you have to leave here if we don't find anything at the house. Deal?"

His expression grew hard. "I can't make a promise like that."

I felt myself begin to crack. I wanted to drag him away right then. I wanted to drag the whole world back to the way it was two weeks before. "Well, then, we're not leaving either. Ethan, you have to come back with us. The police can't charge you for something you didn't do. Every day you stay up here makes it worse."

"She's right," Lacey said.

Ethan's brown eyes flashed angrily at Lacey. "What? Does that mean you're planning on handing me over to Daddy when you get back home?"

She straightened her back, the wind catching and blowing her hair around her flushed face. "Just because I'm a cop's daughter doesn't mean I'm a snitch. I am *not* my father. I hate him, okay?"

He twisted his mouth to one side as though he was thinking. Finally, he sighed. "Okay. After we search the house, we all leave—together."

I exchanged glances with Lacey. I could tell by the look on her face that she didn't quite believe him, but I knew we weren't going to get a better promise out of Ethan.

He reached inside his tent for a checkered shirt and pulled it on. I'd seen Ben Paisley wear that shirt once—I guessed that all the clothes Ethan had in the backpack belonged to Ben. But Ethan's wide shoulders filled out the shirt in a way that Ben's hadn't.

As he stood, he jerked his chin, gesturing toward the forest. "Time to head off."

"Where?" asked Lacey.

"The Fiveash house."

"Wait a minute," I said. "You mean *now*?"

He gave a half a shrug. "Why not?"

Without waiting for a reply from either of us, Ethan turned and stepped off into the woods.

It was easy to track Donovan. He never stopped whistling. We followed him through the trees, keeping a good distance away. I realized we'd traveled back to the mansion when I first saw its long shadow stretching across the ground like skeletal fingers. I stifled a gasp when I sighted the house—it was larger than I remembered, the air around it weirdly still, its wooden cladding and stonework as gray as old bones. Donovan strode inside a shed and walked out with an ax over his shoulder. He disappeared around the other side of the property—but we could hear the sharp whacks as he chopped wood.

Lacey stopped still, drawing her mouth in. "The dogs will start barking if we go any closer, won't they?"

Ethan nodded distractedly. Rifling through his backpack, he produced a pair of binoculars. He aimed them at the dogs' enclosure, adjusting the lenses. "Looks like they're asleep."

"So, what are we supposed to do now?" she asked.

He shot her an annoyed look as he dropped the binoculars over his head. "Stay quiet?" He reached into his pocket and pulled out a small notebook—the same notebook he took everywhere. Seating himself on the ground, he began sketching the house. His fingers made quick movements across the page, sketching the Fiveash mansion in what looked like perfect scale. I knew he must've been trying to map the house's layout in his head.

There was only one place I wanted to be, and that was away from the mountains. But once we'd searched the mansion, we could leave—and never come back. Lacey rested her head against a tree, staring up at the branches with a stony, resigned expression.

Dark shapes moved in an upper-story window. Two people, staring at us. I whipped my head around to face the window directly. The people vanished. There was just the reflection of the swaying trees on the glass behind the metal grille.

"Did you see them?" My words rushed out in a single breath.

"See what?" Ethan raised puzzled eyes to me.

"I saw people . . . up there."

Jumping to his feet, he scanned the house. "I don't see anyone."

"There's nothing there now." I inhaled the cold forest air, calming myself. "Maybe I'm just freaking out."

"Well, try not to. We'll save that for when Donovan comes at us with that ax . . . ." He shot me a thin-lipped smile. "Sorry, bad joke."

I managed to smile back. "Well, if he does, you trip him over and I'll beat him with sticks."

"Sounds like a plan."

Lacey said nothing as she eyed the house, but I could see the strain showing already beneath the cold-stung pink of her face.

A shiver passed through me. Those figures couldn't possibly have been real, could they? I tried to convince myself that they had just been a trick of the light, a trick of my restless mind.

We withdrew even farther into the trees as Donovan appeared with an armful of wood. He deposited the wood in the shed. Afterward, he went into the house for a few minutes, then walked out the door, pulling on a jacket and ski cap.

"Let's follow." Ethan drew his brow down. "If he walks down toward the road where his car is stashed, we'll race back here and scope out the house. If he goes somewhere else, I want to know where and why."

"Okay." I nodded. We didn't have a better plan.

All afternoon, we faithfully tracked Donovan Fiveash's every movement. He trod the woods with an almost nervous energy, always either whistling or muttering scenes from movies, as though he wanted to block any thought from intruding into his head. His dark-blond hair stuck out in a messy tangle beneath his ski cap.

It was a strange, lonely kind of life that Donovan led. Why would someone so young—Donovan could only be twenty-three, maybe twenty-four years old—choose to live all on his own in the mountains?

Ethan grew increasingly frustrated as Donovan walked in circles, seemingly without purpose. Hours later, Donovan returned to the house. I checked my watch. It was already one in the afternoon. We kept watching him as best we could through the windows of the house. At one point, he stood at one of the narrow bottom floor windows, staring out at the forest as though it were his enemy—a bottle of alcohol in his hand.

Then he stepped away from our view. A few minutes later, a deep, droning strain of music carried on the breeze. It sounded awful, as though Donovan had just taught himself to play the piano yesterday.

"It sounds like he's strangling a cat," Ethan remarked. "Some kind of pipe organ."

I recognized the tune—barely. "Lacey, isn't that one of the pieces I heard you play a couple of months ago, at your house?" Lacey had taken piano lessons for years and could make music leap from her fingers.

She nodded stiffly. "Chopin's 'Nocturne No. 20.' Ethan's right— he's murdering it. But why are we even here listening to this? There's no point. Let's head back to camp."

We stepped away into the woods until we could no longer hear Donovan's music.

I held up an arm to brush away the branches of a tree that were draped with enormous heart-shaped leaves. Arms slid around my shoulders and waist. I turned to see Ethan pulling me close to him.

"You were one step away from wishing you were dead." His face was very serious. "That's the Giant Stinging Tree. The leaves have a potent neurotoxin, and it's a bastard getting the needles out."

Lacey glanced over, eyeing Ethan's arms around me, a strange look on her face. He released his grip on me quickly.

I broke away, my heart knocking against my ribcage.

Sitting on the log at the campsite, we ate a quick lunch of squashed sandwiches—Ethan devouring the sandwiches Lacey handed him. She was always making food for people, but barely eating anything herself.

He leaned back on the log, stretching out his legs. "We're going to have to wait Donovan out. Lacey's right—he's probably not going out again today. We'll just have to search the house tonight, while he's sleeping."

"No way!" I said. Terror cracked like ice in my veins. I could not, *would not*, search that house at night.

"We've got no choice." A look of determination steeled his eyes.

Lacey thrust her hands deep into her jacket pockets, puffing up her cheeks and breathing out tightly. "So . . . we're going to search the creepy house of a creepy guy . . . in the dead of the creep-house hours?"

Ethan made an exasperated noise. "You'll both be with me. I won't let anything bad happen. Afterward, we can stay in my tent until morning—it's just big enough for three."

"No." Picking myself up from the ground, I wound my scarf tighter around my neck. "We can't stay. Our parents will be expecting us back."

"Fine," Ethan said, his face hardening. "Go home, then. You should never have come in the first place."

"Cassie, you're staying overnight at my house, remember?" Lacey stood awkwardly, her elbows jutting out at odd angles. "My mother won't check on where I am or what I'm doing—she never does."

"*My* mom will."

"Well," said Lacey, her voice small, "you'll just have to make up some story when you get home. We need to get this thing *over* with."

I had no answer. It'd been my idea to come here. It was at my insistence that we were going to help Ethan search the mansion. There was no backing out or running away now.

Just one night. That's all. Then it was over.

We hung out at the campsite during the next few long hours, watching shadows lengthen and coil into every space around us. Every hour brought a drop in temperature. Night was zeroing in like a hawk on its prey.

Ethan pulled himself to his feet. "I'm heading off for a while. Be back before dark." And he left before either Lacey or I could ask him where he was going.

I was about to see if Lacey wanted to wait inside the tent, but she'd already curled herself up against the fallen tree and closed her eyes. Desolately, I sat on the log, pulling my coat in tight. Another hour passed. *What the hell am I even doing here?*

The wind blustered around us, making the zippered opening of the tent flap crazily back and forward. Ethan's notebook was lying on top of his sleeping bag—the notebook where he'd drawn Donovan's house.

Ethan took the notebook everywhere he went, and never let anyone see it. What was so damned important about it?

Stealing a glance at Lacey to make sure she was asleep, I stepped over to the tent. I knew it was wrong, but I couldn't stop myself. I grabbed the notebook and starting flipping through the pages. There was some kind of ledger, with money and mortgage amounts—as though Ethan had been desperately trying to figure out how to manage the bills at home. I flipped back another few pages. There was sketch after sketch of trees—their surreal roots surging and seething on the paper, trapping small animals and plants. The drawings were angry, ugly.

The next pages held crazy scrawled writings—crossed out and written every which way. I turned the notepad on an angle to read one of the poems:

She, who walks the twisting maze

She, who stalks the silver gaze

She, the only one who'll see

The darkness I hold inside me

The notepad fell open to an early entry. Another drawing, dated a year before. A tremor raced through me. It was a sketch of a house. Not in such detail as the picture he'd drawn today, but a hazy, half-remembered drawing. A drawing that looked terrifyingly close to being the Fiveash mansion. But it couldn't be possible. The first time Ethan had ever seen the mansion was two weeks ago, the day Aisha disappeared. He'd never been that way before. Or at least, that's what he had said….

Was this all some weird, twisted game he was playing?

A snapping twig made me turn. The notebook fell through my fingers. Ethan stood at the river, water dripping from his bare torso—grimy T-shirt in hand. He must have been washing.

He strode up to me, the whites of his eyes clear and large in the deep light, his skin red from the ice cold water and wind. A leaf fell from his tousled hair—I guessed he'd been climbing trees and watching the house. Stooping, he grabbed the notepad from the ground. "Don't touch this—ever."

Swallowing, I scrambled to my feet. "I just wanted to see what you drew of the house."

"Did you?" he said in a way that let me know he didn't believe me at all.

Lacey yawned as she woke. She stared from me to Ethan. "What's happening?"

"Nothing." Ethan pulled the T-shirt over his head. He wouldn't look at me. "It's time we got going." Reaching inside his tent, he picked up a large, sheathed knife and slipped it into a side compartment of his bag. I shivered involuntarily. I could only hope we wouldn't need it.

Night enveloped us as we wound our way through the forest, pounding the life from the trees and pale glimpses of sky. The house loomed ahead, the night shadowing the perimeters, merging the house with the limitless black. My breaths were knives in my chest. I knew it wasn't just my fear of the dark making my chest hurt—it was the house. The closer we got, the more I felt the mansion drawing us in. I stole sideways glances at Ethan and Lacey's moonlit faces. Both of them were serious—Lacey nervous—but neither of them showed the terror that I felt.

Last Halloween, Christina and Evie had wanted to break into an abandoned house on Evie's street and hold a séance. I'd chickened out at the last minute. The thought of being inside that old house at midnight had been too much. But I'd give anything to be there right now instead of here. We skirted the walls, keeping as far from the dogs' pen as possible.

Ethan and I tried a few of the windows, but the grilles held tight. Lacey hung back, her face pale in the moonlight. We moved around to a side door. The blade of Ethan's knife glinted as he inserted it between the frame and the lock. With a dull click, the door cracked open.

The door opened into a dank kitchen. A smell of dust and age hung in the air, together with a greasy odor coming from the twin potbellied ovens. Peeled strips of wallpaper brushed the tops of ornately carved wooden cupboards. Cans of food littered a bench. I closed the door behind us.

Turning our flashlights on, we checked the cupboards. Just more canned and packaged foods. Donovan kept his kitchen well stocked—enough to last an apocalypse. I inspected a large cupboard full of brooms and dusters. Wafts of cleaning fluids caught at the back of my throat and left a chemical taste. I shut it quickly.

We edged around the corridor to a large reception area, leading into what could be a ballroom. An enormous chandelier hung from a long chain in the center of the room. A long wisp of smoke curled upward from the dark fireplace. Ethan leaned on the mantelpiece and peered inside.

To the left stood a wide, red-carpeted staircase—framed paintings hanging along the adjacent wall.

We crept slowly up the steps. Portraits of men and women in the stiff clothing of the 1800s contrasted against newer paintings of a couple in clothing of the early 1900s. A blonde woman with ice-blue eyes and a smug curl to her mouth had her arm draped possessively over a handsome man in a waist-coated magician's outfit. The eyes of the couple pierced straight through me, and I had to look away. A long, spindly corridor at the top of the landing was fixed with hexagonal light shades. I wished I could turn the lights on. The dark closed in everywhere, thickening and congealing.

Ethan reached back and pulled me by the lapel of my jacket, as though he knew I was stalling. His eyes were distant, unknowable. Thin vines of anxiety twisted in my stomach. At the back of my mind, something whispered that if I did find out all the things I didn't know about Ethan, I'd wish I hadn't.

The rooms were musty with a layer of dust over everything. It looked as though the rooms hadn't been touched in a century—but I knew the police had searched them with a fine-toothed comb only two weeks before. Some of the windows were cracked, allowing fine mist to swirl in. A few of the rooms had beds—but most didn't.

It was hard to walk into a room without making footprints on the dusty floorboards. But Lacey had brought along a cloth to try to erase the prints. I hoped the dust would soon settle back where it was before.

Finding nothing on the second floor, we took the stairs up to the next floor.

We stepped into the middle room on the third level. This room looked out toward the river at the front of the house. Yellowed lace dresses lined a wooden rack. Sheer curtains hung over a four-poster bed.

Against the wall, an intricate dollhouse stood—complete with tiny chandeliers, checkered flooring, and wooden stairs. I crouched to see the delicate dolls, beautifully hand painted and dressed.

I stood, flinching as I caught my reflection in a full-length mirror. A curled, handwritten note was tucked to the mirror's frame. *You and always you*, it said in a tall, shaky font. The note looked as though it had been there for decades.

Ethan trained his flashlight underneath the bed and behind the dollhouse. "Okay, next room."

We searched the next seven rooms on that level and found nothing of interest.

The largest room was at the end of the hall. Filmy negligees and frilly pink dresses were carelessly tossed about on the floor and across the gilded, ornate furniture.

Ethan shone his flashlight on a box of old photographs. I picked through them. They were sepia pictures of an era long past. A big top tent. Serious-looking clowns sitting on milk crates playing cards. A magician and his assistant—the same magician from the portrait downstairs?—practicing a magic act with a scarf and a dove. A white-bearded ringmaster standing beside a placard that proudly announced the coming of the Fiveash Circus to New Orleans in January 1920. A name, *Tobias Fiveash*, was scrawled in spidery writing beneath the photograph.

We stepped back into the hall.

An oval mirror reflected our images—my eyes large and anxious in my pale olive skin. A terrible thought crossed my mind. "That was the last of the bedrooms. But we didn't find Donovan in any of them . . ."

Lacey gasped. "So he's roaming the house . . . ."

"I don't think so—or else we would have seen him by now. And we haven't heard any footsteps." Ethan sounded sure of himself, but his eyes remained guarded and worried.

My stomach clenched as two blurred figures—a man and a

woman—flashed past the hall mirror's dark surface. A sound scattered along the corridor—the distant sound of a woman's laughter.

"My God. There are people—." My words caught in my throat, sticking like cement.

Ethan whirled around. "I heard it, too. But maybe it's just the house settling."

I spun on my heel to check the hallway and there was nothing—and no one—there. I'd imagined them. I'd seen shadows and nothing more.

Lacey backed into the wall, breathing hard and squeezing her eyes closed. "You two are freaking me out."

"Sorry . . . ." My voice fell hollowly. I couldn't tell Ethan or Lacey, but my fear of the dark, my night terrors, had often made me see things that weren't there.

"Look." Ethan lowered his voice. "We'll finish this up quick and be out of here. I don't want to let you girls go back to the campsite by yourselves. And we're here now—may as well keep going."

I nodded rigidly. The thought of making my way to the camp through that pitch-black forest alone was almost worse than being in the house. Forcing myself to continue, I followed Ethan and Lacey to the attic and other upstairs quarters. Ethan checked everything thoroughly, looking behind and under furniture.

But still, we found nothing—and no Donovan, either. We headed back to the ballroom. I let a tightly held breath ease from my chest. There wasn't much house left to search. We'd be leaving soon.

A set of French doors led to an extravagant living room, dining room, and library. Beyond the library, a narrow corridor ended in a set of powder rooms.

There was a series of three individual cubicles containing toilets and sinks. The old pipes were cracked and leaking, the stench of an old sewerage system rising from them. A bug climbed up from the sink's drain in the last bathroom, then shot away under the flashlight's beam.

"Blech. Let's go." Lacey held a hand over her mouth and nose.

"Yeah. Nothing to do here." Ethan's face was drawn.

Deep, silvery moonlight fell across us as we made our way back to the staircase. Gaudy plastic flowers adorned an ugly glass vase on a side table on the other side of the staircase. The wooden wall that ran along the underside of the staircase was deeply creviced around a rectangular shape. I ran a finger around the crevice. Ethan frowned as he stared over my shoulder. He pushed against the wood. A door swung open, revealing steps leading down into blackness. I eyed Ethan's tense expression.

"I'll go," he offered.

I nodded, swallowing.

Lacey's thin body trembled as she followed Ethan.

I urged myself to move, to go down the stairs. It wouldn't be fair if Lacey and Ethan went by themselves. Those people I'd thought I'd seen weren't about to jump out at us from the shadows. *Because they weren't real.* People didn't move that fast. People didn't *vanish*.

My feet stepped stiffly one after the other on the concrete stairs.

The air was cold, damp—like standing in light rain on a winter's night, except for the metallic, closed stench of dirt. The temperature was bone-achingly cold down there and I could barely stop my jaw from quivering.

Ethan moved quickly, studying everything. Our flashlight beams crisscrossed each other's as we searched the room. Barrels were lined up on one side of the basement, and a ladder and a big freezer chest stood on the other. I shone my flashlight over the ceiling. It was just a ceiling, a few rusted tools hanging from rough-cut exposed beams.

We checked the barrels next—they were empty.

Marching across the room, Ethan reached for the freezer lid. He went to open it, then flinched and drew his arm back. A weight dragged through my body. I knew what Ethan feared was in there, and I knew why he didn't want to open it.

Lacey cast a sympathetic look in Ethan's direction. Stepping forward, she placed two hands on the lid, and lifted it. I moved closer, peering inside. Heads, legs, and arms—all in pieces. All animal.

She shut it quickly.

None of us moved for a moment, and I knew why. The possibility of finding Aisha like that was too much, too grisly.

We were just kids. We shouldn't even be in the forest.

On the wall behind Ethan, yellow plastic was wound around a large nail. Stepping over, I pulled at a length of the plastic. Big black letters said Police Line Do Not Cross repeatedly on the tape. "It's some of the police tape—that barricade stuff."

"They must have been down here already," said Ethan.

"Guess it makes sense." I dropped the piece of tape. "If the basement was so easy to find in the dark, how easy would it have been for teams of police in daylight?"

I shone my flashlight around the floor again. If you looked closely, you could see different imprints of shoes on the dirty floor.

Two boilers stood against the back wall—one of them larger and newer than the other. Ethan opened their drawers. The new one had drawers filled with sooty coal while the other, though it looked so old it must have been installed when the house was built, looked like it had never been used.

My heart stilled. A low rustle of voices murmured from the ballroom above us. A woman's high-pitched voice trilled above a deeper, male voice. "*Why not now?*"

"Did you . . . ?" I whispered.

Ethan glanced over at me, straightening up from a crouch. "Did we what?"

He hadn't heard.

No longer caring how stupid I seemed to Ethan and Lacey, I raced back up the stairs. They raced after me, their eyes wide and fixed on my face. I shook my head, unwilling to give an explanation beyond a single word—*voices*.

I wanted out of there. *Now*. I wasn't staying in that house another minute.

6. TRAITOR

The poison lingers on your breath
Long after you slip away
Each day, each hour, like a death
Drink the tea, dance with me
Stay with me, inside the dollhouse
Aboard this never ending ride.

—P.

The journey back to the campsite seemed to take a lifetime. The darkness was oppressive, like a coffin slowly sealing us in. But with every step we took away from the house, I felt a little bit better.

Lacey fell into step behind me. Her face was ghostly above the glow of the flashlight. "I've heard that the walls of old houses sometimes hold onto voices—and play them back at odd times."

I knew she was just trying to help. But I couldn't speak. I wanted to run from the mountain. What were we even doing, out in this dark forest, searching for the dead? We hadn't even come close to finding Aisha, but we'd come too close to how we *might* find her.

And whoever or whatever had claimed Aisha was coming for us next. I was sure of it. If we stayed on the mountain, it was just a waiting game. Morning could not come soon enough.

Finally, we reached Ethan's tent.

"We'll bunk here until first light," Ethan said. "Then we'll head straight off the mountain, okay?"

"Okay," said Lacey in a tight voice.

Ethan waited until Lacey and I had crawled inside the tent before he moved in and laid his long body beside mine. I was so numb with cold I could barely feel him next to me—the chill had driven so far into my bones I didn't think it would ever leave me. I knew it wasn't just the cold—it was the sawing terror of that house.

Sounds of the forest grew louder as the night wound on. Layers of screeching bird calls, rustles and crashes through the bush, and a low, raucous baying.

I could feel Ethan's chest rise and fall against my back. His warm breath on my shoulder made my own breathing quiet and slow. He was like a whole world next to me—a world I wanted to escape into and where I could hide. A world better, warmer, brighter, than the darkness of the world I'd somehow fallen into. Almost. There was still a part of Ethan that seemed hidden. Edged with danger.

I woke with a shudder.

A scream arched across the night air. Human, piercing. Bloodcurdling.

Ethan was gone.

Gripping the tent's opening, I slid down the zipper. As I poked my head out, something even colder than the air landed on my face. Flakes of white twirled and danced from the inky sky.

Snow.

A figure sat on the fallen tree, hunched against the wind. He tossed a stone hard into the rocks in front of the campsite.

"Ethan?"

He turned slightly.

Pushing my feet into my boots, I stepped over to him. The scream sounded again—more distant this time.

I clamped my hands over my head. "Did you hear it?"

"That's the Barking Owl. It has a scream like nothing on earth."

"That was an *owl*?"

Sitting beside him, I held out a hand to catch a snowflake. It melted on my hand. *Real snow.* I hadn't seen snow, ever, except in movies and on TV. "I can't believe it's actually snowing."

Through the trees, the patches of night sky were fading to a deep gray. I glanced at my watch. It was close to seven in the morning. I had to wake Lacey and head home. If Mom had found out I wasn't at Lacey's, I'd have to face her. But that was nothing compared to what Ethan was going to face when he ventured off-mountain.

He turned to me with tired, hooded eyes. "I really hoped we'd find something in the house."

Snow licked my nose with an icy tongue. Fishing my ski cap from my pocket, I pulled it on. "I know . . . ."

"But I feel it . . . stronger than ever—there's something everyone's missing. And I know you feel it, too."

I didn't want to admit how I really felt about Donovan's house. "It doesn't matter. We have to get away from here—before things get any worse for you."

"Things couldn't *get* any worse for me. And I've already got black marks against my name. The police could make me look pretty bad if they wanted to."

"That wouldn't be fair." I hugged myself. "I mean, okay, so you stole a car. It's not like you killed somebody."

I wished I could bite back my words as soon as they'd thudded from my mouth. Words could be icebergs—small and insignificant at first, but huge and terrible when they fully emerged.

He kicked out at a shrub. "How'd you know about that?"

I stared up into the bowl of darkness—not knowing what to answer. "I'm just worried about you, that's all," I said finally.

"Because you think I'm some kind of thief?" He shook his head. "Forget it. You wouldn't understand. Besides, nothing I say will change your mind about me anyway. You don't trust me." It was a statement, not a question.

"I do," I lied.

"No, you don't. And did you ever stop and think before you came charging up here that if something happened to you or Lacey I'd have yet more missing girls on my hands?" Ethan studied my face, pain stitched into the muscles around his eyes. "And if something did happen to you, how would I live with myself?"

Neither of us spoke for a minute or so, darkness swallowing us, watching the snow.

How would I live with myself?

His words kept running through my head, warming me, breaking apart all the dark thoughts I'd had about him.

How would I live with myself?

A clear, dark snowflake rested on Ethan's eyelashes. Gently, I brushed it away.

My math teacher back in Miami always liked rattling on about how the universe was made up of fractals—patterns that repeated themselves over and over. Like snowflakes. She said it was evidence of order in nature. Sometimes I wished I could stare down the tube of a kaleidoscope and rearrange the pieces of Ethan and me, and out of every future possibility, find a pattern—a world—in which we fit together.

I tried to force myself to get up and walk away. But I couldn't. The world closed in, grew small and tight—the space within a snow globe. I wanted Ethan with a desperation that terrified me. I was drawn to him like a moth toward a deadly, red-hot flame.

I leaned forward, and my mouth found his. His lips were cold, his body tensing.

I numbed, like my brain had shut down. All I knew was that I didn't want this moment to stop. I wanted him, more than anything.

We clung together for a moment, before he twisted away—a look of anguish and confusion stamped in his eyes

"Sorry." It was the only word that would escape from me.

Stupid, stupid, stupid . . . . I didn't even know why I'd done that—couldn't even explain it to myself.

Jumping up, I turned and raced away—ignoring Ethan as he shouted after me. I stumbled through the woods. I didn't even care if I got lost.

So many times I'd imagined *the kiss*. And hated myself for imagining it. But I'd never imagined the kiss like it had been: on a mountain—with snow freezing us half to death. A sad and lonely traitor's kiss.

Ethan had looked so lost and torn up, and I'd wanted to take all that away. But instead, I'd just made it worse.

The sun's first light streaked red above the trees. Traitor red.

Traces of snow clung to the ground, though most evidence of the snowfall was beginning to melt under the reproachful eye of the sun. Spots of crimson inflamed the trees above. My breath misted the air in front of me. People didn't really mean it when they said they wished the earth would swallow them. But I meant it. I wanted to just drop away. I wanted to hide, to hide everything about myself.

Music—low and plodding—ran through my head. The tune

Donovan had played yesterday. Whatever he'd played that tune on—the pipe organ—we hadn't found it in the house.

That meant there was another room, *a room we hadn't found.*

I stopped dead. My skin electrified.

But where? We'd searched everything.

A hidden room—concealed from us. Concealed, probably from the police. All thought of the botched kiss flew from my head.

A sound edged its way into my head—a distant sound that wasn't the wind or animals of the forest. *Dogs.* Lots of them. The police task force had arrived.

Wheeling around, I charged back to the campsite.

But after only a minute, I began to panic I was heading in the wrong direction. Had I passed that tree, split by old lightning into the shape of a fork?

My stomach turned. I was already lost.

A strong pair of arms caught me as I spun around. Ethan.

"Cassie!" Ethan was furious. Don't ever run off like that—"

"Can't you hear it?" I blurted. "Barking. The police are here."

He stared off past the trees, his jaw clenching. "I don't want you or Lacey hurt. Stay at the campsite. I'll head off."

"What? No! You can't run off. What if they shoot?"

"Let me worry about that."

I sucked in a deep breath. "Ethan, there's something the police might want to know. Remember the pipe organ from yesterday? Well, we didn't find it in the house. And those things are big, right?"

His brown eyes grew large as he realized what I meant.

I nodded. "Once we tell the police, they can go search for it—there has to be a hidden room."

"You think they're going to listen to us? To me? They'll think we're making up stories, or Donovan will just tell them it was the radio," he said harshly. "I'm going back there—now, or I might not get a chance."

"But Donovan—"

"I'll deal with Donovan." There was no hesitation in his voice.

"Then I'm coming, too."

"You sure?"

"Yes."

Gripping my hand, he pulled me back through the underbrush toward the campsite. Lacey was just emerging from the tent, sleepy-eyed.

"We need to get back to the house," he told her. His expression was grim as he grabbed his backpack and dragged a knit cap over his ears.

"What?" She turned to me, her mouth falling open.

I couldn't believe what I was saying either. But the words came anyway. "The pipe organ—we need to find out where it is."

Her bottom lip quivered. "No way. We're not going back there. We were leaving, remember? Let's get out of here while we still can." She froze as she caught the sound of the dogs. "They're here...."

"You can stay here if you want," I told her. I grabbed my backpack and threw the straps over my shoulders.

She zipped up her jacket. "No, I'll come."

We raced through the trees toward the mansion. Donovan's dogs were going crazy, barking and growling at the gate of their pen— they must have heard the police dogs. Donovan came charging out of the house to see what the commotion was. His dogs jumped the gate and ran. With a shout, Donovan followed after them, calling them back. But the dogs were already a long way into the forest and showing no sign of stopping.

"Go!" I said, half out of breath.

We dashed across the grounds to the door that led to the kitchen.

"Okay." Ethan inhaled hard. "When Donovan went to play the

pipe organ, he didn't go upstairs. We would have seen him through the window. So the hidden room has to be downstairs."

Wordlessly, we spread out. The mansion was a different place during the day. The darkened, expensive-looking furniture and gilt-edged fittings showed what the mansion must once have been. We peered behind large paintings and inspected the bookcases, which were filled with musty books from the late 1800s.

Frustrated, we gathered again in the center of the ballroom.

"There's nothing here." Lacey fiddled with the strap of her backpack. "And Donovan might be back any minute."

Ethan stared past her, into empty space, seemingly as though he hadn't heard. Then he turned slowly, away from us. Lacey and I watched him walk toward the fireplace. He stood in front of it, his gaze fixed downward. A thin tendril of smoke wound through the air.

"Last night," he said, "something was bothering me. I mean, there's supposed to be smoke in a damned fireplace, right? But the wood doesn't look like it's ever been lit."

With uncertainty, we crossed the room to join him. He was already crouched down, moving aside logs of wood. Underneath the wood, there were no embers, no ashes—just a blackened wooden grate. Still, smoke trailed upward—from somewhere.

My heart glitched in my chest. What the hell?

Reaching inside his jacket, Ethan pulled out a flashlight. He trained the beam into the grate. The light shone down a long stone hole—like an underground chimney. He tugged on the grate. It was bolted down securely.

Cursing, he moved back onto his heels. "There's a fireplace down there—and another room."

A chill sped along my spine. "But the only floor lower than this one is the basement."

He shook his head. "The room down there is deeper than that. A hell of a lot deeper. But maybe there's access through the basement."

Lacey was visibly shaken as we made our way to the hidden panel that sat below the side of the staircase. My heart was a fist hammering against my ribs. Ethan lifted the panel aside and dim daylight spilled onto the steps. The earthy smell and darkness of the basement slipped over me like a glove as I headed downstairs with the others.

Desperately, we checked the same walls and floor we'd checked last time. Ethan slammed a hand against the stone wall. "There's got to be a way down."

Lacey was inspecting the second boiler. "Why don't they just get rid of this old thing if they've never used it?"

I glanced over. The boiler was coated in greasy dust, save for the four knobs on each of its metal drawers. The knobs were worn and free of dust, which didn't make sense if the unit wasn't in use.

I moved next to Lacey and opened the boiler's drawers. They were as clean and free of coal as before. As I closed the first drawer, the knob retracted. Perhaps that's why they never used the boiler— it was defective. I pressed two of the other knobs, and like the first, they pushed in completely. Shrugging, I pressed in the last knob.

A loud knocking sound reverberated underneath us.

Lacey jerked her head around to face me, her eyes huge and fearful.

Ethan bounded over to us. "What the hell was that? What did you touch?"

Shaking, I pointed at the boiler. "Just that."

He stared at the pushed-in knobs.

We were thrown to the ground as the entire floor shuddered. With a mechanical groan, the whole floor began to descend.

Cold, stale air met us.

We were descending into a deep cave, shadowed light coming from an unseen source.

I bit my lip to keep from screaming. Ethan stared about with grim anticipation.

The floor settled onto the ground level below. The ceiling of the basement was now horribly high above.

Around the cavernous room, just about every available space was crammed with circus paraphernalia and weird curios. Broken carousel horses littered the floor near big-wheel tricycles and penny-farthings. A store dummy wore a blue, Victorian dress. A car that looked like it belonged to the early 1900s sat in one corner. Two long racks held antique dresses and costumes. Massive shelves were filled with puzzles, masks, clowns, theatre posters, game machines—and a thousand other things.

Donovan's family must have been circus people.

My stomach knotted as our flashlight beams moved across a line of lofty, thin figures. Then I realized they were wooden clown statues—taller than Ethan.

Venturing over to the shelves, I picked up a set of wedding dolls, accidentally twisting the heavy wooden base they stood upon. A droning wedding march played for a few seconds.

Lacey winced, placing a slim hand over her face.

"Lacey hates dolls," I told Ethan. It sounded stupid when said out loud. But it was no more stupid than my fear of the dark. Perhaps less stupid. Dolls have faces whereas darkness has none.

"Maybe he comes down here to play with all his toys." Ethan pulled the cord on a small, waist-coated metallic monkey. The monkey clattered up the pole it was attached to.

"Like a collector?" I said. "Maybe."

Ethan sat on a clown's tricycle. "I was sure this was it. I was sure this was going to lead somewhere."

I eyed him sympathetically. I had felt it, too. Although I desperately didn't want to find Aisha's remains, at the same time I ached for resolution.

Sighing heavily, he stepped toward a large piece of machinery that had a metal wheel and motor. He inspected it, then frowned at me. "Why's he got a generator running down here?'

Frowning, I shook my head. Then something caught my attention. In a recess in the adjoining wall, the pipe organ stood on a wooden platform, its pipes disappearing into the rock behind it. Running to the organ, I picked up the crackly, yellowed sheet music sitting on top. The faded title read "Chopin Nocturne No. 20 in C-sharp minor."

Ethan walked alongside me, placing both hands on the pipe organ and rocking it. It barely moved. Rusted bolts held it to the platform.

Beside the organ, a metal panel was set into the wall, about two square feet. Stepping over to it, I slid up a small door in its center.

"What the hell is that?" Ethan said.

I gave him a shrug. "Not sure. Looks like one of those dumbwaiter things they used to have in old houses."

"A what?" Ethan stared at me.

"They used them to take food up and down floor levels," I said.

"Well, this goes *down*. Does that mean there's another damned level below this?" Ethan blew out hard.

Lacey shivered, even though sweat was glistening on her temples. "I hate this place."

Ethan looked like he was about to snap at her, then changed his mind. "Why don't you and Cassie leave?" he said quietly. "Go home. Call the cops. Lacey, call your dad. Maybe this cave is too big to search on our own. I'll stay here and keep looking."

I wanted to say I'd stay and keep looking, too, but really, I wanted to run, and keep running. Then I froze. Straight ahead of me, set in the opposite wall, was a rounded area darker than the wall around it. A passage.

Ethan hooked his chin up questioningly at me. Turning, he looked in the same direction.

"Oh my god," Lacey breathed. She had seen it, too.

Without hesitating, we crossed toward it. Too late to go back. Too late to do anything but keep searching.

Bitter air snaked toward us. The passage before us was the still, cold black of a granite coffin. Our combined flashlights barely penetrated the darkness as we took our first steps inside. I barely made out the sketchy outline of a rounded rock ceiling and walls, spearing down into a winding passage.

My foot slid on something that was not rock—something rubbery. I bent to snatch it up. It was one of those gel phone cases. I turned it over. My heart dropped through my chest. The pop-art image of Marilyn Monroe colored the back of the case.

"That's Aisha's," Lacey breathed, her face stretched tight across her high cheekbones.

Ethan took stiff steps over, seizing the case.

Lacey pressed her back into the wall. "What do we do now?"

Ethan stared at Aisha's phone case with a dazed expression. "We find her."

"Okay." Her voice squeezed tight.

Words dried inside me. Ethan looked at me for confirmation. I wanted to run. But Aisha was here. *She was here.* This was proof. This is what I'd come here for. No, this was more than I'd come here for—much more.

I nodded, my fingers digging into my flesh inside my pocket.

No one spoke as we moved along the passage. No sound but the sharp intake of our breath. The black air stuck to me with a tar-like grip, claiming me.

Were these the last steps Aish had taken in her life? Were these the last steps we'd ever know, too?

7. NOCTURNE

Her ghostly heart knows no sorrow
Human fear held fast in chains
Surrender all you once held dear
Dance and dream again tomorrow.

—P.

Something big blocked the passage up ahead. I shone a shaky light over the large mass—the beam of light barely reaching it.

Lacey stepped forward, running her flashlight's beam around in a circle. "It's got . . . lots of heads . . . ." She turned back to us.

We moved in slowed steps. Murky shapes solidified. The heads belonged to gargoyles and unicorns—on a circus carousel. The carousel was old, antique—like everything back in the cavern. It entirely blocked the passage. A metal panel had been fitted across the middle of the carousel—from platform to ceiling—completely cutting off our view of whatever was on the other side, and stopping us from getting any farther. We couldn't climb over the top of the carousel either, as its circular roof was fitted into a recess in the cave ceiling.

We tried heaving the carousel around, but it didn't budge.

Lacey shook as she climbed on board and shone her flashlight over a red-eyed unicorn near the strange metal dividing wall.

Tiny red and yellow lights flickered on along the center column. With a cranking whir, the carousel, and the metal wall, began to rotate. Lacey cried out, rushing forward.

Ethan's shout echoed. "Get off!"

She was gone in an instant—around to the other side.

The carousel made a complete turn. And returned empty.

My heart hammered against my chest wall. The carousel made three more turns, but Lacey didn't come back.

"Lacey!" I cried out.

Ethan panted heavily. "Okay. Okay. So this thing works by jumping on board. I'll get her. Then you girls have got to go. I don't want anything happening to you."

"I'm coming with you." I didn't want to be left alone, even for a second.

We stepped on the carousel together, and once again, it began to turn.

Shadowy light closed over me as the carousel reached the other side and ground to a halt.

The lights were *on* on the other side. Someone *had* to be in the curving rock tunnel ahead.

Lacey sat on the floor below us, rubbing her ankle. "I panicked. I fell."

"Are you okay?" I said, jumping off the platform and kneeling next to her.

Ethan and I helped her to her feet. She winced as she placed weight on her right foot. "Yeah, I'll be okay."

"We'll help you back on," I told her, "and we'll get out of here." I glanced at Ethan. "Right? All of us. Lacey's going to need our help to get off the mountains now. And what if someone's down here?"

The carousel shuddered to a stop.

Ethan shook his head, looking frustrated. "We know Donovan can't be here. I want to see where this tunnel goes—just for a minute. Wait here."

"This is my fault," said Lacey in a small voice. "I say we all go and look, together."

I wanted to push them both back onto the carousel with my bare hands. But neither of them was budging. Maybe they thought I was weak. We'd come to find Aisha and we'd found proof of where she was, or at least, where she'd been. Now all we needed to find was *Aisha*. "Okay," I breathed. "But I'll hold you to that minute."

Ethan glanced down at Lacey's leg. "Can you walk?"

"Think so." She smiled tightly.

Lacey stepped gingerly forward on her hurt ankle. Slinging an arm around her, Ethan helped her walk. Sucking in a deep breath, I followed them. Together, we edged around the rock wall and peered around into a long corridor. It flowed steadily downward— the walls and ceiling almost perfectly round. Fluorescent lights ran along bare wiring along the length of the corridor, fixed at a high point in the wall. The lights sparked and buzzed, flashing on and off. Terror gripped me at the thought of those lights going out. Strange dark spaces, like open doorways, had been cut into the walls.

"The tunnel looks like the volcanic tubes sometimes created by flowing lava," Ethan mused. The stale air of the tunnel closed in around me. I didn't want to walk any farther into this place. The long corridor ahead seemed a trap.

But the sooner we looked around, the sooner we could leave. Stepping forward, I ducked my head around the first open space in the wall and looked inside. My heart squeezed tight in my chest.

It *was* a doorway. Inside the cavernous room stood an enormous kitchen. The wooden benches and chairs came up to my chest—a setting made for a giant. An antique bear and doll were seated on two of the ten chairs—the dolls much bigger than us. The bear was jointed at his legs and arms, and stiff. The doll had light-brown, waved hair, her head and chipped hands made of porcelain—or bisque, like the dolls my grandmother used to have. Beneath her lace collar, I saw a peek of a wooden body.

An oversized kettle sat in the center of the table. For a moment, I was glad the dolls' backs were turned to us. But that was crazy— the dolls couldn't *see* us.

Lacey grabbed my arm. Her fingernails dug into my arm. "This can't be real," she whispered.

Ethan stepped inside the room, snatching up a heavy meat cleaver that hung from underneath a cupboard. He turned and gestured for us to keep moving.

The next room consisted of two interconnected spaces, and seemed to be used for storage. One space held suitcases, drawers, and racks of dresses that were both enormous and girl-sized. Lace-up boots were arranged on the floor. The other space held nothing but a headless dummy holding a dusty, black antique dress.

Adjacent to the storage room were two metal-barred doors. The doors looked like those I'd seen crypts guarded behind in old churches. *Cells*, I thought, and felt the hysterical desire to laugh. *Twin cells*. Across from these were yet another door, this one unlocked. Ethan pushed it open. Fetid air seeped out—the airless, urine-soaked bathroom smell just like in subways. The room was tiled, with taps and a shower. Ethan closed the door quickly.

We rounded the next bend in the corridor—almost missing a natural crevice in the wall. The crevice was barely large enough for a human to pass through.

Lacey stiffened as we passed, flinging herself back against the wall. She opened her mouth either to scream or to tell us something, but was unable to do either.

Ethan and I peered inside. Ten huge beds were lined up in two rows. A giant Raggedy Ann doll occupied the bed nearest to us, and a wooden clown doll had been laid in the bed opposite—both of them had to be over eight feet in length. Smaller dolls with bright red cheeks occupied the beds farther in, but the room was so dark I couldn't see more. Apart from the beds, no pains had been taken to make this room look like a bedroom—the walls had been left as natural rock, the room smelling of moisture and damp moss.

I reached out to take Lacey's hand as we continued down the corridor. The sight of the creepy dolls would be even worse for her than it was for us.

The end of the tunnel branched into two uneven corridors—the left tunnel tapering into darkness. We headed right, and were deposited in another massive chamber. White-and-black linoleum tiled the floor. *Another* carousel stood pride of place in the center of the room, except this one had horses instead of monsters. It still amazed and baffled me that someone had even *built* all of this, had managed to get both carousels this deep in the earth.

Wall-to-floor shelving held harlequin dolls, wooden puzzles, games, hoops, monkeys riding unicycles, and dollhouses complete with tiny figurines. A library filled with old books stood on one side of the chamber—consisting of three eight-foot bookcases arranged in rows, with aisles in between. School desks were lined up in front of the library—ten of them just like the beds in the bedroom, so large they would dwarf a child.

A chandelier hung from the rock ceiling, but the lights weren't on. I guessed it was just decoration. All the lighting seemed to run off the same wiring.

A fireplace stood against a far wall, embers glowing. Its square, stone chimney soared upward—twenty feet or more to the ceiling.

"Finally, the missing chimney," said Ethan, exhaling. We were standing directly below the ballroom of the Fiveash house. "But still no Aisha," Lacey said, in a trembling voice. "This is crazy," Ethan said. "It's like the whole place was made for giant children. He ran his hands over his head, messing up his waves. Even here, in this terrible place, I had the sudden urge to run my fingers through them.

More than anything though, I just wanted out of there. I craved a shower—the slimy cave moisture clung to my skin. I stepped over to one of the huge wooden desks that were positioned near the library of books. The desk's lid creaked as I lifted it. The cavity was filled with pencil drawings. Carefully, I carried them out and onto the desktop. The drawings were childish—those massive balloon bodies and stick limbs that young children always seemed to draw. On one of the pages, a more mature hand had drawn birds and butterflies, and the child had tried to copy—the child's smudgy, lopsided creatures rising up the page.

I replaced the drawings, and then opened the desk beside me, expecting to find more of the same. But the drawings in this desk were exquisitely drawn—scenes of forests and dolls and horses. One of the pictures—a drawing of a young girl riding a horse— seemed to have been deliberately ripped.

"Either Donovan has multiple personalities or the drawings are by different people," I said slowly. I traced a finger over the heavy lines of the pictures.

Ethan came to look. Lacey stayed where she was, arms wrapped around her waist, shivering.

Bending, Ethan studied the ripped pieces of the drawing in the second desk. He scooped up the bits and assembled them on a desktop. The picture depicted a tiny red-cheeked girl riding a horse through sunlit clouds. Every muscle and sinew of the horse was expertly drawn, the horse's mane rippling. You could almost see the muscles working under the horse's flank and sense the horse reveling in its freedom. The child had her head back—her hair ribbon flying loose—far away in the wind. A name was penciled-in on the ribbon—Philomena.

Why would someone rip such an incredible drawing and keep the childish ones intact?

There was a mess of red paint in one corner of the drawing—maybe that was why.

I rubbed a finger over the waxy red stuff on the corner of the page. A faintly penciled *Aisha D.* revealed itself.

The blood in my veins slowed and froze.

It couldn't be. It couldn't—

"Oh my god," I gasped. "What if one of the dolls sleeping in those beds . . . is *not* a doll?"

Ethan looked straight through me, his eyes wide, hollow. Without a word, he turned and raced to the corridor.

"Lacey!" I gestured wildly to her. She still wasn't moving. "Come on."

She shook her head. "No. No way." Her fists were tightly clenched. "I can't go back there! Don't make me go there!" Her voice rose to a shriek.

I backed away. "It's okay, Lace. Stay here. We'll be back, okay? We'll be right back."

I turned and ran after Ethan, leaving Lacey alone.

8. WAKE ONCE AGAIN

Tomorrow morning, if God wants so,
you will wake once again.

—Brahms's Lullaby

When I caught up with Ethan, he was standing before a bed at the far end of the bedchamber. In the dim light, I only just made out a form under the blankets. I squeezed my eyes shut for a moment, trying to adjust to the darkness.

I moved inside the dark crevice. Cold and damp surrounded me. I forced my legs to keep going. I stepped past the massive Raggedy Ann and wooden clown figures that occupied the first of the beds. Farther in, five smaller dolls rested under their thin blankets. *Human-sized dolls*— with pallid faces and red-painted cheeks that looked like bruises in this light. Their arms were crisscrossed over their chests. All wore thin, yellowed nightgowns and ribbons in their hair. Only one didn't wear makeup—the girl in the bed next to the Raggedy doll, her blonde hair falling in tangled waves around a waxy complexion.

My heart clenched and thudded.

They were real. Not dolls. Not playthings.

Only the crazily oversized bed had made them seem doll-like before.

The smallest of them couldn't be more than five years old.

Someone—Donovan—was keeping these children down here. Revulsion coursed through my body. We had to get them all out of here—if any of them were still alive.

Ethan bent to touch a dark ponytail bound up in a reddish ribbon. A high ruffled collar hid her face from this angle. Delicately, he moved her chin so that he could see her face in full.

Aisha.

So strange, with the doll's makeup and slightly hollowed cheeks. But Aisha.

Ethan seemed to throw off the covers and scoop her up in one motion. Aisha's head flopped onto his shoulder, as if she really had been transformed into a doll.

He ran with her and I followed, terror drumming through me, a scream caught somewhere in the cage of my chest. Dim light from the corridor streaked across the Raggedy Ann doll's face. The light shifted slightly, making the doll's face seem like it turned a little. Of course it hadn't.

Did the doll's hand just twitch?

You're in shock, I told myself. Like Lacey. Just get out of here—breathe.

I fled and followed Ethan to the carousel with the monsters—the one we'd jumped onto when we'd come into this place. *The way out.*

Ethan laid Aisha carefully in one of the chariots. He turned back to me with wild eyes. "It won't turn, this damned thing won't turn!"

I wanted to ask if she was breathing. But I couldn't. Maybe Ethan was fooling himself and wanted to pretend she was okay. Stepping forward, I bent down to Aisha. A vein in her neck pulsed when I touched it.

She's alive.

I could scarcely believe she was there before me. Solid and whole.

"Go get Lacey," said Ethan between clenched teeth. "We need to get out. Now!"

I rushed away back down the corridor. Once we had Lacey, we could get out of this nightmare.

The room we'd left Lacey in was totally empty.

Overhead, something moved across the ceiling. Heart pounding, I slowly raised my eyes. A shadow—a shadow that shouldn't be there—slithered. A shadow that pierced and clung to me—to merely look at it was to take it inside of me, like a reflection on a still, dark lake.

I forced my eyes shut. I was losing it. Trauma was causing me to see and hear things. Finding Aisha alive—that was as shocking as finding her remains. My mind was spewing out bile.

The shadow was gone when I opened my eyes. But traces of the shadow remained inside me, suffocating and poisoning.

I took frantic steps to the kitchen and bathroom. They too, were empty. Lacey had vanished. I knew there was one more place to look—that deathly dark tunnel we'd skipped over earlier, the tunnel branching to the left.

I turned and nearly screamed. A blonde girl about my age was standing in front of me, pressed against the wall, her face so pale it was ashen. The girl who'd been in the bed next to the Raggedy Ann doll.

"Are you here to hurt me?" She trembled in her thin, knee-length nightgown.

"No," I said. "No. We're here to help."

The girl nodded. But she recoiled as I moved closer.

"It's all right. Just come with me." I attempted to smile, but I was sure it looked like more of a grimace.

She hesitated—then followed me to the carousel, stepping silently against the stone.

"I can't find Lacey," I told Ethan breathlessly. "She disappeared."

"What do you mean, *she disappeared*?" He straightened up. His eyes clicked to the girl. "Who're you?"

"Jess-uh-min," she answered, and then, brightening suddenly: "My father named me after the town of Jessamine in Kentucky. We were passing through there when I was born. A pretty name for a pretty girl, he said." Her expression darkened again. "I used to be prettier, though, before the bad thing." She tugged the collar of her nightgown across, exposing ugly dark gashes on her neck and shoulder.

My back stiffened. "Who did that to you?"

"The bad thing did it."

"What is the bad thing?" I wasn't sure if I wanted the answer.

Her eyes turned clouded. She covered the scars again. "Please don't ask."

"Okay," I breathed. There would be time to find out what happened to these girls later when the police investigated. Right now, we just had to get them all out of the mansion.

"She's coming with us," I said to Ethan.

Ethan didn't argue. "I still can't get this thing cranking. Maybe if we all get on it, it will kick-start. Like before."

The girl shook her head. "I'm quite sure you cannot start it."

He blew out a frustrated breath. "Do you know how I *can* get it going?"

The girl stared at Ethan as though he'd said something stupid. "You're asking completely the wrong question."

I tried jumping up on the platform next to Ethan and Aisha, but nothing happened.

"Get on," Ethan ordered the girl.

She shook her head. "It won't help, I'm afraid."

Ethan jumped to his feet. "There has to be a lever or switch, or something. He felt around the wall. The rough, rounded wall seemed not to have anything resembling a switch. I joined Ethan in searching the tunnel's surface.

"Maybe there's another way back to the house." Ethan eyed me desperately, and then turned to Jessamine. "Do you know if there's any other way out?"

She stepped backward. "You're planning on leaving me, aren't you?"

I shook my head. "You can trust us. We just don't have much time. We had a friend with us—a girl named Lacey."

Jessamine tilted her head. "Is that a doll?"

The question stunned me so much I nearly couldn't answer. "She's a real-life human being. And she's here—somewhere."

Jessamine raised her fair eyebrows. "There is no one else here. Of that I am quite certain. Except the Toys, of course," she added.

"Toys?" Ethan shot her an exasperated glance. "Look, tell us how Donovan gets in and out—is it the carousel, or somewhere else?"

She hesitated, threading her fingers together. "There is no coming and going here. There is only patience."

Ethan turned away as though he'd given up on her. I guessed she'd been here for a long time and traumatized in ways we couldn't begin to fathom. She spoke weirdly, with a very proper accent that half-sounded English, though I knew she'd been born in America.

"I'm going to look for myself." Jumping back on the carousel's platform, Ethan touched Aisha's shoulder. "Aish," he whispered, "I have to leave you here for a moment. I'm sorry. I'll be back as soon as I can."

"Oh, she won't hear you," Jessamine said calmly.

"Why not? Why won't she wake up?" I asked her.

"She's had her special tea. She'll sleep for hours."

Ethan's face lengthened as he stared down at Aisha. He turned to Jessamine. "Please—look after her. We'll be back. Cassie, come with me—two will be quicker than one."

Ethan and I raced to the first room—the kitchen. I comforted myself knowing we were searching for both another exit and also for Lacey.

Ethan placed both hands on a square metal object set against the wall. He pushed at it—a cover slid up. Sticking his head in, he tried to see upward. "It's the bottom end of that dumbwaiter thing."

I wished desperately that we might spirit ourselves upward inside of it. But it wasn't big enough for even a dog to travel in. Bits of chipped bark were scattered in the bottom tray. I guessed that Donovan sent logs for the fire as well as food down this way.

Kneeling, I checked the cupboards. A makeshift system of pipes wound from the sink to the floor. I wondered if the water came directly from a river. A wooden crate held empty cans of food.

Cupboards above the benches held a large selection of cans and packets of dried fruits.

For a moment I was hopeful that the next time Donovan came down to deliver food or collect the trash, we could overpower him—but then I thought of the dumbwaiter. Long periods of time might pass without him physically coming down here.

Ethan exhaled hard. "How stupid was I? That trash we dug up in the woods came from here. That was way too much garbage for one man to be putting out. I should have known that."

"None of us could have imagined this place," I said firmly. "We'd better keep looking."

We sprinted down to the large chamber with the chandelier, searching behind and under everything. We found nothing.

"Lacey!" I cried, no longer worried about staying quiet. "Lacey, where are you?"

We looked in the storeroom next. Curious, I opened the drawers there. Neatly folded inside were jeans and jumpers, a tiny pair of purple shorts, runners, and a cell phone. Aisha's Marilyn Monroe T-shirt sat on top of one pile.

Everything Aisha had come in here with was here in the drawers. The drawers probably held the possessions of all the girls.

"Let's check the bedroom." Ethan's neck muscles strained.

Curling my fingers tightly around my flashlight, I followed Ethan.

We squeezed through the crevice of the bedroom. The rest of the girls still slept—if they were sleeping at all, and not lifeless.

I shone my flashlight onto the Raggedy Ann doll. It was still. My fear had made me imagine crazy things when I was in the room before. Ethan trained his light onto the high ceiling, possibly hoping for some kind of escape hatch.

"The beds must have been built in here," whispered Ethan. "There's no way they could have been moved in here from outside—the entry isn't big enough."

Nothing down here made sense, I thought.

We checked beneath the beds and around the walls. A dark stain sat on the rotting linoleum floor beneath the last bed that we checked. I forced myself to look closely. Whatever the stain was, it was old.

We shone our flashlights around the room for one last look before we stepped toward the exit. Our beams flickered over the pasty faces of the girls. They stirred, rising one after the other to a sitting position—only three of them now that Aisha and Jessamine were no longer there, nightgowns loose around their bony bodies. Wide eyes stared out from thin faces, red makeup on their cheeks and lips—like a set of Russian nesting dolls.

The small child hugged a bear that was missing its head. She rubbed an eye as one of her long ponytails fell loose from its ribbon. "Did you come to play with us, too?"

An older one, about seventeen years old, put a finger to her mouth, long red hair spilling over her shoulders. "Philomena, they're new. They probably don't know yet."

The third girl just stared, the deep pits of her eyes void of emotion. Of Indian descent, her thick black hair hung around a pointed, darkly olive face.

In my peripheral vision, something *moved*.

Vomit hit the back of my throat as I turned.

The Raggedy Ann doll twitched and sat bolt upright in the bed. It twisted its head to the clown. With a sickening rattle, the wooden clown levitated from its resting place and settled against the exit— barring us from leaving.

"What the hell?" Ethan was shouting. "What's going on?"

The small girl bent her head. "He won't let you out unless you know the password. Sometimes Clown plays this game with us."

"To hell with this." Ethan charged at the clown. The clown held its ground, barely swaying from the impact of Ethan's shoulder.

Ethan picked himself to his feet and hurled himself in a rage at the clown again. The clown slanted backward, but sprung straight up again, like a punching toy.

"Don't hurt him," cried the small child. "Or he'll hurt us."

Ethan pulled his fist back, breathing heavily.

"What do we do?" I pleaded at the oldest girl.

Her wide eyes implored me, "If you don't guess the password, you'll never get through. The password is only ever a single word."

"This is crazy. Let us out!" I screamed the words out to the air itself.

"I'll drill a hole right through you if whoever's operating you doesn't move you." Ethan stared upward, above the clown. "Whoever you are, you're not that smart. When I find you, I'll beat you to a damned pulp."

Something primal chugged within my brain. *Survive.*

Password. Single word.

"Clown," I said quietly, "Is that the password? Clown?"

The clown figure swayed from left to right.

"That's a no?" I said. The desire to laugh bubbled up in my throat. I was going crazy. I had to stay calm. "What about . . . bed?"

It swayed again.

I racked my head for a password. It could be anything. Far off, in the kitchen, the kettle boiled and hissed.

"Is the password . . . tea?"

The clown moved grotesquely forward and backward in a *yes* motion. It slid across the floor with a heavy scraping sound, leaving the entry open.

My whole body trembled.

The girls each pulled a dress from their bedpost and pulled it on over their slips. Then they tugged old-fashioned lace-up boots onto their feet.

Ethan and I edged out of the room, looking repeatedly from the doll and clown—Ethan jabbing the clown with his fingers as he passed it.

We raced back to the carousel.

Jessamine sat stroking Aisha's hair, singing a lullaby. I knew the tune—it was the old Cradle Song my mother used to sing to me. But the words were different from the one I knew:

Good evening, good night,

With roses adorned,

With carnations covered,

Slip under the covers.

Tomorrow morning, if God wants so,

you will wake once again.

"Why is she still asleep?" Ethan rushed to Aisha's side.

Jessamine lifted her eyes to Ethan. "It's tea time, of course. I've given her a nice cup of tea. She woke feeling dreadful. I made her better." She wiggled a finger at a large cup of steaming tea just behind the chariot.

"Why," Ethan demanded, "did you give Aish more tea? What's in that stuff anyway?"

Jessamine tilted her head. "You guessed the password. You should have been clever enough to guess that it's tea time, too."

I tensed, icy fingers brushing my spine. How did Jessamine know what password I'd spoken? How did she even know what happened in the bedroom—was she playing games with us?

The three girls from the bedroom stepped up behind us.

"Why are they calling Angeline, *Aish*?" whispered the tiny girl to the tall red-haired one.

Jessamine jumped lightly to her feet. Then I noticed that she had changed into a knee-length dress with a dropped waist and faded ribbon posies around the bottom. Her stockings bore holes. "Let's all have a tea party. You two can dress properly, too. You'll find a variety of attire in the dressing room."

Confusion and anger rose inside me. "What? No. We are not going to dress nor have a tea party with you. We are going to *leave*. Now, do you know where our friend Lacey is? Have you been giving her cups of tea, too?"

She frowned. "I'm sure I don't know who you mean."

"Lacey came in here with us. She's my age but smaller, with

blonde hair and . . ." My voice trailed off as I watched Jessamine prance away, her dress swishing at her knees. The other three girls looked nervously over their shoulders at me, but quickly scurried after her.

"Jessamine," said Ethan darkly, "has no intention of escaping from here." He held Aisha's limp hand. "I don't know what Donovan's done to her—or any of the girls here—but he's warped in the head. I mean, what the hell *is* this place?"

"Don't you get it?" Cold settled in my whole body, like an invading fog. "It's an enormous dollhouse. And we're trapped in it."

9. TEA WITH JESSAMINE

Won't you have a tea with me?
A picnic lovely by the sea.
Won't you play a game with me?
Skip to my Lou
I'm coming for you.

P.

"I haven't introduced everyone to our guests." Jessamine, seated at the head of the table, let out a cooing sigh. "How rude of me."

Ethan and I exchanged a glance. We'd decided to play along for the moment. We had no choice. The carousel wouldn't budge, Lacey was missing, and we could find no other exit. So we had agreed to join Jessamine's "tea party."

"I guess it's best to start with the youngest first," Jessamine said, turning to the youngest girl. "They do get restless, you know. Well, this is our Philly—Philomena. She likes to draw flowers and princesses—and she rides tricycles at terrifying speeds along the hallways. You must watch out for her, or she'll send you flying."

Jessamine smiled brightly at Philomena. Philomena eyed us coyly, sucking her lips in. She looked like any other five year old who suddenly had the spotlight on her. Her honey-brown hair and wide brown eyes matched the photo of the girl I'd seen in the police photo, only that photo had been a year old.

Jessamine then turned her gaze to the olive-skinned girl, who handed out cracked plates to each of us, her deep-set eyes giving nothing away. She walked with a limp, her legs hidden under her long dress, and wore her black hair in braids on top of her head— her slim fingers clasped firmly together. She looked around fifteen or sixteen years old.

"Now this is Sophronia. She's our quiet one. She's a mute. She'll knit you a fine scarf, if you ask nicely. It does get chilly down here. She writes poetry in another language sometimes—she's from the Indian sub-continent, I believe."

Sophronia didn't look at us at all, even after she placed the food out—a spread of moldy bread and thin soup. Even the bear and doll that were seated at the table got a serving. The girls ate slowly, in petite spoonfuls. I shot Ethan a sideways glance. We pretended to eat the food, but didn't let a speck of it pass our mouths. Who knew what was in it?

"Of course," Jessamine continued, "missing from the dinner table is our Angeline—or, Aish—as per the odd pet name our visitors have for her." She gestured to Aisha, who was curled up on a plush chair in the corner of the room, where Ethan had deposited her. "She's a sleepy girl tonight. She's still finding her way around here, but she's an excellent artist and she has developed a great interest in the photographic books. She may say some quite odd things at times, but like all artists, she's prone to fancy."

It was weird hearing Jessamine talk about Aisha. And the girls didn't merely tolerate Jessamine—they seemed to allow her to *control* them

"And lastly, but certainly not the leastly, we have Missouri," said Jessamine. "She may seem too mature to be any fun, but she'll whip you at chess so you'd best have your wits about. She mostly likes to read, sometimes draw—though she's not as good as our Angeline, of course. It might be churlish to mention that she can be a fibber at times, but it's all in good fun and you just have to ignore her pranks when they get bothersome.

Missouri cast a furtive look my way then returned her eyes to her plate, carefully cutting the mold from the bread. She had bound her red hair up in a loose bun.

Mentally, I tried to remember the details from the police folder. Could the thirteen-year-old runaway be this girl? The runaway would have just turned seventeen, so the five-year time period since she vanished was a match. The girl in that photo had her shoulder-length strawberry-blonde hair streaked purple. If her hair color had deepened to red, this might be Molly. The full lips and steel-blue eyes were eerily similar.

Turning to me, Ethan mouthed the word "leastly" and pulled a puzzled expression. I nodded in acknowledgment. Jessamine spoke in such a weird way. And she actually viewed us as guests. I tried to imagine what my mother would say if she were here. Mom used the term "coping mechanism" a lot. Perhaps this whole act was Jessamine's coping mechanism. I couldn't imagine the horror of being trapped down here.

I wanted to find out for sure who they all were, but it was impossible to ask them anything at this crazy tea party. Missouri and Philomena's accents sounded more English than Australian to my ear—but that could be because they'd been forced to live in isolation with crazy Jessamine all this time. Sophronia hadn't spoken a word—Jessamine had called her mute.

If Missouri was really the girl who'd run away five years ago—Molly Parkes—then someone had made her take another name. I looked closely at the smallest girl, Philomena. It was hard to tell, but she could be the three-year-old who had vanished at a family picnic—Frances Allanzi. Maybe *none* of the girls' names were real.

"Why aren't you eating, Jessamine?" Ethan glared at her pointedly.

"I'm the host," replied Jessamine. "My priority tonight is to make sure all my friends and guests are comfortable. But forgive me. I haven't introduced myself, not properly. Of course, you know my name already—Jessamine. I believe in patience as a virtue, and I do like to practice good manners. I'm partial to dancing and clever stories—and you must tell me all about yourselves when you've had ample time to rest, perhaps in a day or two."

My stomach sank when Jessamine said *a day or two*. There was no way we were staying another hour, let alone *days*, not if I could help it.

The girls ate every scrap of their dinner. It was hardly enough for a night's meal, but I guessed they had to ration out the food Donovan sent down here.

Jessamine beamed around the table benevolently. "We must now thank our Provider for this meal."

The girls bent their heads and murmured. "Thanks to The Provider."

"Wait—who exactly is this Provider?" Ethan's eyes scanned the table of girls. "You mean that Donovan guy?"

"Of course not." Jessamine laughed, as if the suggestion were a silly one. "The Provider gives us our food and he supplies our needs."

"Where can I find him?" Ethan's eyes were intent, his shoulders straightening against the back of the chair.

She shook her head. "Oh, you cannot find him. He can only come to you." She smiled. "But I've told you as much as you need to know. I realize you are guests and can't be expected to know the rules here. But please, it would border on rudeness for you to enquire further."

I looked at Ethan and shook my head. He plunged into a sullen silence.

She tilted her head, seeming satisfied that he wasn't going to ask her more questions. "I would be indeed remiss if I didn't also introduce our friends. We have Clown and Raggedy—whom you met in the bedchamber. And Bear and Clara, who of course are here joining us for supper. You must mind your manners about them, as they're good fun, but they won't take any nonsense."

I stared briefly at the bear and doll she indicated. Jessamine blinked at me, as though expecting me to wave my hand in greeting or acknowledge them in some other way. But I refused. They might be over eight feet tall, but they were a stuffed bear and a ceramic doll.

Fortunately, Jessamine let it go. "And now . . . I think we should give our guests a display of our best dancing."

Immediately, the two oldest girls, the silent Sophronia and the tall red-haired Missouri, jumped to their feet and cleaned up the dinner plates, depositing them in the sink.

Jessamine fixed intent blue eyes on Ethan and me. "And you two must dress for the occasion. You'll find appropriate clothing in the dressing chamber. Missouri can show you the way."

Ethan gaped at her. "No way. Sorry, but we're not watching your dance. You've already wasted enough of our time with your games."

Jessamine's smile didn't falter as she stood up. "I know you must be very tired after your journey," she said stiffly. "But good manners are *very* important here." Without another word, she left the room.

Sophronia followed obediently after her.

Missouri turned to us. "Please. If you don't do as she wishes, it will only get worse. For all of us." Her voice was as taut as the skin of her high cheekbones—words half-whispered, half-urgent, and full of dark things I didn't want to think about. I couldn't guess what she'd been through.

"Missouri," I pleaded, "who controls the dolls—the man you all call The Provider? Tell us and we can help you."

"Please don't ask questions." She shook her head, seeming on the verge of tears.

"Then tell me—who is Jessamine? And what is this place?"

"I can't tell you any of that." Her voice was edged with warning.

"Please." My voice cracked. I was growing desperate. "We have a friend with us—Lacey. She's missing here somewhere. We need to find her. Do you know where she could have—?"

"Jessamine's waiting in the ballroom." Taking the youngest girl's hand, she left before I could say another word.

Ethan and I eyed each other.

"We have to play along, Ethan," I said. My voice sounded foreign, even to me. "We have no choice."

Sighing heavily, he nodded. Together, we supported Aisha between us, and helped her down to what Jessamine and the girls called the ballroom. Ethan sat with her on the daybed.

A fire had been started in the hearth, red flames leaping. Already, Missouri had changed: her long hair was held back with a matching pink hairband. The dress was slightly too short for her long frame, reaching mid-calf.

Sophronia rushed to put on a gramophone record, which played some classical music I didn't recognize. The tune screeched through the air, the needle skipping and sputtering. I would have rather listened to nails across a chalkboard.

Jessamine clapped while the girls twirled about the room in some kind of waltz that didn't require partners. Philomena seemed to enjoy it, sashaying in her lemon dress.

"It's 'Hotel California,'" Ethan remarked.

"It's the what?" I said.

"Never mind. Just some old song."

Sophronia didn't dance like the rest—she seemed to hop from one foot to the other in a lopsided way—almost hobbling. Jessamine danced next. She moved around the dance floor expertly. Philomena watched her in awe.

I excused myself, saying I needed to go to the bathroom. I needed a chance to look for Lacey.

Jessamine scowled but waved me away.

I ran past the bedchamber, half expecting Clown or Raggedy or Clara to leap out at me—and dashed inside the bathroom.

The freezing air bouncing off the tiles made the bathroom a refrigerator. At least the cold air made the smell tolerable. I suspected that if the room had been warm, you'd gag coming in.

I inspected every wall, every floor tile—even pressing every tile—hoping for something to happen. Lacey had to have gone somewhere. Perhaps she'd leaned against a secret door or fallen down a trapdoor. Many of the tiles were cracked and chipped, and a few were loose, but there was nothing of interest. I put my ear to the floor—it sounded like water rushing underneath—broken pipes maybe.

The showers had only one tap each. I turned one of them on—icy water spurted from the wide nozzle. There wasn't any hot water in the bathroom at all. A chill went through me. The girls had to be washing themselves in this freezing water.

Threadbare towels had been washed and wrung out and hung over a dressing screen. A single mirror hung above a wooden dresser, with tiny light bulbs running along the top of it. Ethan and I had already checked the dresser. I gripped one side of the mirror and tried to see if it could be removed. It was stuck fast to the wall. Another dead end.

When I returned to the ballroom, the girls were at the desks, drawing. Jessamine had fallen asleep in a rocking chair. Rising from the daybed, Ethan whispered to me that he was going to check the other tunnel—the dark one. I closed my eyes in a silent *yes*, relieved I didn't have to go back down there. Sophronia raised dark eyes to me, then quickly looked away. Only the small girl—Philomena—stared openly at me. Missouri scrawled quickly on her drawing paper. She held the piece of paper up to me. It said, *Sit down. Don't Speak. Draw*.

Holding Missouri's tense gaze, I dropped onto a desk seat. I'd use the time to think until I figured out our next move.

I took out some paper and pencils from beneath the desk's lid. If Ethan didn't find a way out in the tunnel, we'd have to find another way. I drew a quick sketch of the underground area. It was roughly a rectangle in shape—mostly just one long corridor, with hollowed-out rooms—a kitchen, a bathroom, a storeroom, and a ballroom—leading off it. Carousels stood at either end—at the entry and in the ballroom.

Somewhere, we must have missed something. There had be another way out. Either Lacey had found it or she was still in the tunnels. Either way, there must be a hidden corner we hadn't yet found.

The picture of the horse and child that Aisha had drawn entered my mind. On the ribbon had been a name—Philomena. I understood the drawing now. The drawing meant escape. It had obviously angered someone enough that they had ripped it in pieces. Ethan returned less than ten minutes later, shaking his head. "It dead ends in a wall. Nothing there."

Jessamine's eyes snapped open. She glared at Ethan.

"What are you doing?"

Ethan shrugged. "Stretching my legs."

"You would've had the opportunity to stretch your legs had you joined in the dance. Sit down."

Ethan sprawled his lanky body on the daybed beside Aisha.

"You must sit at a desk unless I tell you otherwise." Jessamine's tone was strident. "I think you and our other guest are over-excited."

As though Jessamine had given some kind of signal, Sophronia headed out from the room—returning within minutes with a trolley of steaming tea.

As Sophronia passed me with the trolley, she furtively snatched up the map I'd drawn, screwing it into a small ball in her fist. I was about to protest, but Missouri shot me a tense look, glancing sideways at Jessamine. What was so terrifying about Jessamine that the girls would do anything to appease her?

"It's been a most pleasant day." Once again, Jessamine's mood seemed to shift, as though controlled by inner tides. "But the time has come for sleep to refresh ourselves for the coming day."

I startled. They were all going to bed? I tried to calculate how long we'd been here. It had been early morning when we first found the place, and surely not more than three hours had passed since then. My watch refused to work and it was still stuck on 7:12 am.

Jessamine eyed Ethan reservedly. "It wouldn't be proper for a boy to retire to the same bedroom as the ladies. I trust you won't mind if you stay here in the ballroom?"

"I'm staying with Ethan," I said quickly. "And Aisha—Angeline—will sleep with us, too. We'll all sleep out here."

"I'm afraid that won't do." Jessamine smiled thinly. "The Toys won't allow it either."

"We're not sleeping in there with that clown thing," said Ethan in a harsh tone. "Get that straight. We'll stay out here—I hope that won't offend anyone."

Jessamine sniffed, turning her face away. "It's not the done thing—but very well. I'm too tired to debate. But I must have Angeline."

He stood. "She stays with me. And her name is *Aisha*."

"Boys are so insolent," said Jessamine. "It's a great shame you found your way here."

"What is this place?" he railed. "Why are you all being kept here? Let us help you—we can all get out of here!"

Missouri shook her head slightly at Ethan and me.

Jessamine folded her arms and walked about in a slow circle. "I don't like your tone."

Immediately, as one, the girls backed away, Missouri cradling Philomena under her arm.

Jessamine flung a hand in the air, her expression light once again. "Silly me, I'm forgetting that you're just guests, and you can't be expected to know how to behave. Those who come here need instruction—otherwise they wouldn't have come."

"What does *that* mean?" Ethan stared at her.

"You need *lessons*. When Missouri first came here, she was like a wild animal in a cage. But look at her now!" She gave a satisfied nod. "I'll honor your requests. You may stay in the ballroom tonight. Angeline may stay with you—she's had a frightfully good sleep after all, and she may need to eat her dinner and such. But you mustn't make a good deal of noise, for our girls must have their rest."

The muscles in Ethan's jaw and neck grew taut, but he bowed his head.

I sighed in relief that he didn't challenge her again—we weren't going to get anywhere with Jessamine. We needed time alone to keep looking for a way out.

Missouri and Sophronia trailed Jessamine out of the room. Little Philomena curtsied to us before she left. I was grateful not to have to sleep in that creepy bedroom.

Silence fell, except for the maddening ticking of the grandfather clock—I hadn't noticed the sound before. The clock claimed it was just after eight in the evening. There was no way that was the real time.

Aisha murmured in her sleep but didn't fully wake.

Ethan straightened up next to her. "We need to find out how those Toys are operated. Someone must be watching everything that happens down here."

I shuddered. "I haven't seen any cameras."

"Hidden cameras can be very small. Hidden in the toys maybe."

Ethan and I exchanged glances. Together, we moved to the massive shelves of toys. Grabbing anything with a face, we poked at eyes and yanked heads off. I squeezed the soft bellies of the stuffed toys, looking for anything hard that could be a camera or a microphone.

We found nothing. Behind us, Aisha moaned. She half-rose, rubbing her forehead with one hand. Ethan rushed to her side. Her eyes widened at the sight of him, her lower lip trembling.

"Aisha," Ethan said. "Don't worry. We're going to get you out of here."

She gripped his arm, and then stared up at me. "How?" she whispered. "How did you get here?"

I knelt next to her. "We found the way in." I reached to squeeze her hand. "I can't believe we found you."

"You've been asleep for hours," said Ethan. "I've been out of my head with worry."

Aisha swayed slightly, disoriented. "I woke on the carousel. Jessamine gave me tea. I didn't know what had happened . . . ."

Ethan helped her to sit up properly. "We're with you now."

"Are the police here?" She stared past us, to the hallway.

"The police don't know we're here," I told her. "No one does. But they will," I said, with slightly more force, as if I could help myself believe it.

Aisha's eyes grew moist. "Not even Lacey?"

Ethan opened his mouth and shut it.

"Lacey came with us," I said slowly. "She's down here too— somewhere."

Aisha bent her face down onto Ethan's head. "If no one knows you're here . . . then it's hopeless."

"My tent is still out on the mountains." Ethan gave a firm nod. "Lacey said her dad was sending out some kind of police taskforce to find me. They'll find the tent and track us here."

He sounded so certain, and I desperately wanted to believe him. I pulled chocolate and muesli bars from my pocket. "Dinner," I said.

Aisha smiled grimly and took the food. She ate everything, especially savoring the chocolate.

We told her about the rescue effort, how hard everyone was searching for her, and how her family was doing—leaving out the part about her brother beating up Ethan. And I told her how much everyone at school had missed her. She listened like she was hearing tales from a past life, even though she'd been missing just over two weeks. She looked different, too. The peachy conch-shell complexion was replaced with a sallowness, and she was already thinner. "We looked everywhere we could."

"What happened to Lacey?" she asked finally.

"I don't know." I eyed the dark ceiling. "The last time I saw her, she was here in this room. But then she just . . . disappeared."

Pain entered Aisha's eyes. "Disappeared?"

"We looked *everywhere*. But we can't find her. Maybe there's a hidden room . . . ?"

Aisha shook her head, looking troubled. "Jessamine talks about the *Toy Box*—a place for bad Toys. It's somewhere down the tunnel across from the ballroom."

Ethan straightened. "I looked down there—I didn't find anything."

"There's some way in," she said. "I know that Missouri knows how."

We sat in silence for a moment, with the grandfather clock marking time—only not the right time.

Ethan took her hands. "What happened? I mean, what happened when you went missing in the forest?"

Aisha's forehead tightened. "I don't know. I only remember a hit to my head—and the next I knew I was being dragged along a long, long black tunnel. I thought . . . I thought I was dead. I was so . . . groggy. Then I was on the carousel. And then I was here."

"We walked that tunnel," said Ethan darkly. "I'm going to kill Donovan for dragging you down here."

I couldn't help but stare at Ethan. He *knew* Donovan couldn't have kidnapped Aisha. Donovan had a rock-solid alibi. Who else could have dragged Aisha down here? One of the girls? No. Aisha was tall and athletic. A frail girl couldn't have lifted her down into the cave and then dragged her all that way.

Still, Ethan persisted. "What does Donovan do down here?" Ethan said. "Has he hurt you?"

Aisha closed her eyes, resting her head against the cushion. "Donovan's only been down here once since I've been here—to fix a broken tap. I haven't seen him apart from that."

"Tell us about *here*," I asked her. "I don't understand any of it."

"I don't understand it either," Aisha said helplessly, looking as though she might cry. "Every day we get up and do what Jessamine tells us to do. We drink the tea and we sleep a lot. And there's never enough to eat. It drives me crazy trying to imagine why we're being kept down here."

Her voice broke and grew dry. I went to fetch her a cup of water. Thoughts stormed my head. Who was Jessamine to have command of the girls? Could Donovan have been using a false alibi?

And would the police really find us, as Ethan had promised they would?

Or were we on our own?

10. ON A WHIM, ON A WISH

One, two, buckle my shoe
Three, four, bolt the door
Five, six, a bag of tricks
Seven, eight, it's already too late.

—P.

The echoing gongs of the clock crashed through the air.

I realized I'd been dreaming—of dolls and suffocating underground passages and growls and the bloodcurdling screams of an unseen owl.

I woke into a worse nightmare.

I was still in the underground. Panic rose inside me. Why hadn't we turned back when we'd found the secret cave? We'd found Aisha—alive—but we hadn't managed to save her. We were stuck now, just like her. And Lacey was gone.

The clock's hands said midnight.

I stood awkwardly, stiffly. Sleeping in the chair—big as it was—

hadn't been comfortable for my back and neck. The heat of the fire had seeped away and an intense chill had ushered in.

Aisha slept with her head on Ethan's lap—he sat with his head back, also sleeping. The lights were still on. I guessed the lights stayed on all the time.

My muscles tightened. Something heavy scraped along the passageway.

I concealed myself behind a rocky column at the entrance of the chamber. My view of the passage was hampered, but at least I couldn't easily be seen.

Jessamine, clad in her nightgown, stepped down the passage, holding a lamp out in front of her. I stifled a scream as I caught sight of what walked behind her. The doll and clown moved side by side—the doll's legs plodding heavily and the clown dragging along on its wooden base.

The trio continued, turning to walk down the unlit passage and disappeared from view.

I pressed my back against the rock, trying to breathe through a feeling of suffocation. Was I losing my mind? Had I already lost it? It was just a nightmare—and soon I'd wake up and the nightmare would end.

Another dark figure ran tentatively along the corridor in a nightdress.

Missouri.

Was she heading into the tunnel, too? I remained still.

But she came into the ballroom instead.

I stepped out from my hiding place. "Missouri?"

She jumped. "I have to talk with you," she said, her voice low and rushed. "I had to wait until Jessamine was gone."

"Where is she going?" I asked her, my breath tight in my chest.

"I don't know where she goes, not exactly, but she does the same walk with the Toys every night at midnight." She glanced toward the dark tunnel.

"Missouri isn't your real name, is it?"

Missouri shook her head.

"You're Molly Parkes. You were the thirteen-year-old runaway . . . ."

"Yes."

My stomach dropped. That was five years ago. "You've been here all that time . . . ."

"I didn't even know what year it was, until Aisha came. Sophronia has been here maybe three years, and Philly—almost a year. But Philly was only three years old then, and didn't know the year or date."

"Who is Sophronia?"

"I don't know. She doesn't speak."

"I think Philomena's real name is Frances."

"Yes. She might be four by now—or five. She didn't know what day her birthday was." She blanched. "But you must never, ever call us by our real names. Don't even think of us in terms of who we really are. You need to trust me on that."

"I understand."

She crossed her arms. "Why are you here? There's never been more than one at a time brought in before."

"We weren't brought in. We found our own way in. We were looking for Aisha—Angeline."

Her eyes widened. "Does anyone know where you are?"

I didn't know whether to say yes or no. Telling her that no one knew we were here seemed a bad idea.

"I think so," I said carefully. "Police will be looking for us right now. We have a tent out in the woods. They'll find the tent soon, and track us here."

Missouri's eyes sparked with hope. "I had no hope of rescue, none at all—until you came along."

Questions sharpened in my mind. "Why won't the carousel work—the one that blocks the way out of here?"

"Have you seen how the other carousel works?" she said bitterly. "It works on a whim, on a wish."

I didn't understand. But I sensed there was nothing further she could tell me about the carousel.

"What about Jessamine? *Who* is she? And those horrible marks on her neck and shoulder—who did that to her?"

"Jessamine isn't who she seems," Missouri said darkly.

"What's her real name?"

"Jessamine *is* her real name. I've seen it engraved on her locket."

"Her locket?" I shook my head. "I haven't seen a locket."

"She keeps it hidden for the most part. I know the locket is painful for her—it reminds her of who she used to be."

Behind me, someone stirred. Ethan.

I turned back to Missouri. "Who's The Provider? Is it Donovan?"

She shook her head. "I've only seen him a few times. The first time was not long after I came here, just after…." She trailed off, her face draining of color.

"What happened?" I asked.

"I don't want to talk about it," she said quietly. Her face went tight with fear, and she reached out and grabbed my wrists. "Listen to me. If you hear voices, or something that sounds like voices— don't give in to them. No matter what they tell you." She leveled her gaze at me. "Do you understand?"

"Voices? What do you mean? Is someone . . . trying to scare us?"

"No." She withdrew her hands. "The voices are real. Trust me, they're real."

I touched her arm. "Why?" My throat was thick. "Why are you here? Why are any of us here?"

"I only know small pieces of the whole. I suspect The First One knows everything. If you want to know the answers to your questions, you'd have to find out all she knows."

"The First One? You mean the girl who was brought in here first? Is that Jessamine?" I asked.

"Yes, but she's not Jessamine. The First One isn't here any more."

"Then how can I find out anything?" I cried desperately.

"I don't know. I've only seen her briefly. I've tried to find anything I can of hers—writings or drawings. But I've never found anything." She angled her head toward the corridor. "I can't stay. If Jessamine catches me, there'll be trouble for all of us."

"How do we get into that place called the Toy Box?" I said, a last-minute plea, remembering what Aisha had said.

She shook her head. "You don't want to go in there. I won't tell you how." Turning, she fled down the passage—her white face turning back to check if she was being followed.

Minutes later, the sound of wood dragging on rock returned. Jessamine was on her way.

I didn't sleep the rest of the night—the grandfather clock ticking off each second.

In the morning, the girls lined up in the bathroom, cleaning off the red cheeks and lips from the day before and reapplying them. Sophronia bent to apply red circles to Philomena's cheeks.

I splashed my face quickly at the basin and dried it with one of the thin, scratchy towels.

Breakfast was lumpy porridge, steamed in a huge cooking pot out in the kitchen. Sophronia tried to fix it as best she could—

frowning with the effort of pushing the spoon through the mixture.

Sophronia and Missouri served the porridge. Ethan and I put our hands up to refuse a plate, but we were given plates anyway. Raggedy and Clara sat at the table this morning, and were also served porridge.

Evil-looking black things spotted the porridge—dead bugs. The girls casually picked the bugs out and put them on the table. Aisha flicked a bug from her spoon. She briefly looked up at Ethan and me with a look of shame—as though to say, *this is how I live now.*

Ethan and I pretended to eat.

After breakfast, Jessamine announced it was time to sketch. She instructed that the guests were to join everyone else. Without having eaten, my stomach ached. Raggedy and Clara walked behind us as we headed down the corridor, their plodding steps making my skin crawl.

"We need to get into the Toy Box," I whispered to Ethan. I closed my mind to all thought of the darkness that was surely at the end of that tunnel. It was the only possible place that Lacey could be.

He moved his head close to mine. "I was thinking the same thing. This place might work on some kind of grid. *Something's* operating those toys. Maybe that's where the control box is."

Aisha's eyes narrowed slightly. "What are you two whispering about?"

Ethan kept his voice low. "We want to get to that place you called the Toy Box. Any clue?"

She inhaled sharply. "You have to do something really terrible to get put in there." Turning slightly, she glanced back at the Toys behind us.

Ethan drew his brow down, a fierce light in his eyes. "I'm prepared to do something really terrible."

In the ballroom, the girls busied themselves getting paper and pencils from their desks. I sat at a spare desk, pulling out paper and pencils, too. Aisha sketched mechanically, raising her eyes every now and again to Ethan, as though she wanted to reassure herself he was really there. She risked a quick, thin smile in my direction—but her expression was guarded.

Philomena drew the fuzzy outline of a girl with strange black hollows for eyes. Missouri's expression grew tense when she noticed what Philomena was drawing. Reaching out her hand, Missouri turned the page over. Quickly, she drew a family: parents, a baby boy, and two girls. The sketch had the family surrounding the smallest girl, stretching their arms out to her. I guessed Missouri was trying to take Philomena's mind off whatever terrible picture she'd been making before. The little girl ran a finger over the sketched figures, giving a small smile.

Jessamine stormed forward, snatching the drawing of the family away. She tore the paper to shreds, letting the pieces fall to the ground. "I *told* you to stop drawing those awful pictures!" She whirled around to face the rest of us, eyes blazing with fury. "You are to put down your pencils. You will no longer be allowed to sketch if you insist upon drawing things that serve no good purpose. You will spend the next hour on other pursuits. Be sure to choose wisely."

Sophronia tucked her drawing away, but not before I'd seen the giant eye she'd drawn—evil and reptilian.

Philomena jumped onto the carousel. Automatically, the carousel began turning. With her headless bear tucked under one arm, she rode a pink and white horse with a missing eye. Restless, she climbed from that horse onto a royal blue one. The old Greensleeves tune came mournfully from the speakers underneath the carousel roof.

"Philomena!" Jessamine called. "You know no one is allowed on that horse."

Chastened, the little girl jumped down and sat on the edge of the platform dejectedly.

The blue horse was different than the others—the only one that had a jeweled saddle and an ornate crest of carved cherubs. Like the others, the tail was made of real horsehair, but the tail on the royal blue horse seemed plusher—as though great care had been taken with choosing it.

It was hard watching this carousel move so freely when the one that led out wouldn't budge.

Jessamine sat watching the platform spin, her eyes growing glazed and distant. Within minutes, she was asleep.

Aisha looked across at Ethan and me, her eyes widening in silent question.

The three of us stood and stepped away from our desks. Missouri caught my eye over the top of her book, desperately shaking her head. But I couldn't stay in the ballroom. Turning, I followed the others.

Ethan and I pulled out the flashlights we still had in our pockets. My legs trembled as we stepped into the tunnel that led to the Toy Box. Black air closed over me. My heart pumped crazily against my ribs. I stopped pretending to myself that I was searching the cave and kept my gaze in Ethan's direction, reassuring myself that he was there with me. That familiar feeling of dread that I always felt in darkness stole all reason from me.

I tried to swallow the lump in my throat. "Missouri told me that if we hear voices, we're not to listen to them."

Aisha nodded. "She told me that, too."

Ethan twisted his mouth wryly. "Missouri's probably half-nuts. Anyone would get that way in this place."

We hadn't gone four yards when towering figures moved out from the black air. And someone walked in between them. Raggedy, Clara, and Jessamine stepped into view. I stopped, stunned. There must be a hidden passage from the ballroom into the tunnel.

So there were secret places where Lacey might be hiding, or stuck.

Jessamine's face was a cold mask. "*What* do you think you're doing?"

Ethan's fists clenched in anger. "None of your damned business."

"Ethan," I hushed him quickly. "We were just taking a walk," I said from between my teeth. "You said we could do as we wished."

"But this is out of bounds. You must know that by now. You are not to go near the Toy Box—do you understand?"

"Why? What's in there?" Ethan demanded.

For a second, a smile flitted across her face. "Nightmares and dreams," she answered.

The Toys moved out from behind her and advanced on us.

Jessamine held up a hand and the Toys stopped in their tracks. She smiled brightly. "But perhaps you're looking for your friend. And in that case I must give you some understanding"—her eyelashes fluttered downward—"for we should not leave those we love alone and lost."

The girl was seriously unhinged.

"And in that case, you'll be pleased to know I have good news." She clapped her hands. "Your friend is with The Provider!" Jessamine searched our faces for reactions. "She's having a nice visit, and she'll be back with you later today."

"What do you mean, *she's with The Provider*?" Ethan burst out. "If he hurts Lacey—"

"Why ever would he hurt your friend?" Jessamine interrupted. "He's not like that at all."

"Well, who hurt *you*?" I said. "Who made those marks on your shoulder?"

"I told you—it was the bad thing. I don't wish to discuss it."

"Maybe you *should* discuss it. Because something very wrong is happening here but no one wants to talk about it!" Frustration boiled inside me.

"There is no need to talk about the past," Jessamine said firmly. "Refixerating what I was saying before, your friend will be brought back here quite soon. You and the boy need to prepare for your friend's return."

I guessed she meant to say, *reiterating*.

"What do you mean, *we need to prepare*?" I crossed my arms.

"She'll be our guest of honor, silly. All of you must dress for the occasion." She glanced meaningfully at Ethan and me.

"We're not changing clothes," Ethan told her.

"Then you won't see her."

I thought fast. "Will The Provider be bringing Lacey down here himself?"

"Of course," said Jessamine. "She won't come unescorted."

"Okay." I nodded. "We'll dress in whatever you want. But we want to be there when he comes down here—it's a very special occasion after all."

"It's all settled then." Looking pleased with herself, Jessamine gestured toward the corridor. "Go and change. Your clothes are waiting."

"Waiting?" Ethan echoed.

"Of course," she replied. "Everything here's been waiting for you—and if you'd just pay attention, you would see that."

He opened his mouth wide as though to unleash a barrage of words, but then turned his head away.

"Not you, Angeline," called Jessamine. "You don't need to go with them. Get back to the ballroom please."

Aisha hesitated, shooting Ethan and me an uncertain glance, then headed off in the opposite direction.

"Good thinking," said Ethan under his breath. "We need to talk to The Provider—whoever he is. We need to find a way to convince him to let us out of here."

In the dressing chamber, a dress had been laid out over the back of the chair—the dress kind of a sepia-orange in color. And a gray jacket and pants were folded on the seat—I guessed those were for Ethan.

Picking up the gown, I moved to a corner of the room. Jessamine hadn't seemed to realize she'd just asked a girl and boy to dress in front of each other.

Ethan snatched up the gray clothing. "This is insane." But he turned to face the wall to allow me to change.

I unbuckled my jeans and stepped out of them, then peeled off my jacket and T-shirt. A slip hung beside the gown—which looked exactly like the nightgowns the girls wore—and I guessed I was meant to put it on first.

I pulled the slip on—it was too tight—but there wasn't another one there to try. The gown was stiff and cumbersome as I wriggled into it. It was as constricting and uncomfortable as the slip. I attempted to lace the gown behind my back.

Ethan was dressed already. He looked a different person in the jacket and waistcoat. For the first time since we'd entered the Dollhouse, a grin spread across his face. Taking my shoulder, he turned me around and laced the back of my dress. I could scarcely breathe in the strangulating clothes.

Jessamine appeared at the door, her expression approving. She held out the red face paint to me. "You must look your best."

I knew it was useless to argue. Taking the makeup, I moved to the gilt-edged mirror on the wall. I stuck a finger in the paint and applied it in a circular motion on my cheeks, and then rubbed some on my lips. The paint tasted waxy and old. I now resembled the other girls. I looked ridiculous. Ribbons had been laid out on the dresser below the mirror, along with a huge wooden hairbrush. I dragged the brush through my tangled brown hair, plaiting it on both sides and then fixing the plaits at the top of my head with the ribbons.

Already, I barely recognized myself.

"Don't worry," Ethan whispered. "It's only for an hour or so. Then you'll be back to being you—beautiful without makeup."

I glanced at him in surprise, my stomach knotting at the unexpected compliment. But he was already looking past me to Jessamine, his face set in a defiant expression.

We followed the waiting Jessamine to the ballroom.

Aisha and the girls stared in open-mouthed surprise when Ethan and I entered the room.

"Announcing Calliope and Evander," said Jessamine to everyone.

Philomena giggled. "Cal-eye-oh-pee."

"Why did you call us by those loopy names?" Ethan said, frowning at Jessamine. "I'm Ethan. This is Cassie."

Jessamine shot him a warning look. "Evander is Greek for good man. There is hope for you, however dim. And it is important to have such a name to live up to—otherwise you might well turn to darker past-times." She paused, staring at me. "Calliope, I could not see who you *really* were before you fixed your face and clothing. But I see you now. You are Calliope. Calliope, of course, was born of the pool of Mnemosyne. Do you know Mnemosyne and the myths? My governess taught me them all. The Greek myths are just follies, but it is important to have a well-rounded education."

I shook my head. "What or who is nee-*mos*-uh-nee?"

"Mnemosyne is a deep spring within Hades. If you drink from its water, you will remember everything as you go to the next life.

You must never drink from it, for surely it is a torture to remember such things." Her eyes clouded and she gazed at me for an extended time, as though she didn't think the myths were follies at all.

I glanced at Ethan. Jessamine was completely around the twist.

Jessamine clapped her hands and announced that we were to begin dance practice now—to prepare for Lacey's return.

Ethan and I were to complete the first waltz. Jessamine had us bow and curtsey to each other, and then do a kind of skipping motion along the width of the floor, while holding hands. I was sure this wasn't a real waltz and that Jessamine was just making it up as she went along.

"Can't wait to pound The Provider's head into the wall as soon as he steps foot in here," Ethan whispered into my ear.

"I'll be right beside you," I said fiercely.

Ethan raised a lopsided eyebrow at me. "Go, Girl Wonder."

He held my hand as I spun out and in again, melting against the hard frame of his body. My body began to heat up. Being so close had felt comfortable and sweet at first.

But now . . .

Aisha's face tightened as we waltzed past her. She drummed her fingers on the armchair rest as she watched. I moved away from Ethan, keeping him at arm's length.

Jessamine clapped her hands for the waltz to end, and I sat with a thudding heart, keeping my face angled away from Aisha.

Ethan didn't get to sit down. Jessamine declared that each girl was to waltz with him.

Sophronia leaned heavily on Ethan, dancing awkwardly for their waltz. Something seemed wrong with her body, as though her spine was bent or one leg was longer than the other.

Missouri blushed when Ethan took her hand to lead her around the dance floor. If she'd only just turned thirteen when she came here—she had likely never even been kissed. I'd only kissed one boy—a neighbor back in Miami—a cute Puerto Rican boy who I later found out had made a mission of kissing every girl over the age of twelve in our neighborhood.

Ethan bent down to waltz with the tiny Philomena next. She giggled through the entire dance, staring up at Ethan as though he were something magical.

Aisha's turn was last. Everyone stared as Ethan offered her his hand. Aisha pulled him against her.

"Do move apart and dance properly," Jessamine protested.

Seeing them together made my heart squeeze into a ball of stone that sat so heavily in my chest I didn't know if I could bear its weight.

The last waltz ended, and Jessamine directed Sophronia to go and get the tea trolley.

"Wait!" Ethan practically shouted. "You said we were getting Lacey back. We've dressed up and danced your dumb dances—now where is she?"

Jessamine hesitated for a second. "First we need to recover from our exertions. The ladies must fix their hair and makeup again. Then you shall eat. Afterward, your friend and The Provider will join us in the ballroom for tea."

"Fine," Ethan said. "But no *tea* until after they get here."

Missouri moved alongside me as we all moved into the corridor—her face chalky. "I'm worried," she said. "The Provider hardly ever comes down here."

I exchanged taut glances with Aisha.

We fixed our hair and faces in the bathroom, then made our way to the kitchen. Ethan sat there already, shifting in his seat. Two of the Toys—Bear and Clara—sat on the other side of the table from him. We all seated ourselves, waiting for Jessamine. She appeared minutes later, having changed her clothing—a white lace dress with a matching headband.

Missouri served what Jessamine had called supper—even though it consisted of jam tarts and some kind of custard slice and nothing else. My stomach knotted up with hunger as the tarts and slices were put on plates. But I was determined not to eat. It felt as if eating and drinking in this place would bind me to it. I'd become part of the flesh and bones of the underground.

Jessamine seemed to fuss a lot with her food, without actually eating anything that I could see. After everyone had eaten their jam tarts and custard slices, Jessamine pushed her uneaten portion away. "I have some difficult news," she said, with a sigh. "The party is postponed. Our guest of honor had a terrible fall today—a flight of stairs I believe, and she had to be taken off to the hospital."

Ethan and I met eyes.

He sent his plate flying across the table. "What?"

"It's natural for you to be concerned. She's suffered a confusion. I do hope she'll come 'round."

"You're playing with us!" Ethan roared. "She's been dead for days, hasn't she? Well, hasn't she?"

"I told you all I know. Don't take your anger out on *me*."

Ethan jumped to his feet, grabbing a large knife from the plate that had held the custard dessert. "You made up the fall on the stairs. *Confusion* isn't even the right word. What did you mean to say? Concussion? Contusion?" His eyes blazed. "Telling us Lacey was coming down here was just a trick—just so you could get us to wear these stupid clothes. You're just a little girl playing make-believe, aren't you?"

Ethan charged at her and leveled the knife at her throat. "You tell your Provider to get himself down here—now!"

"Ethan!" I shouted.

Jessamine's expression darkened. "You—are a vile, horrible boy."

Aisha stood up, knocking over her chair. "It's *you* who imprisons us! You're the vile one! Let us out!"

Missouri took Philomena by the hand and rushed her from the room. Sophronia sat stunned.

Bear and Clara moved from their seats.

I heard scraping coming from the corridor.

I felt a sudden, hysterical fear. Clown was on its way.

Then Clara leapt and toppled Ethan to the ground. Aisha screamed.

I tried to drag the doll away. It was strong—much stronger than something made of ceramic and soft material should be. Sickeningly strong.

The doll turned its attention to me—shoving me. I sprawled to the floor. It laid itself down on me. Then it pushed down—and down—*and down*—with a terrifying pressure.

My bones will crack, or I'll suffocate . . . .

11. EMPTINESS IS A PLACE

Clock hands spin and whir
Like winged, fanciful birds
Stealing your hours and stirring your sleep
They fly you away in a dreamless haze
To the Theatre of the Absurd

—P.

Suddenly, the doll lifted itself from me. It climbed back on its chair—as though nothing had happened. I sucked deep breaths into my lungs, choking down sobs.

Ethan and Aisha were rounded up and herded by the other Toys—Bear, Clown, and the Raggedy Ann doll. They were taken from the room, Ethan yelling with rage. I heard a metal door slam shut

Nothing—no circus tricks or magic—could have toys doing those things. They were alive, yet not alive. They were inanimate, until they had a job to do.

Sophronia stared at me, her dark eyes wide but expressionless.

I stepped out of the kitchen and into the passage. Jessamine stood there—waiting for me.

"This is what happens to rude, bad Toys." She pointed toward the two cells with the metal-barred doors. Ethan and Aisha were locked away in them. "They must sit up on their Toy shelves and wait for forgiveness."

Had she just called them *Toys*? The only places to sit or lie down in the cells were barren lengths of wood, like rudimentary benches, which Jessamine had called *toy shelves*. When we'd first seen them, the cells had reminded me of the underground crypts I'd once seen in an old church. I could never have imagined what these cells were used for here.

"They are to stay here, without dinners or breakfasts until they learn better manners," she added. "And you would do well to remember their fate." Jessamine turned on her heel and left in the direction of the ballroom. Ethan shook the bars, but they barely rattled. There were no visible locks. They were somehow just automatically locked.

"I'll get you out," I whispered hoarsely.

Jessamine turned around to glare at me. "Calliope?" she said icily.

There was nothing to do but walk after her. If I got put away, too, I was no help to anyone—especially not to Ethan and Aisha.

In the ballroom, Missouri rocked Philomena in the big rocking chair, singing "Hush, Little Baby." Her words faltered as she saw us.

"You are to read in silence," Jessamine instructed. "I am very tired."

I took a random book from the library. My mind turned in on itself as I sat on one of the empty chairs. Even if I could figure out some way to open the cells, Jessamine and those monster Toys would just put Aisha and Ethan back inside—and me, too.

Blankly, I stared at the girls. None of them had come to our aid. None of them had said a peep in our defense.

Soon, Jessamine announced that she was retiring to the bedchamber. Clown and Raggedy stationed themselves at the entry to the ballroom as she left.

I felt dazed, like I was drifting from my body—hunger gnawing like a lion at my stomach. I ached for a shower, I hadn't had one since the day I'd come up to camp in the mountains. The clock said the time was seven in the evening. That was crazy. Had I fallen asleep? As the clock began to chime, Clown finally moved toward the sleeping chamber and Clara returned to the kitchen.

Missouri continued to read her book, Philomena asleep on her shoulder.

"It's seven o'clock," I whispered to Missouri. "Surely that can't be right?"

"I'm afraid it is," she told me.

"It's time for dinner already?"

Missouri's eyes were heavy. "There won't be dinner tonight."

"Because of what Ethan and Aish did?"

She gave a slight, slow nod.

I looked away. "I'm sorry."

She stared around her as though checking to see if Jessamine or any of the Toys were watching. She gestured toward the chair next to her. I stepped over and dropped into it.

"I know what you're going through," she told me in a low voice. "I was like you when I first came in here. But don't try and fight. Her punishments get much worse. And she'll make us *all* suffer."

Giving her a guilty grimace, I wanted to ask what those punishments were. But a sick feeling in the pit of my stomach told me I'd find out anyway if I were imprisoned long enough.

Desperately, I wanted to get Missouri on my side. There were things I needed to know that only she could tell me. I had to find out more about her, and let her know she could trust me. "Can I ask you something?"

She eyed me with a blank expression, and I knew that she might not answer.

"How did you even survive here for five whole years? I can't imagine."

"I've always been a survivor. That's been my life." She glanced down at Philomena. "Every morning when I wake and see Philly's face, I see hope. She *is* hope. And I keep going—for her and for Sophronia."

"Who brought you here?"

The muscles around her brow constricted. "I brought me here—most of the way."

"I know that you ran away from home." I smiled grimly. "What made you run away?"

She shrugged her free shoulder, running her hand along a length of Philomena's hair. "I was a foster child—I'd just turned thirteen—and my foster family threw a party for me. But I couldn't stay."

"Why couldn't you stay?"

She eyed the ceiling, as though trying to remember a former existence. "I needed to settle a score. That's all."

"Please . . . tell me what happened."

She breathed deeply. "I escaped through a window, the night of my birthday. I slept in a supermarket parking lot, and the next day I caught a bus. But I couldn't go straight to where I wanted to go. My foster care parents would have told the police, and the police would have known exactly where I was headed."

"What do you mean, *you had to settle a score*?" I remembered the photo of the almost thirteen-year-old Molly Parkes with her fierce eyes.

She shook her head gently, stroking the sleeping Philomena's hair. "It doesn't matter. Anyway, I needed somewhere to hide out first. So I decided to catch a bus to the mountains and hide out for a while. I arrived at Devils Hole and headed off into the forest. I had a backpack full of food, there were fresh water rivers, and it was summer. I thought I'd be okay." She stared off into the distance. "All I know is I went to sleep in the forest," she turned eyes to me, deep as a well, "and woke up here."

Again, I slept on the daybed in the ballroom. This time, completely alone. Hunger and fear tore through me like raging beasts.

Part of me refused to accept that I was even there. It was like I was in two places at once—underground and also standing upstairs in the main Fiveash house. I couldn't conceive that one simple decision had led us to where we were. Surely I could still turn around and walk away at will?

At the stroke of midnight, Jessamine and the Toys repeated their walk to the dark tunnel. I closed my eyes, trying to shut out the bone-chilling sound of the clown.

My only solace was that dim lights remained on day and night in the ballroom.

I watched as the hands on the grandfather clock reached seven in the morning. If I had slept at all, it had only been in snatches. Gasping, I watched the clock's hands spin backward, around and around. They stopped at one in the morning.

No. *No, no, no.*

A whole night had passed by, but now the clock had reset itself to an hour after midnight. And who knew how many times the clock had reset itself while I slept?

I wanted to scream out loud. I rose stiffly from the daybed.

A figure moved out from the library—Clara—her smiling mouth macabre in the darkness. I sat down again quickly. She bobbed her head in a nod.

My breath sucked from my chest. That *thing* had been there all night. Watching me.

Drawing my knees up to my chest, I began waiting out the long hours again.

I woke in the same position.

Jessamine stood before me, her expression unreadable. "Go wash up and make yourself presentable."

I didn't argue or protest. My limbs were rigid, paining from the cold and sleeping in that position for so long. I made my way down the corridor. The other girls were still asleep in the bedchamber. Ethan and Aisha lay curled up and sleeping on the cold floors of their cells.

I stepped into the bathroom and shut the door behind me.

Bending over the sink, I scooped water into my mouth. My stomach griped and twisted. I felt the water run all the way through my stomach and into my intestines.

My insides were completely empty.

Emptiness is a place—an abandoned town—a bottomless hole.

And this was only three or so days without food. Maybe it had been four—it was impossible to tell.

A terrible thought entered my head. We were at the mercy of The Provider.

What if he decided there were too many of us and stopped sending down supplies?

I studied myself in the mirror. My body stood there, but my mind was locked within a box. My expression was one of frozen fear. Only a small part of me still functioned—I had to grasp tightly onto that part or I'd slip completely away.

In my heart I knew something terrible had happened to Lacey. But I couldn't let myself think about that anymore, else I'd curl up and want to die.

I had to find out who The First One was. There had to be traces of her somewhere. Perhaps she had left a note in one of the books. I planned to search the library as best as I could.

I pulled off the dress and undergarments that Jessamine had made me wear and stepped into the shower.

Freezing water pummeled my body as I wrenched the faucet around. I rubbed myself up and down with the soap in a frenzied motion. But I couldn't bear to stay underneath the water long enough to wash the soap off. I reached for the damp towel. Breathing hard, I tried to dry myself. The cold made my body react as though it had just run a marathon. Giving up on getting dry, I wrapped the wet towel around myself and padded out into the hall and to the dressing room.

My clothing lay folded in a drawer, just as the other girls' clothing did—the stuff they were wearing when they first came. I pulled on my jeans, T-shirt, and sweater, and returned the towel to the bathroom.

In the ballroom, Sophronia knelt by the fire in her nightdress, her black hair swinging as she prodded a log deeper into the flames. I crouched beside her, letting the fire's warmth seep into my flesh— but I was cold to the bone and it didn't penetrate very far.

Her almond-shaped eyes surveyed me, looking over my clothing.

"Sophronia . . . I'm sorry. It's our fault that no one gets to eat."

Silently, she stood and walked away, her foot limping as before. It wasn't hard to see that she was angry with me.

Jessamine stepped up behind me, her blue eyes livid. "Calliope, you may not wear your men's attire here. Get yourself changed into something decent."

"These are my clothes," I told her in a small voice. "This is all I have."

"There is an entire dressing chamber of suitable clothing. You will dress properly, and you will do your face."

I stood to face her. "Will you allow the others to eat if I do what you ask?" Something told me not to ask about releasing Ethan and Aisha—I needed to get on Jessamine's good side first, if she even had one.

From their chairs, Missouri and Philomena stared over the tops of their books at me.

"If *you* show obedience, I will consider reinstating food privileges." Jessamine yanked me back to the dressing room.

"Fine, I'll wear whatever you want." I pointed at the black velvet dress on the mannequin. "This?"

Her eyes clouded. "No. You are never to wear that. Do you understand? Choose something else."

Without another word, she left the room.

I selected the simplest and warmest clothing I could find—a long-sleeved, high-necked top and a plain pinafore. I wriggled into the too-tight dress and struggled with the stockings and boots.

There was no breakfast served. We were sent directly to the ballroom for reading. Missouri, Sophronia, and Philomena were already curled up on chairs with books in hand. Stepping over to the library, I pulled out a murderously thick book. I'd heard of the title—*War and Peace*, but didn't know anyone who'd read it. No wonder—the thing weighed a ton. Handmade paper bookmarks fluttered from the back jacket of the book. Missouri's and Sophronia's bookmarks.

I replaced the book, and continued my search for any clue of The First One—flipping through book after book and then replacing it.

"My my, you *are* having trouble finding a decent read," said

Jessamine. "Just choose one and have done."

Quickly, I pulled out a book—this one filled with the ancient poetry of someone named Virgil. I sat and read for a short while, but my mind raced. If I couldn't search the library, I wasn't going to just sit and read for endless hours. The thought was intolerable.

"I have stomach pains," I told Jessamine politely. "May I be excused?"

She waved me away.

I crept down the corridor, but not to the bathroom. I eyed the wardrobes and drawers. Maybe The First One—whoever she was— had left some belongings behind. But I had to be quick. If I wasn't, I knew Jessamine would come looking for me.

A corner of thick, green material protruded from a large bottom drawer. There hadn't been anything in that drawer the last time I checked. Frowning, I tugged it open. Large reams of the material had been folded and forced inside. Straining, I pulled at the thing— falling backward with it as it wrenched loose.

The taste of bile hit the back of my throat.

Ethan's tent.

Behind me, someone gasped. I turned. Missouri stood with her hand over her mouth. I hadn't even heard her follow me.

Ethan and Aisha had their fingers gripped around the bars of their cells as I stepped woodenly back into the corridor.

"Cassie, what's wrong?" Ethan called.

I tried to speak, but could only manage two words. "The tent. . ."

His hands dropped to his sides, his shoulders sagging. I could tell from his devastated expression that he understood.

I ran back to the ballroom and curled up into a chair with trembling legs. Missouri followed, sinking stiffly into the chair beside me. Our only hope of being found had just been shattered into tiny pieces.

Philomena was sprawled on the middle of the floor by herself—a doll in each hand—humming.

"Philly, do stop that rowdiness." Jessamine's eyebrows stitched together in annoyance.

She clutched her stomach. "My belly hurts. It hurts!"

Missouri knelt beside the little girl, raising her eyes to Jessamine. "She's hungry, she needs food. You promised food if Calliope changed her clothes." Her voice was low, faltering.

Jessamine rose to her feet. "You know exactly why there's no food. You can only blame yourselves."

Missouri's eyes blazed. "Philly doesn't deserve to be punished."

"Nevertheless, she has to learn," said Jessamine. "Surely it's not that bothersome to do without for a few days."

Sophronia rose from a dark corner—I hadn't even noticed her sitting there in the shadows. She hobbled from the room, and returned with a trolley of cups and steaming tea.

"I can always rely on you, dear Sophronia." Jessamine bowed her head. "Tea is precisely what we need."

I knew even before I was given the cup of tea that I was going to drink it. It wasn't food, but it was *something*. And it was going to put me to sleep—take me away to a place where I wouldn't feel this clamoring hunger. It would take me away to a place where I didn't know that police wouldn't ever find the tent—or us. I sipped the hot liquid quickly, even as it burned my throat.

Guilt crushed into me—I should've been doing all I could to stay awake, to figure out what to do next. But the next moment, heaviness dragged through my body, and sleep came down over me like a wave.

Slipping straight into a dream, I saw intense sunlight. I was back in South Beach, Miami—back when I was ten or eleven, on a class trip with my school. Waves washed over my feet, and the sun—big as a satellite dish—dazzled my eyes.

But soon I lost the school group and became hungry. I went pleading to strangers along the beach for food. They were eating cakes and ice cream, French fries and doughnuts. But no one, not one person, would give me so much as a bite.

12. EVERY HEARTS' DESIRE

Light the candles
Grant her every desire
For birthdays come but when you wish
Extinguish every other light
Come gather 'round the pyre
Hear her choir sing
Of forgotten things, this requiem of night.

—P.

I woke into dim, spidery light. Air so cold my breath whitened the air. The smell of wet moss clung everywhere. My arms pained stiffly as I tried to stretch them—they'd been crossed over my chest. My heart clutched as I realized I was in the bedchamber. I sat bolt upright, musty sheets slipping away from my body. I didn't remember leaving the ballroom.

I'd slept in the bed with the dark stain beneath it. I sensed the lingering presence of the last occupant of the bed. A wave of grief and pain enveloped me, so intense that nausea rose in my stomach.

Missouri and Philomena began to wake at the same time. When Philomena tried to get up, she was too weak, and collapsed back onto the bed. Sophronia roused. She gazed at me with dull eyes.

Jessamine stood at the door. She wore a deep purple dress—the fabric grayed and stiff. "Come on lazy bones. All of you. No dilly dallying—I have the most delirious news to tell you all."

Missouri's eyes were ringed with dark shadows. "Philly needs food. You're starving us."

Jessamine glared. "You and your impertinent accusations. Get up."

Philomena dragged herself obediently out of bed, wobbling on unsteady legs, then collapsed on the floor.

Missouri rushed to pick her up and placed her back in the bed, brushing hair from her forehead. Missouri bowed her head into the bed beside Philly. It was the first time I'd seen her cry—or any of them cry.

"Now that you're all awake, I'll tell you my news," Jessamine said happily, as though she hadn't even noticed. "We have strawberry cake! Today is my birthday!"

Missouri looked up with a wet face, as if she didn't quite believe what she'd heard.

"Is there really cake?" Philomena said faintly.

Jessamine scowled. "Why is everyone still in bed? This is a day of celebration—get up and follow me! Come Sophronia!"

We were herded out to the kitchen in single file, still in our nightgowns. Aisha and Ethan were each curled up on the benches in their cells. I vowed to try and sneak them some food—they must be even hungrier than I was.

On the kitchen table, a large, elaborate, pink-iced cake sat in pride of place. Fifteen candles circled the edge.

The sight of food made my mouth literally water. Clara and Bear moved into the kitchen, standing at the door. Raggedy and Clown took standing positions at the head of the table. Sophronia stepped on tippy toes to fetch a box of matches from the cupboard. She lit the candles one by one while Missouri placed plates on the table.

Jessamine eyed us all expectantly.

Missouri began the Happy Birthday song—her voice thin. Philomena and I joined her, the song a mournful dirge.

Sophronia cut the cake, giving Jessamine the first slice, even though she must have been desperate to tear into it herself. I could hardly control my impatience.

Jessamine practically glowed with excitement. "I wish that all my friends have a delightfully delicious day and that for celebrating this day with me they all have their hearts' desire granted."

Sophronia pushed slices of cake in front of each of us. My heart dropped to see pieces given to Raggedy and Clown—pieces that would only end up in the trash.

The cake tasted rich and wonderful. Sugar hit my brain like a speeding train. Philomena smiled broadly—icing all around her face. She wiped every bit of icing off with her fingers and ate it.

Jessamine declared that games were to commence in the ballroom now. I wanted to stay and eat more cake—at least one more piece. But she had already left the table, and I knew I was expected to follow. I snatched and bundled two pieces of cake into the large front pocket in the skirt of my pinafore.

Ethan and Aisha were awake now, standing with their hands on the bars as we filed past. Jessamine didn't acknowledge them. I tried to send them a silent message as I passed—*I have something for you*.

I continued to the ballroom with the others. "This has turned out to be the best birthday ever." Jessamine flopped into a chair, pulling

Philomena onto her lap. She *did* care about Philomena, at least in some sense—but only as a toy, a plaything. Perhaps she cared about all of the girls in some sick, twisted way. How long had she been down here? What had The Provider done to her, to make her this way?

Clown guarded us, ensuring we didn't communicate with each other. We were allowed bathroom breaks, singly. When it was my turn, I curtsied to Clown and left the room.

Aisha was again asleep on the bench. Ethan sat with his back against the wall, staring up into nothingness.

I slid down to the floor, sitting in front of Ethan's cell. "Hey, Captain Thunderbolt."

His face pulled into a taut grin. "Hey."

"Been on any good raids, lately?"

"Yeah. I raided the bank and took off with their stocks of gold."

"Try raiding the local grocery store next time."

"Good idea. I'll put that on the list."

I pulled out the cake slices from my pinafore pocket and slipped them through the bars. Ethan nodded gratefully, secreting the squashed offerings inside his jacket. He ate his slice quickly, stuffing it down his throat in a few gulps.

I laced my fingers through the bars. "Every time I come by here, I'm afraid you or Aisha will be gone, disappeared into the walls. Like Lacey."

"I know. I have the same thoughts."

"We have no control here. And the clocks—they keep crazy time. We don't even know how much time is passing."

He shook his head. "Don't worry about that. Time isn't linear, anyway. My people on my mother's side are Aboriginal. They believe in circular time. Science is just starting to catch up." He smiled thinly. "Besides, that's the least of our problems." Then his smile was gone. "Hey, it's dangerous for you to be here."

"Yeah. I know." I stepped backward. "See you on my next trip into town."

"I'll be here." He pretended to tip a cowboy hat.

I rose and stepped away into the corridor.

"Hey, Girl Wonder." He silently jerked his chin upward, indicating for me to come back.

I turned around, moving close to hear him.

He was gripping the bars of his cell. "I just want to thank you. You were my wingman in the forest. You were . . . brave."

I gave a short, sad laugh, moving my hand over a bar so it was next to Ethan's. The forest, the mountains—they seemed like scenes from a different lifetime.

Something intensely sad and sweet visited his eyes. "Cassie . . . ."

"Yeah?"

"I didn't get a chance to tell you . . . ." His dark eyelashes lowered and his fingers touched mine.

My heart was beating fast. "Tell me what?"

"What's going on here?"

I flinched. Aisha had woken, and was staring rigidly at me. I hadn't noticed her awake. Not that I was *doing* anything with Ethan, but still, I felt caught out, exposed, and I pulled my hand away from his.

"Aish . . . we were just talking," Ethan told her.

"It didn't look like *just talking*."

He opened up his jacket. "Look. She brought us something to eat."

I wanted to say something. But the look on Aisha's face told me it was better not to intrude.

Her pale eyes glazed. "I—I've been down here all this time," she told Ethan, "wondering what was happening . . . out there. Wondering who you were with. Wondering when you were going to forget about me."

He let the jacket fall closed. "And that's never," he said seriously. "I was never going to forget you. I would have searched for you forever."

Suspicion flickered across Aisha's face. "Did you even think I was alive?"

Ethan went to answer, but hung his head instead.

Aisha went silent, hugging herself. "If you thought I was dead, then you weren't really looking for me. You were just looking for . . . an ending."

"I hoped. But I'm a realist. It's who I am. I still thought about you every second of every day."

"Because you were trying to prove that you weren't responsible. Isn't that right? That's what you told me before, that the police were trying to pin my disappearance on you?"

"Aish, c'mon. Yes that's true. But I still wanted to find out what happened, for your sake and for your family's sake."

Her eyes were cold. "But not for your sake. Not because you missed me or thought I might still be alive."

"That's not how it was. I care about you."

It was time to step away—to let them talk. I turned to go.

"How do I even know Lacey was with you in the forest?" she said, her words sharpening in my back.

I knew her words were meant for me. I turned around to face her.

"Lacey was there," Ethan said quickly. "Of course she was there."

Aisha met me with a level gaze. "You were sleeping out there in the forest with my boyfriend, weren't you? Tell the truth. Did anything happen?"

Heat flew to my temples. The kiss had been numb, stupid—it didn't count, surely?

Her eyes grew round and intense. She glared at me then at Ethan.

"Nothing happened," said Ethan with a note of finality.

"It wasn't anything—" My words rushed out at the same time that Ethan spoke, then trailed off guiltily.

"I knew it," Aisha whispered. Her knuckles grew white. Suddenly, she lunged forward, grabbing the bars of the cage. "Help!" she screamed. "Please! Help!"

Almost immediately, Jessamine appeared in the corridor. Raggedy Ann lumbered behind her.

"That girl," Aisha said quickly. Her eyes were glittering, as if she had a fever. "She kissed the boy. She kissed the naughty Toy. And she gave him food—check his pockets!"

Ethan backed away in his cell, shock and hurt registering on his face.

"You, Evander, will stay in there an eternity if you do not repent." Jessamine eyed Ethan with repulsion. She whirled around to me. "And you, Calliope, if you wish to drink from the cup of darkness, so be it."

Ethan mouthed a single word to me. *Run.*

But I couldn't. I wouldn't get five feet before Raggedy pinned me, suffocated me. Besides, there was nowhere to go.

Jessamine sighed. "I had high hopes for you, Calliope. Let's hope with sufficient . . . *education*, you can learn the discipline you need. Come."

And then I knew. I knew even before she advanced down the passageway and turned not right, but left.

I was a bad Toy.

I was about to be put in the Toy Box.

13. THE TOY BOX

Arrange them all, a pretty collection
High on a shelf, for your admiration
Dead of eye, ceramic faces
Give them correction and education
Disobedience brings a clock that stops
The eternal darkness of the forgotten Toy Box.

—P.

The mouth of the passage was a giant black mouth ready to swallow me. Jessamine slipped inside the darkness. I stopped, unable to move. But the Doll pushed against me, sending me forward.

My spine froze. *Not in there. Please, not in there.*

Not alone.

Jessamine bent to pick up a lamp. I shuddered with relief as light streaked through the passage. Up ahead, the lamplight showed the dead-end wall Ethan had described. My legs quaked.

Jessamine seemed to pull some kind of lever on the wall. A bone-crushing sound echoed in the tunnel—the sound of rock grinding against rock—immensely heavy rock.

The light now illuminated a cathedral-like arched corridor through the rock. A hidden passage. Whatever lay on the other side, I didn't want to see it.

Jessamine turned to me. "You must spend time in the Toy Box, to learn how to conduct yourself. It is dark and lonely in the Toy Box and not at all pleasant."

Rigidly, I followed Jessamine's slight frame through the corridor. Raggedy plodded behind me. Drips from the ceiling landed on my neck, dribbling wetly down my shoulder.

The slope of the passage wound around and down—ever down. It seemed this journey would never end, and I'd be walking this path forever. My heart was clay, clamped to my ribcage. The lamplight touched something deep red in the distance: Velvety folds that hung vertically, like curtains. It almost looked like a cubicle—or like the confessionals you saw in old churches.

Jessamine stopped to face me then, her face in a shadowy glow above her lamp—her eyes hard like stones.

"You will stay here for some time. As I told you before, this is a place of dreams and nightmares. It is a place where you must search your soul and repent." She indicated the makeshift confessional.

She stepped away from me. Terror struck as Jessamine retreated toward the passage, taking Raggedy—and the light—with her. Without turning around, she stopped dead. "We must stay exactly as we are, Calliope."

Then she continued into the darkness.

I crept close to the wall as all light deserted me. I backed myself up against the rock. Were there more giant Toys in here, waiting to jump at me and pin me to the wall? I felt out of control—panicked.

I had to find my way back. I felt along the rock, my fingers scratching and scraping at the wall. Water streamed down the rock face. My hands slid on slime.

The sound of scraping rock filled the air, echoing hollowly.

The doorway was closed. I was trapped. I struggled to control my ragged breaths. Cold and wet penetrated my entire body. This darkness was deeper than anything I'd ever experienced. Already, I was losing myself—my mind.

I had run from darkness all my life, only to end up in the worst darkness imaginable. *Was I going to die here?* Scenes from my past bled through my mind. I was so far away from everything from before. Away from my mom, school, my old life in Miami. So, so far away. Desperately, I commanded my body to stop trembling. It refused.

My legs moved woodenly forward. There was no point of reference, no break, in the black that surrounded me. Not even a pinpoint of light.

A heavy material enveloped me. My heart gripped itself. My arms flailed as I pushed it away. I knocked into something— something wooden. A chair. A normal-sized chair—not the enormous ones of the kitchen and ballroom. I sat, grateful to have something solid—an anchor—something that wasn't made of oily darkness.

I slowly explored the space around me with my hands. Musty drafts rose in around my ankles, seeping underneath the curtains. Directly in front of me was just a rock wall. But smoother. My hands blindly felt around the surfaces. Smoother than rock. Carved, maybe. A stone face, a stone arm.

A lamp.

My fingers shook as I lifted the lamp free from the stone arm. I twisted the knob. A hazy light took hold in the glass.

The light traced the curves and creases of a stone statue—a man. A saint. In his eyes and mouth, pieces of clear glass. Wet moss covered half his face and shoulders. The statue was set into the rock wall, beneath an overhanging rock—like a grotto.

"Help me," I whispered.

I held the lamp with both hands, turning to see around the cubicle. It was simply made of four wooden posts, with curtains hung between them. The chair behind me was old and worn, and had a carousel horse carved into the wood.

Out there, in the blackness, a breathy rattle disturbed the quiet. An *inhuman* sound.

A high, terrified keening fled from between my teeth.

The distant sound came through to me in waves, in whispers, in staccato. Missouri's words punctured my mind. She'd said that if I heard voices, I shouldn't listen to them. If these were voices, they were like nothing I had ever heard in my life.

Cold sweat coated my body beneath the dress.

I crawled inside my mind, trying to find a thought, a memory— something to take me away from this, to shut out the whispers.

Remember. A picnic with Mom. In a park with old trees. I am five. My bike is new and green. Silvery-green, the best green anyone ever saw. My first bike without training wheels. And I can ride it. I just need one more try. One more try with Mom holding the back of the bike, as I wobble forward. But the trees are wrong. They're slipping straight down, straight into the earth, clods of dirt flying in the air. . . .

I couldn't hold onto the memory.

The whispers seeped into my mind, like the cold air snaking through the curtains.

I had to let it go. Find another day, a day in the sun.

Remember. I'm at school. First day here. Heat burns through the asphalt into my shoes. I hate the uniform, hate the looks the other students give me. I hate the town. This wasn't what I was promised by Mom and her boyfriend, Lance. I see Ethan. He smiles his uneven smile—not like a boy smiling at a girl—more like a brother-in-arms, a comrade, an acknowledgment. He doesn't want to be there either. He keeps smiling, grinning as he throws something casually over his shoulder—a jacket. No, larger, heavier than a jacket. He turns and walks into darkness. He has a girl on his shoulder—an unconscious girl . . . .

No, this was wrong. My mind was seeing only darkness. Go back, go back, go back.

Go back to the last time you were truly happy.

Remember. I am three. There's a brand new swing set in our yard, a birthday present. I'm swinging so high that my face touches the sun. I stay out there all day, pretending I can fly. Gray clouds roll fast across the sky. Mommy says a storm is coming but I refuse to come inside. Dark falls around me and rain spatters my cheeks. I think Mommy must have forgotten me. I hear voices—angrier than the thunder. Mommy and Daddy. Mommy sees me, grabs my hand. And we're running, running out to the driveway and into the car. Lights glow through the rain and the night—red and green and white. We're on a road where the colored lights go away. Mommy is crying. There's a terrible noise—a crunching, squealing noise. Our car lights shine on the bark of a tree. And we slam into it. My body tears away from the seat and I'm thrown out, tumbling into the night . . . .

My eyes flew open.

No. That never happened. There was no car accident. *There was no car accident.*

My parents had divorced when I was three—my dad moving to L.A. I'd barely seen him in the years after that. Neither he nor Mom

138

had ever mentioned an accident. But my mind refused to let go of the image, throwing the scene of the accident at me again and again, battering me with it relentlessly. I heard the high-pitched siren of an ambulance. I saw my mother's face, her eyes closed and her cheek streaked with dark blood.

Stop it. This isn't true. It didn't happen. Why was I imagining such things?

I jumped to my feet and pushed free of the curtains, keeping tight hold of the lamp.

"Jessamine!" My voice echoed through the cavernous space. "Jessamine! Let me out!"

The eerie whispering sounds stopped. A heavy silence blanketed me.

I blundered forward. I needed to get away, to escape the nightmare playing in my mind.

Panic rushed through me in waves. The walls of the cave seemed so far away I couldn't reach them. Running through shrouds of darkness, I held my free hand out in front of me, trying to find a compass, a wall to follow along. But there was nothing.

The lamplight shone weakly over the mouths of three tunnels up ahead. My breath came in short stutters. There had been no tunnels before, *had there?*

I raced into the first tunnel. My heart thudded. Could one of these passages be a way out?

The walls here were different than the cave walls on the outside— smoother, with whitish, crystalline seams running through them. The transparent minerals gave off a soft glow.

The tunnel twisted and plunged downward, curving sharply.

I ran, holding the lamp high.

The passage opened up into a small chamber. It seemed to be a dead end. I was about to turn and leave when I noticed a desk in a dark recess, the same kind of desk as in the ballroom.

A moldy, wet piece of cake sat on a plate on the desktop. Pink icing and candles had melted off the top of the slice, like a surrealist painting. Jessamine's birthday cake.

A vase with a plastic rose had been placed beside the cake.

I set the lamp down near the desk, breathing hard.

It had to be the desk of The First One.

With trembling fingers, I took the plate away and set it down on the floor. As I lifted the desk's lid, wafts of moldy air made me gag. Inside, damp papers sat decomposing.

Drawings and writings—just like in the other desks out near the small library in the ballroom.

The papers were all too damp to handle, the writing too smudged to read.

A book sat beneath the papers. Carefully, I lifted it out. The gilt-edged book had a latch on top of it. I flicked the latch open. The book was of Greek gods and myths, the pages filled with a raft of impossible characters, each illustration rich with reds and golds and deep greens. Someone had gone crazy scribbling things into every blank spot, on every page—most of it hard to read as it seemed to have been written fast, unchecked, like the person had been compelled to keep going until they exhausted themselves. Most of the writings were signed with a simple "P."

I paused on a page about Mnemosyne—hadn't Jessamine mentioned her?

The illustration showed a milky-blue pool in a deep cave, softly lit by crystalline rock walls. A waterfall poured down from an unseen source. I ran a finger beneath the accompanying text.

Drink of the pool of Mnemosyne at the time of your death, and you will remember all from your past life as you go into the next. But drink of the river of Lethe and you will remember nothing. Mnemosyne presides over the pool of memory in Hades. She bore nine daughters to Zeus, the eldest of whom was Calliope — the muse of poetry.

Why had Jessamine thought to call me Calliope, born of the Pool of Mnemosyne?

I was about to close the book when I noticed more writing scrawled on the opposite page.

I've seen her since before I was born
Her long dark hair and eyes like pools
Of memory
Cassandra, Cassandra I sensed you torn
Between innocence and remembrance
Don't seek the hollow night
Of Mnemosyne
Don't follow me
For I am long gone.
—P.

A cold hand reached inside my chest and clutched my heart. Cassandra. My name.

But it was just coincidence. Had to be. Snapping the book shut, I dropped it inside my skirt pocket.

I closed the desk and replaced the plate, afraid that at any second my trembling fingers would drop the plate and smash it to pieces on the rock floor.

I sensed something, some kind of presence — a vibration. The whispering voice returned, slithering through the tunnel.

I raced away, back toward the mouth of the tunnels.

The whispering echoes retreated. But the sensation that I was being watched crawled through my veins. I came around a bend in the passageway and froze. In the murky light ahead, a figure stood. A man wearing a top hat and cape. He made a deep bow, then strode toward me. At first I thought it must be Donovan. But his hair was a much lighter blond. And he moved with an arrogant, straight stride, unlike Donovan's slightly hunch-shouldered gait.

"Please, help." My voice rose in panic. "Can you show me the way out?"

He stopped, his mouth curling into a half-smile, his eyes fixed on me in a way that made me shiver.

He didn't speak or offer any help. What did I expect? I was alone and lost in the underground maze. He was completely at ease, as though he belonged there. Another thought came to me—could he be The Provider? Was he the one who had taken Lacey? Had he hurt her and was he about to hurt me, too?

Turning sharply, I stepped the other way, my feet tripping over each other, then broke into a run.

I was back in the Toy Box.

A piercing voice cut through my head. Sharp, scolding. A hand closed around my shoulder, stopping me from running any farther. "Calliope. Answer me."

Jessamine's face was before me, her brow furrowed.

"They're coming . . ."

"Who is coming?" she asked me.

"The voices. And the man . . . in the tunnels." I glanced back over my shoulder. The tunnels had vanished, as though they'd never been there.

Jessamine eyed me strangely. "There are no such things here."

Impossible. I couldn't have imagined them. "There were," I said, but my voice was trembling, uncertain. "I swear, they were there before."

"Listen to me." Jessamine gripped my shoulders. "You must never speak of them, or the man, or the voices, or any such fancy. Do you understand?"

I nodded, my mind spinning. Too late I remembered the book in my pocket. I clasped my hands in front of my skirt, praying she hadn't noticed it there. I could feel its bulky outlines—so I hadn't imagined everything.

"I can see you are quite shaken," she told me. "You must have been dreaming. Dreams come easily here, to those who seek them. That is the purpose of the Toy Box, of course."

Taking the lamp from my frozen fingers, she extinguished the light. I followed behind her as she made her way back to the statue and replaced the lamp on the statue's arm.

Raggedy moved out from the shadows. Jessamine stepped away into the passage ahead. I ran in front of the doll, relieved for once to have it near me. We walked silently along the passage, my body numb. I didn't want to think, didn't want thoughts trespassing in my head. But I knew something within me was different, changed. It was as if a door had opened at the back of my mind—a door with vast reaches behind it. A door that could never again be closed.

14. LORD OF MISRULE

To the hammer of your heartbeat
He keeps time as he waltzes you
Through moonless nights and starless skies
The Provider denies his deceit
Behind a masquerade, a serenade
All light fades and too late do you learn
From this dance there is no return.

—P.

My eyes drifted open in the bedchamber. The wet rock walls seemed to close in on me, forming a funeral crypt where nothing living could possibly survive.

My head felt as heavy as an iron ball. Jessamine had forced me to drink tea directly after returning from the Toy Box, and I'd fallen into a deep haze. I didn't even know how I'd made my way to the bed.

Missouri was the only one awake—the others slept in their beds.

The Toys and Jessamine were gone. An anxious smile slipped into Missouri's pale features. "Are you okay? I've been so worried about you. You've been asleep for two days."

"*Two days?*"

She nodded somberly. "Jessamine must have given you a very strong dose of tea."

I tried to swallow, but my throat felt raw and dry.

"My friends, are they—?"

"They're both okay," she said quickly, glancing over her shoulder.

I nodded, relieved. I must have been underground at least a week. My stomach knotted as I thought of Mom and all she'd be going through. The police must be looking for us. But no one knew Lacey and I had gone to the mountains. Would Ben Paisley confess he knew where Ethan was?

Please, please, find us.

Something poked sharply into my hip. I looked down. I still wore the pinafore from yesterday—Jessamine must have ordered me straight to bed. A rectangular object sat inside the skirt pocket. I pulled it free.

As I stared down at the book I now held in my hands, I remembered. I remembered the Toy Box and all that had happened in there. It wasn't a nightmare I'd woken from—it was real. I held the evidence in my hands.

Slipping from my bed, I padded to Missouri through the chilly dark air. "I heard things in the Toy Box," I whispered. "And saw things."

She turned around, checking for Jessamine. She moved her blanket across, gesturing to me to get in. I climbed into the bed beside her.

Tendrils of dark red hair fell about her pale face. "You . . . you heard the voices?"

I nodded, trying to shut out the memory of those sounds vibrating in my ears. "You've been in there too, haven't you?"

"Yeah, lots of times. At first, it was always because Jessamine thought I was misbehaving. And then later . . ." —she lowered her voice—"to try to find a way out."

"Did you ever come close?"

"No." Her breath misted the air white.

"What's in there—in those tunnels? I was only able to go down one of them."

Her pale, smooth forehead wrinkled. "Tunnels?"

"Behind the saint statue."

She tilted her head in confusion. "But there are no tunnels. The statue is in front of a solid wall. You must have been dreaming."

I stared at her. "I wasn't dreaming—they were there. I even brought something back . . . ."

Her eyes widened in the dark light. "Only one of us ever saw the other side of the wall. But she could only see it in visions, she could never actually go there . . . ." Her gaze moved to the object I was pulling from my pocket, her jaw tightening.

I opened the book, showing her the scrawled, manic writing. "This is what I found, in a desk, at the end of the first tunnel."

A gasp fled her lips, her fingers trembling as she touched them to her temples. "Prudence."

At least now I had a name. The mysterious "P." was Prudence. The First One.

"How can I find her? Will she be somewhere in the tunnels?"

Missouri's face went chalky. "You must forget her."

"What?" I shook my head desperately. "No!" I flipped the book to a strange poem about a serpent. With the dim light coming from the corridor, I could barely see the letters. "What do all these poems mean?"

"I told you to forget her. And you have to forget you ever saw this." Her voice drew down into a tight, small space. "Don't tell the others, okay? Not a word." Missouri twisted in the bed, taking the covers with her and leaving me out in the cold.

I flinched as though I'd been stung. Missouri had told me I needed to find out about The First One if I wanted my questions about the dollhouse answered. She'd even said she'd tried and failed. But now that I'd found The First One's desk, she had completely shut down. So far, Missouri had been the one I could trust, the one who could help me figure this place out. Why was she pushing me away? I hadn't even had a chance to tell her about the *man* I'd seen in the tunnels.

I returned to my bed, a desperate loneliness tightening in my stomach. Everyone was hiding something.

I knew it was up to me to find the way out of there.

I hid the book securely beneath the mattress.

With a start, I noticed Sophronia lying in her bed silently, her eyes open. Had she been listening to our conversation? Had she seen where I'd hidden the book? If so, I would have to move it, soon. I didn't trust her at all.

Crashing sounds boomed along the corridor.

The pipe organ.

Philomena woke sleepily. She glanced over at me, seeming to sense how lost I felt. "Don't be afraid, Calliope," she said, yawning. "It's just Donovan. He plays that awful noise to let us know when he's sent something down."

My heart leapt. Could this be my chance? To plead with Donovan? To overpower him? To get out. But then I remembered the dumbwaiter, which I guessed was how he sent things down.

Jessamine entered and gave us the command to wash and clean ourselves in the bathroom. I would have to move the book later. She seemed nervous. "Today is the winter solstice, and we are to celebrate." But her eyes were flat—like stones in a riverbed, as though this were no celebration at all.

Missouri and Sophronia exchanged glances. I guessed they'd had these celebrations before, whatever they were.

An idea shot through my head. "Surely we can't have a celebration if two of us are missing . . . ?" My words trailed off. I wanted to ask about Lacey too, but I didn't want to push too far. And I feared something terrible had happened to her and she was never coming back.

Jessamine bowed her head imperiously. "Evander and Angeline will be joining the festivities. I do hope that you will *all* be mindful of your behavior on such an important occasion."

I exhaled a silent breath of relief.

Rising from our beds, we headed down the corridor. Ethan roused from sleep and frowned at me questioningly. He seemed to sense that I had something to tell him. But I couldn't risk stopping to explain everything that had happened in the Toy Box—I wouldn't jeopardize his chance of getting out of there.

Dresses awaited us in the bathroom—five new, shiny dresses, hanging on hooks over the shower railing. Philomena gasped, running to touch the smallest dress—a white one with tiny angel wings on the back of it. New face paints sat in a basket on the floor.

Missouri turned to Jessamine, who stood at the bathroom door. "These are for us?"

"Yes, The Provider chose them especially for you all, and Donovan sent them down a few minutes ago. You are to take special care with your makeup today. The theme is birds and butterflies. Everything must be *perfect*." Stepping away, she let the door close behind her.

"You'd better get ready," Missouri told me in a taut voice.

Pulling Philomena's hair back with a hairband, she started cleaning yesterday's doll makeup from her face.

Stepping over to the basin, I scrubbed my face with a sliver of soap.

Sophronia selected some of the new paints from the basket while Missouri propped Philomena up on the bench. Sophronia drew a stylized butterfly across Philomena's eyes and temples, and colored it in with bright colors. She then drew gaudy blue and purple bird motifs on Missouri and me, tracing sweeping V-shapes around our eyes. She painted deep red color on our mouths.

"So this 'celebration' happens every year?" I asked, directing my question at no one in particular.

Missouri nodded. "This is the Feast of Fools, held each year on the winter solstice. It's meant to be a day where the masters serve the servants. All it really means to us is that we get fed—and fed well. And then Jessamine plays games with us. But she's never had us go to *this* much trouble before—we normally just wear our best gowns and use our old makeup."

I was relieved that she was talking to me again, but there was an undercurrent now, a distance. We'd become strangers again, and I couldn't figure out why Prudence's book had provoked such a strong reaction. She hadn't even asked me about the tunnels. It was as if she wasn't really interested in finding a way out at all.

Sophronia began painting her own face. Missouri took over the styling of our hair—braiding it and winding it around our heads.

Missouri's red hair was startling above the purplish face makeup. Sophronia looked like some kind of rare and exotic creature with her makeup on.

Philomena smiled broadly as Sophronia placed a leafy gold crown on her head. Sophronia then fussed with fixing feathers and baubles in our hair. She wrapped a gold ribbon across my forehead, like a headband.

Missouri checked the lengths and sizes of the gowns and handed me one. The two longest gowns had to be for Missouri and Aisha. I dressed quickly. The sequined green gown exposed my shoulders and plunged down at the neckline.

I turned to face the mirror. I didn't look like a young girl anymore—I could easily pass for seventeen. I decided I liked the makeup—it was something to hide behind, pretend I wasn't me. All of this, being down in the underground, could be happening to someone else—happening to this strange girl with the intense eyes and vivid makeup.

The door opened, and Aisha stepped into the room. Her lips parted as she caught sight of me.

"Aish!" I cried. "I'm so glad you're—"

"Don't," she said icily. Without saying another word, she turned her face away from me. Collecting her dress from the hook, she moved to a corner of the room, keeping her back to me. She was furious at me and there was nothing I could do about it.

The rest of us made our way out and down the corridor, Philomena swishing about in her new dress.

Ethan was gone from the cell. I felt an intense wave of relief. So I wasn't *all* alone then.

The light coming from the ballroom was brighter than usual. I gasped as I rounded the entry.

The kitchen table had been moved to the ballroom—piled high with cakes and French pastries and puddings and plates of hors d'oeuvres and exotic fruits.

"Where did all of this come from?" I whispered.

"The Provider must have brought it," said Missouri in a hushed tone. "But they've never done a spread like this before."

Philomena's eyes grew large in her elfin face. She took in a big gasp of air. I expected her to rush forward, but she didn't. She hung back, waiting.

Raggedy plodded into the room. Ethan and Aisha followed.

Aisha also wore extravagant makeup and a brilliant blue gown. Ethan had donned a suit and birdlike theatrical mask. Ethan bowed to the room and Aisha curtsied. Jessamine and Bear strode in after them, the top half of Jessamine's face painted in the circular motifs of peacock feathers.

"You all look wonderful indeed," said Jessamine, but the expression beneath her makeup was apprehensive. She hesitated a moment, seeming to debate within herself what to say next. It was the first time I'd seen her as anything other than sure of herself. "Do take care today," she said finally. She had us arrange ourselves about the room, either sitting on chairs or standing, as though we were characters in a play, taking our places and waiting for the curtain to lift.

Clown and Clara stationed themselves at either end of the ballroom entry.

Jessamine stepped stiffly over to the gramophone and selected some music. I recognized the tune from the piece that Donovan had played—Chopin's "Nocturne No. 20." But it sounded so different— not heavy and plodding the way Donovan played, and the gramophone record wasn't one of the scratchy ones. The classical music filled every space in the underground, each note a measure of grief and sadness.

Above the music I could hear rustling—murmurs of many voices at once, out in the corridor. I turned sharply to Missouri. Her eyes were large and confused as she listened. Blood drained from my limbs and I suddenly felt dizzy.

A figure strode in: a man. His face wore the harsh painted lines of a clown, but over his nose and eyes a huge cone-shaped beak jutted out. Dressed in a black suit, a theatrical white cape hung from his shoulders. The eyes behind the mask gazed with cold satisfaction about the room.

Missouri and Sophronia stared at each other, unbelief and fear etched on their faces. Their expressions told me who this man must be. The Provider. My whole body felt as if it had been filled with ice water.

He was the man I'd seen in the tunnels. I was sure of it.

Missouri had told me she'd only seen The Provider come down on rare occasions—when something important had happened. What had compelled him to come down this time? Muffled sounds gathered out in the corridor.

A dozen or so people swooped into the room, men and women dressed in extravagant costumes—the men wearing the same beak-like masks as The Provider and the women wearing bird-themed makeup similar to ours. All of them with cold, searching eyes. Vulture eyes.

I shrank back in my post near the library. Philomena drew her legs up on her chair, sinking her head into her knees.

Jessamine stood with one hand clasped over the other, her eyes cast downward. I sensed her fear of these people—but was she afraid for herself or for us?

The Provider strode to the center of the room, tossing his cape behind his shoulders. "Welcome, one and all. What a merry occasion. This day marks a time-honored tradition stretching back centuries." His accent was American—rich and cultured—rising and falling in slow, deliberate beats. "A day in which the servants rise to become the masters." He cast his gaze over us. "As your Provider, I give you . . . The Feast of Fools!"

The crowd of people behind him clapped riotously and stamped their feet.

The Provider stepped over to Missouri, smirking a little. "Ah, the one with the hair and heart of fire. So pleased you made your way to us. You were lost before we found you."

Her face was frozen as she took the hand he offered. He led her into a waltz around the floor.

A prickling sensation crawled over my skin as I watched the party guests look on, their mouths stretched in wide grins but their eyes needling and cold. The Provider's cape flew behind him as he took Missouri into a series of flamboyant spins. He bowed and returned Missouri to her seat, her temples flushing with relief to get away from him. The waltz had at least been quick, only lasting half a minute.

Finding his way over to Sophronia, he produced a white rose from inside his jacket. "The little Indian flower. Our adventuress. You grace us with your silent presence."

She accepted the rose, showing no emotion.

The Provider's eyes alighted on Aisha. He strode to offer her his hand. *Enchanté.* The girl who sought more than her pale world, more than the dirge of the ordinary." He turned and stared purposefully at Ethan. Aisha trembled as she took his hand. She was weak from her days in the cell. He had to hold her up as they moved into a slow dance. He whispered something to her, and her expression fluttered like a leaf—to my shock, she actually *smiled*.

Ethan shook his head in disbelief.

The Provider walked her back to her chair. She curled up with her legs beneath her, refusing to meet Ethan's stare.

On bended knee, The Provider brought his face to Philomena's eye level. "Dear me, tiny butterfly, you flittered away from those who didn't give you all your heart desired. No one ever neglects you here." He produced a pink rose from his jacket, and gave it to her.

His gaze fell on me.

"Ah, the newest arrival. Stand up so I can see you."

I obeyed. I had no choice. The strange guests around the room fell suddenly silent.

The Provider grinned. "What an exquisite sweetness—to witness the bud that didn't wish to bloom. The sun in the world above was just too bright, was it not?"

He extended a hand to me. I took measured steps over to him, my heart like a wild bird in a cage. Mesmerizing blue eyes centered on me. He was much younger than I'd at first thought—not more than twenty—the face, beneath the mask, what my friends Christina and Evie would call *hot as hell*.

As soon as my fingers touched his, he pulled me into a twirling waltz, so fast I grew faint—so fast it seemed the ballroom had disappeared and we were dancing in a darkened space.

His arm tightened around my waist. His lips brushed my ear. I tensed. "How is it that you found your way into the tunnels?"

"I . . . I don't know what you're talking about." My voice faltered.

"Don't lie. It isn't attractive. Not in one quite so lovely as yourself." He drew himself back to study my face. "You saw me. And regrettably, you ran away from me."

A thought flashed through my mind. I steadied myself with a long breath. "There's a way out—through the tunnels—isn't there? That's why you guard them."

Laughter rose from his throat. "Oh my dear, you are amusing. No one needs to guard them. The tunnels will only lead you back to where you started. I'm afraid *out* is a concept you must put from your mind. There is no longer any *out*. There is only here."

Releasing me for a moment, The Provider turned back to the guests and gestured them onto the dance floor. Pairing off, they moved into the waltz. Aisha accepted the hand of a stout, beetle-like man. Missouri, Sophronia, and Philomena tried unsuccessfully to turn down the men who approached them. A svelte blonde woman in a black dress and the makeup of an eagle draped her arms around Ethan's neck, dragging him toward the dance floor. I hated her on sight.

The Provider once again pulled me toward him. His coat smelled of greasepaint and dust. "You should feel honored—you are the reason I ventured down to this dreary hole tonight. I had to meet the one who can step through cave walls."

Fear coiled inside me. "You came here because of *me*?" My voice rang loud—too loud—in my ears.

A slow smile inched across his face. "Dance with me. You can't stall like that in the middle of the dance floor."

I realized then I was standing there frozen. It was as though everyone in the ballroom had heard me and stopped still, too. Ethan and Aisha stared at me open-mouthed. Missouri and Sophronia eyed me in shock as their masked dance partners waltzed them away—their expressions confused and questioning.

Jessamine stood by the grandfather clock, staring over at me with pitying eyes.

The Provider flicked a hand toward the guests, indicating that they should keep dancing. I moved back into the waltz, my steps wooden and dazed.

He touched me beneath the chin with a finger. "Don't disappoint me. Tell me how you managed to *step through*. Only one of you has been able to see through the wall before. But no one has reached the other side."

"I don't understand what you mean. I don't understand anything about this place." Desperation rose inside me. "You have to let us go. The police know exactly where we were headed—I wrote it in my diary."

He rose an eyebrow, as though he knew I was lying. "Did you now? How amusing."

A sob caught in my throat. "It's not too late. We won't tell. Let us go. Let all of us go. From this *dreary hole,* as you call it."

"But my dear, you came here quite unbidden, uninvited."

"That was a mistake."

"There are no mistakes," he said, lowering his voice. His eyes were smoldering. "There is intent behind everything we do. You are here because you want to be."

"Believe me. I don't want to be here."

"Don't you? Look deeper. All the girls here were once running from something. Oh, I know all their dark secrets. Missouri was fleeing from her terrible family. Angeline was running from her ordinary life. Little Philomena, she wandered off in the woods that day so she no longer had to see the baby brother who had taken her place. As for Sophronia, well, she was fleeing from something—a twelve-year-old girl doesn't make her way into the depths of Devils Hole alone for a picnic." He paused to stare at me. "So what is your story?"

"Didn't you say I was the bud who didn't wish to bloom?" I lifted my chin.

"Oh, you *are* that. I can see it in the awkward way you carry yourself in that very grownup dress. But you do have a story, and I intend to find out what it is." He leaned a little closer. "I intend to find out who *you* are."

He smiled. He had perfect teeth, a perfect face—angular and sharp, as though carved from stone. He'd noticed me, in this dress. I became uncomfortably aware of my own body. Chopin's "Nocturne No. 20" grew loud in my ears, its vaulting, tragic-beautiful notes reverberating through my chest.

I took a deep breath. "Why are you keeping us here?"

He sighed. "Life operates on a system of predators and prey. You see, there needs to be small sacrifices for higher aims."

My heart caught in my ribcage. "And we are the sacrifices?"

He shook his head, and looked vaguely annoyed. "This is a day of celebration. You're boring me."

"You said before that this is a day where the masters serve the servants. I demand the masters do as we ask."

He stared at me with a cold interest.

Boldly, I met his gaze. "I propose a game. You let us out, into the forest. We get to run and you all get to chase. But you all must be blindfolded."

He laughed. "My dear, you don't have the barest notion of who we are, do you? We would have you in our grasp within seconds. Where is the sport in that?"

All breath sucked from my lungs. What did he mean, *they would have us in their grasp within seconds*?

No, I didn't know who they were. I had no idea who they were.

"Then just . . . let us go." My voice shrank to a whisper.

His hand tightened on the small of my back. "You're a frightened child, and nothing more. I will find out how you gained passage to the tunnels, if it's the last thing I do."

Aisha spun past in the arms of the beetle man. He moved in to kiss her, but she shook her head. He grabbed her arm, telling her something I couldn't hear. Struggling from his hold, she quickly turned and fled the ballroom, her hand pressed to her lips.

Ethan's blonde dance partner finished her waltz with him. She marched up to The Provider and me. "He's mine, Sweetpea." She gave a cold smile and stepped in between us, throwing her arms around him. Up close, she looked around eighteen years old. The dress she wore—it was the same black velvet dress from the mannequin in the storage chamber. Dust sat in the folds of the gown.

"Audette," he sighed. "You are so possessive."

"Just the way you like me." She nuzzled his neck.

I retreated into the library, catching my breath between the bookcases, hoping I could stay hidden in the shadows.

The waltz ended. The guests stopped and clapped.

The Provider held his arms out. "My friends," he said expansively, "we mustn't neglect our new masters on the Feast of Fools!"

He waved a hand in the air, and the people surged forward to the table. They heaped decadent selections of cakes and hors d'oeuvres onto plates, and began offering them around to the Dollhouse captives.

The Provider brought a plate to me, bowing as he did so, with a flourish of his cape. "An *amuse-bouche*, just for you."

Tentatively, I took the plate, staring down at a rectangular prism of savory jelly. It had some type of globe-shaped food trapped inside it—something that looked like an animal's eye.

None of the guests were eating. Their eyes seemed hungered, but not for the food.

I turned away from them. I *had* to eat. My stomach ached. Jessamine brought another plate over to me—a plate of tiny, delicate cakes and profiteroles.

Ethan tried to cross the room toward me, but each time, he was stopped by the guests, and given food.

At last, hunger gave out. We ate until we could eat no more. I watched Ethan wolf down entire plates of devilled eggs and stuffed olives and cheeses.

Philomena pushed yet another slice of gooey caramel fudge into her mouth, and let out a groan, then collapsed onto the floor, holding her stomach.

Jessamine clapped her hands. "Up Philomena. Ladies do not make spectacles of themselves during dinner."

The little girl rolled onto her knees and crawled along the floor like a puppy to her chair. Jessamine clucked in distaste, but The Provider threw back his head and roared with laughter.

A cry started up among the people. "Lord of Misrule! Lord of Misrule!"

Two men and a woman heaved an old, wooden puppet theatre into the room.

An elderly woman stepped in front of the theatre, her vivid makeup smeared on her face, the lines around her mouth like spider's legs. "For those who don't know me, my name is Faustine, and I am a patron of the arts." Her accent was heavy, French, her voice husky. "Now, friends, enjoy the antics of the naughty boy Punch who does all the things we wish we could do and get away with." She paused. "Well, in our case, we actually *do* do all the things we wish could do."

The people appeared to find this riotously funny. They laughed and tittered.

"Punch is the Lord of Misrule," she went on, raising a pair of pince-nez glasses to her face, "and the centuries-old tradition of celebrating his reign shall continue!"

The guests clapped as three of them positioned themselves behind the puppet theatre. They acted out a simple play of slapstick retribution with the ugly marionette puppets.

Cackling laughter bounced around the room as Punch, left to babysit his own baby, hit the squalling baby with a rolling pin. A passing policeman saw Punch hitting the baby, and Judy and the policeman rushed in to hit Punch with a baton.

The play finished to uproarious mirth. Philomena had sat enthralled through the whole thing. Next, The Provider called Philomena to play a game with Clown. He instructed Missouri to wind a scarf around Philomena's eyes as a blindfold. The wooden clown moved to the center of the dance floor. Philomena had to find

Clown, with Clown being allowed to tilt to avoid her grasp. The people laughed hysterically and clapped her on. After a few minutes, Clown tilted forward to make it easy for Philly to grab him. She wrestled her blindfold down, relieved to have found him.

The Provider bent down to her. "You won, butterfly. And here is your prize." He handed her a long wooden box, painted with clown mouths.

She fixed her gaze intently on the box, her small fingers scrambling to open the lid. She shrieked as a jack-in-the-box leapt out. A round of sharp laughter hit the air.

Philomena turned and stared at Missouri with wide eyes, as though to check if it was okay that a toy should jump out at you from a box. Here, toys did a lot of unexpected things.

The Provider clasped his hands, smiling at her benevolently. "And now you may choose the next game."

She stepped away from the toy. "Hide and seek," she said shyly.

Missouri shook her head vehemently, trying to catch Philly's attention.

The Provider bowed. "As you wish, my lady. Ladies, you are to hide. The games ends when we find you all."

One of the men held back Ethan's arm when he started to move. "Got to give the ladies a sporting chance, eh? You can wait five minutes."

Missouri took Philly's hand and left for the corridor. Sophronia followed. I knew where they were all headed—the bathroom. It was the only room with a door. None of us wanted to be found by The Provider or his guests—though I knew we would be found eventually.

I went to hide on the carousel that should have led to the exit. Aisha was already there, curled up under a chariot, staring up at me.

"Get in," she hissed.

I crouched on the floor of the chariot beside her.

Her eyes were almost glazed, red-rimmed and filled with terror. "The man who I was dancing with," she whispered. "He told me we would never get out of here. None of us."

I inhaled a shuddering breath. "The Provider told me the same thing." I cleared my throat. "But they're just trying to scare us."

She shook her head. "There's something wrong with those people." She squeezed her eyes closed. "I mean, not just because they're keeping us here. I can't explain it. Their eyes . . . *change*. Like they have dark pits instead of eyes."

My insides compressed into a tight ball. I didn't want to voice the dark thoughts in my head. Swallowing, I listened for footsteps and the jingle of their ornate jewelry.

"I'm sorry . . ." she breathed.

I put a finger to my mouth.

Her voice lowered to a whisper I could barely hear. "No, I need to say this . . . in case . . . in case we die tonight. This thing tonight— these people—has made me see how stupid I've been. I was angry when I told Jessamine you kissed Ethan. I swear I didn't know she'd send you to the Toy Box. We need to stick together, not fight each other."

A sharp finger prodded my side. I jerked my head up to see the woman named Faustine bending down to peer at me.

"Found you." She clapped her hands gleefully, raising her pince-nez glasses to eyes that looked as cold as a predator's. "Now we must find the others. What fun!"

Aisha and I stood. But already, Faustine had vanished.

The stout man that Aisha had been dancing with jumped onto the carousel platform. "Booooo," he roared. "Run, little girl. Run!"

He chased Aisha out into the corridor, running with his arms out like a gorilla's. I raced after them. The man caught her, wrapping his arms around her and lifting her high. Aisha screamed.

Ethan bolted from the other end of the hall, leapt onto the man's back, and closed his hands around his neck.

"Ethan!" I shouted.

But he didn't listen. He squeezed tighter and tighter, his mouth determined under the mask. The man stumbled, then fell to the ground with Aisha. The bird mask fell away. His face was dark purple around bulging blue eyes, his hook-nose pointed upward. Aisha crawled out, whimpering, from beneath the limp man.

My lower lip shook. *Ethan had killed one of them.*

But then the man on the ground turned his head toward me and winked.

Terror drilled through me. Aisha was right. There was something very, very wrong with these people. Racing into the kitchen, I grabbed a kitchen knife. As I ran back to the corridor, I saw that Raggedy had pressed Ethan against the wall. The beetle man had vanished. Without thinking, I plunged a knife into Raggedy's back. I ripped into her soft stuffing, tearing the blade downward.

With a grunting yell, Ethan pushed Raggedy from him. She fell onto her back with a heavy thud.

He took the knife from me and sliced the blade across Raggedy's neck. "I'll see how you damned dolls move!"

Stuffing burst from inside her. Reaching a hand in, he felt around inside her chest cavity. He threw handfuls of stuffing on the floor. Raising the blade again, he cut across the top of the doll's soft head and pulled the stuffing free. Her smiling face deflated.

Ethan moved back, panting, face distorted with confusion and terror. "There's nothing in there!"

"Quick!" Aisha pulled his arm. "Before the other Toys come."

Down the corridor, Missouri appeared. Her hand covered her

mouth at the sight of the disfigured Raggedy lying on the floor. She raised terrified eyes to us. "They came for us in the bathroom and Philly got scared and ran. But I can't find her! Or Sophronia—she's missing too!"

We raced after her. The bathroom, bedroom, and ballroom were all completely empty. *Where had they all gone? Had the guests left?*

We stepped back into the hall. There was only one place left to search: the Toy Box. My heart rattled as we ran toward it. I saw a flash of white material in the darkness ahead of us. Philomena had been wearing a white dress.

"Oh no," Missouri breathed. "I have to get her out of there."

"Let's all go." Ethan gave a short nod.

With arms wrapped around myself, I took stiff steps down into the passage.

"Philly?" Missouri whispered. "It's me, Missy. Don't be scared."

Silence.

Then the sound of rock scraping on rock.

"Someone's opening the Toy Box." Missouri's face was taut.

The black air crawled over me as we ventured farther in. The dress flared out in the darkness ahead.

"Philomena!" Missouri called.

Again, she didn't answer.

"She must be trying to hide," said Missouri tightly.

"We have to go after her." My voice trembled thinly. I couldn't allow what had happened to me to happen to a five-year-old child.

Sticking closely together, we crept through the Toy Box and inside the crypt-like entrance to the hidden cave. I was back, back in that black void where nightmares become real. The door scraped behind us with a dreadful note of finality—closing. Despite the chill, a thin trail of sweat wound down my spine.

Missouri had said she'd been in the Toy Box many times by herself—

she must know the way out again. I held onto that thought.

Far ahead, a lamp illuminated the cave wall—the lamp that Jessamine kept on the statue's arm.

Footsteps rang out against the stone. We hung back, even though the weak light didn't quite touch us. The Provider strode into the light, swishing his white cape over his shoulder. We watched as he stepped inches from the wall—and disappeared.

"It was his *cape* that we saw," Missouri gasped. "Not Philly's dress."

Aisha and Ethan crossed the cave floor to the far wall and began moving their hands over its surface, wedging their fingers into every crack and fissure. Missouri and I ran after them.

"What the—?" Ethan pounded his fists against the rock.

Missouri turned to look at me. "Calliope found her way through there yesterday."

"You did?" Ethan turned to me. "What is it? A switch or something?"

"No," I said, my voice cracking. "I-I don't know how I did it."

"What do you mean, *you don't know how*?" Missouri fired back. "You must."

I held her gaze. Why did she think she had the right to question me like that when she wouldn't answer my questions about Prudence? "I'm telling you the truth."

"We all heard what The Provider said to you," she told me, her voice cracking. "He said he had only come here because of you. Those people have never come here before, but now they've taken Philly and Sophronia—"

"We don't know that," Ethan cut in.

"Then where are they?" Missouri demanded.

Ethan exhaled a loud, sharp breath, turning back toward the wall. "There's got to be a panel or something."

A rush of whispering vibrations swept through the cave.

Ethan clenched his jaw. "What the hell is that?"

"Shut the voices out," said Missouri quickly. "Don't listen. Remember what I told you."

An immense shadow crept across the cave wall. At first it seemed just a play of light caused by the lamp. But it moved with its own energy, writhing and slipping.

My legs turned wooden. I'd seen the shadow before—it had been in the Dollhouse when Lacey vanished. The voices and the shadow—they were one and the same.

"Stay strong," came Missouri's voice. "No matter what. Don't listen to it."

I tried to block it out, to shut out my fear and the sound that echoed in my ears. But the whispers edged inside my mind.

Come with me.

Come with me.

My breaths were shudders and gasps. The voice, *that voice*—low and alien—penetrated my being, burrowing into my core. Once again, I tried to think back, before the Dollhouse, before the mountains, before leaving Miami. I tried to see Christina and Evie and my old school. Sunshine and kids on skateboards and bikes racing out the school gates.

But rivers of black ink rushed through every part of my memory, pouring from school windows and streaming along the sidewalks, until everything was stained black.

An acrid stench entered my nostrils—an odor of something burning. And all around, the scent of rain-soaked woods. Cold rain fell on me—sheets of it visible through the headlights of a car.

I was pulled back inside the scene of that accident—the car accident that had never happened. But so real, so vivid I could feel the rain falling on my face, could smell the burn of tires that had just screeched across a tar road.

A car door swung open on its hinges, letting the rain in. And someone sat slumped at the car's wheel.

A gasping cry brought me out of the dream. Aisha's cry.

I snapped my eyes open, not realizing I had closed them. We were on the other side. All of us.

15. THE ENDLESS CAROUSEL

The carnival calls
from behind the wall
They spin and turn
here in the underground
And watch you with eyes that burn
A dark dance on the carousel,
this parallel nocturne.

—P.

Three tunnels lay ahead—the same tunnels I'd seen before. The crystalline seams in the rock wall gave off just enough light to see. I sucked in a deep breath of stale air. The others stared about wide-eyed, their limbs trembling with shock.

"We're here . . . ." The words dropped from my lips. I pointed to the first tunnel. "That's the one I went down last time. All I found was a desk, and a dead end." I glanced at Missouri.

"Not that way," Missouri said quickly.

I'd known before I spoke that Missouri wouldn't want to go to where I'd found Prudence's desk.

"Okay, let's try this one." Ethan gestured toward the tunnel next to it.

We moved cautiously into the passage. The air was suffocating, thick. I couldn't escape the feeling that we were walking into the belly of a beast. Just like the first tunnel, this one curved around.

Holding out a hand, Ethan touched a transparent seam of crystal. "I didn't know that any caves in these mountains looked like these."

Beyond us, the tunnel plunged into darkness, the glowing seams disappearing. I cursed not having the lamp with us. Dread combed my back as we felt along the wall, moving farther and farther into the black air.

"Listen," whispered Missouri.

Was it possible? From ahead, I could make out the distant, tinny sounds of a carnival. We rounded a bend in the passage. Far ahead, multi-colored lights decorated the blackness—the lights of a Ferris wheel and carnival stalls.

The cave walls disappeared as we stole farther along. Dark trees rustled around us. *Trees.*

"My God," I breathed. "We're out of the Dollhouse. We're *outside . . . .*"

A reddish light washed over Ethan's wide-eyed face. "Let's stay far away from that funfair. We need to get to a road. We need to find help."

Staying close together, we threaded through the trees, Missouri reached out and crushed a leaf in her hand, a look of wonder on her face.

We were walking away.

Away from the mansion.

The night was moonless and so dark I could barely see what

stood just a few feet away, but I knew I was one step closer to getting back to real life. Hot showers, my clothes, my *mom*—hell, even my homework. My heart pounded so hard I thought it would puncture my lungs.

"Wait," said Ethan quietly. "I'm going to scout ahead a bit. If anything should happen to me, I want the rest of you to run—and keep running until you're so far away they'll never find you."

"We still need to find Philly," cried Missouri softly.

I swallowed. "The best help you could be to Philly is to bring rescue."

She hesitated. "I can't leave her. But you three should go." Purposefully, she stepped away toward the funfair, being careful to stay out of sight.

Ethan stepped off into the black night. Aisha and I waited a minute and then, hearing nothing, no shout, followed cautiously.

Suddenly, Ethan collided into me.

"Ethan!" I gasped.

His dark eyes stared into mine. "How did you get ahead of me?"

"We couldn't have," I answered. "You must have gotten turned around."

A floodlight from the carnival turned our way, the light almost reaching us as it flashed through the trees. "They know we're here," Aisha cried.

Giving up all notion of sneaking away, we fled.

But the second that we ran, the carnival lights were in front of us again. We were running *toward* the carnival instead of away from it.

Turning sharply, we headed in the other direction. But once more, somehow, the carnival was before us. From behind a circus tent, Missouri stared at us, not understanding.

Cursing, Ethan raced away, faster. Aisha screamed as the back of Ethan morphed into his front, and he raced back toward us.

With shaking steps, I moved forward and reached out an arm. I watched my own hand reach back to me, as in a mirror image. I snatched my arm away, revulsion rising in my stomach.

Missouri's eyes grew round as she stepped across to us, the whites of them shining in the darkness. "It's some kind of trick."

"No!" I breathed. We'd been so close, *so close*, to escape.

"Spread out," said Ethan. "Don't let them catch you!"

I dashed across the grounds, this time heading straight toward the fairground. If we couldn't *escape*, then maybe the only way out was the last place I wanted to go. And if Molly had been able to walk this way, then we could too.

I ducked behind a stall and stole a look around it. A man dressed as a court jester was tied spread-eagle to a spinning wheel. People threw knives at the wheel as it spun, shrieking with laughter as the blades narrowly missed the man's limbs. Guests who'd been at the Feast of Fools strolled around the grounds arm-in-arm, watching magic acts. A woman on teetering high heels stepped past me with two large wild cats on leashes—panthers. Carnival-goers sat inside Ferris Wheel pods, still wearing their masks, waiting for the ride to begin.

No smells of popcorn or candy drifted in the air at this carnival—the air was as stale as it had been in the tunnels, only warmer.

I had to keep moving. There had to be a way out. Fortunately, no one seemed to be running around looking for us. Maybe we hadn't been spotted, after all.

I crept onto a carousel—yet *another* carousel—sticking close to the shadows, and crouched behind the body of a fiberglass horse, my heart thudding. Where to next?

Fingers brushed my shoulder. I backed away, turning slowly.

The Provider's mouth twisted into a smile. "So, you visit us again, Cassandra."

"Leave us alone." My words sounded thin and childish.

The carousel began to turn. I stumbled backward and tried to run to the other side of the ride, concealing myself behind a chariot.

He was there, almost instantly. "But you came here to us, my dear."

Anger rose inside of me. I couldn't run. I couldn't hide. "Who are you?"

He smirked. Light blond hair brushed his collar and fell about his face—giving him a deceptively angelic look. I stared at him. I knew then I'd seen him before, with the woman who had claimed him as hers at the waltz—Audette—in a painting hanging in the Fiveash house. But no. That was impossible. The portrait had depicted a couple from the early 1900s.

"My name is Henry, if you must know. Raised in the Fiveash Circus, heir to the fortunes of *Le château sur la falaise solitaire.* Everything you see around you." He spread his arms out. My muscles tensed when I caught sight of the dark outline of a massive building in the distance. Not the Fiveash house, but a larger house, a thousand times larger. A castle.

"This is a terrible place," I told him, refusing to sound impressed.

"Ah, but you have seen but a sliver of the pie. Come, let me show you around." He offered a hand. "And you will tell me how you managed to pass through to here, and how you brought your friends with you this time."

My stomach clenched. So they did know that Missouri, Ethan, and Aisha were there.

"Are we just toys to you people?" I demanded, ignoring his words. "Toys to come and play with?"

He shrugged nonchalantly. "Toys are Jessamine's little hobby. I assure you, I am not here to play." He leaned closer, so close I could feel his breath on my temple. "But we can play a game if you wish."

He produced a deck of cards from inside his jacket pocket. "Pick a card, any card. If it's the Jack of Diamonds, you must tell me how you got through the wall. If you choose any other card, you may go free."

"I won't play stupid games with you," I spat back at him.

A girl in a black mini-dress and striped tights stood watching me from beside a circus tent. A butterfly mask concealed her face. But she hadn't been at the Feast of Fools as far as I could remember. Almost imperceptibly, she shook her head. Was she telling me not to trust Henry? If so, I didn't need the advice. Then she turned and ran in the direction of the castle. Was that the way out?

Without another word to Henry, I turned and chased after her.

I hadn't gone a hundred feet when a hand reached out and pulled me behind a fountain, where four stone gargoyles looked out from each corner. *Ethan.* Aisha and Missouri crouched behind him. Relief flooded me at seeing them again. I turned, but the girl in the striped tights was already gone.

"We've been looking for you," Ethan fixed anxious eyes on me. "We're heading inside that monstrosity." He indicated toward the castle. "We've tried to leave the grounds, but it's the same story everywhere—we can't get out. Maybe the way out is in there."

"They know we're here," I said quietly.

Wisps of red hair blew softly around Missouri's pinched face. "We didn't find Philly or Soph yet. We have to go back."

"We can't," I said. "Our best hope is to get out of here and get help." But even as I said it, I couldn't believe these people would let us find Philomena or Sophronia unless they wanted us to. The lights of the fairground blurred as I stared beyond the fountain, the Ferris wheel becoming like a pinwheel of fire. This wasn't real. None of it was real— at least, not what we understood to be real. Henry wouldn't have let me run from him if there was any danger of actually getting away.

A spray of fountain water flicked across my face, leaving a briny smell and taste in my nostrils and on my tongue. Even the water was wrong.

Across the grounds, I saw Henry conversing with an elderly butler in a suit. The butler pointed in the direction of the castle. Henry's shoulders hunched, as though suddenly carrying a great weight.

It was time to go. Under the cover of a long, rose-covered tunnel, we raced toward the castle. Keeping low to the ground, we crept around bushes and trees. A low arched door, only two feet or so high, stood at the base of the castle wall—the smell of stale alcohol drifting from it.

"Must be a cellar," Missouri said quietly.

We lifted the heavy wooden door and crawled inside.

Metal and wooden barrels were stacked in rows. Carefully, we moved between them—if we caused any of the barrels to fall it'd make a huge noise. The air was warm as we made our way out of the cellar and along a passageway. A single lamp cast a circular light over the crumbling walls and floor.

At the end of the passage stood a huge set of doors made of some kind of gleaming black stone. A carving of a strange tree spanned the doors—a tree with roots that looked almost the same as the bare branches. The image reminded me of the twisting tree roots and branches that Ethan had drawn in his notebook.

I watched Ethan's face as he ran a hand over the carving, a frown stitching itself between his eyebrows. "I've seen this before . . . ."

"Where?" Aisha asked.

His jaw tensed. "In dreams."

Frowning, his hands grabbed the metal rings. As he pulled back hard, the doors heaved open.

Heat rushed over us. The doors opened into a room with stone walls and a heavy mahogany desk. A fire roared in a cavernous fireplace—the warmth seeming like an illusion after the cold sterility of the Dollhouse. A smoky scent mingled with the musk of old rugs and books. Books and papers were stacked in high columns on the desktop.

Ethan closed the doors carefully behind us.

Outside the crosshatched metal of the arched window, dark rain lashed. *Rain*. It hadn't been raining out on the fairground. Was *this* the real world? Or was this all just image-on-image, all of it some vast distortion?

I moved a wooden chair beneath the window. I held fast to a lungful of air as my fingers fumbled to undo the rusted latch and push the window shutters open. I reached out an arm and cried out as water poured over my skin.

Aisha stared at me wonderingly. "Your arm is wet. There's no trick this time."

Tears sprang to my eyes. I turned back to Aisha, shaking my head. "It's a waterfall, with a rock wall behind it. It's not rain. We're still underground."

I shut the window quickly.

There was no other way out. Cursing, Ethan eyed the large room in frustration. Aisha stepped over to the desk and started rifling through the books and papers there, as if there might be a clue.

Missouri brushed her hair back from her face. "We have to try another way."

"Look at these," said Aisha softly. She held a handful of old sepia photographs—the same kind of photographs that had been in the Fiveash house, all featuring the Fiveash Circus.

"Henry—The Provider—grew up in the circus," I said. "Those must belong to him."

Missouri's eyes shadowed with suspicion. "How do you know his name is Henry?"

I met her gaze. "He told me, a short while ago, when he found me outside on the carousel."

Someone rattled the rings on the outside of the door. Ethan whirled around. We all dipped behind the desk as the door opened. I heard two sets of footsteps cross the stone floor and another door slide open.

We peeked up just as the door was shutting again—a concealed door that looked like an ordinary bookcase.

"Old castles are full of secret doors—I should have guessed," Ethan whispered.

"We should follow them," I said. "If we stay here, they'll only find us. It's our only hope."

We waited a few moments, then gathered by the bookcase, listening. We could hear nothing except the crackle of the fire and the waterfall pummeling the window. Carefully, I leaned against the bookcase to push it open. We stared down a long passage—an ancient-looking corridor with oil lamps along one wall dimly illuminating the stonework and paintings of somber people in medieval gear. Softly, we slipped into the hall and Aisha closed the door.

I felt exposed as we stole along the uneven flooring.

We passed dark rooms, thankfully empty of people. Each room had the same type of window—high and with a crosshatched metal grid. Each window had nothing but a rock wall behind it. The only exit was a set of large wooden doors at the end of the corridor.

Ahead, a wide arc of iridescent dark blue light swooped through the gloom. It was like nothing I had ever seen, pinwheeling out from the crack in the double doors. We crept down the passage, and took turns peering into the room beyond the doors. It contained nothing except a vast and intricate machine emitting the bright indigo light in a circle.

Henry was there, his face deep in concentration. The man I'd seen him with earlier—the butler—stood beside him.

I'd seen a device like this only once, on a school excursion to a museum. They'd called it an astronomical clock. Only that clock hadn't been the size of a car and hadn't been anything near as complicated as this one. This one had gears running within gears, a panel of dials, and a spinning globe suspended in its center.

Henry moved a hand over the globe. Tiny spinning balls rose in the air in clusters—millions of them. Backdrops of brilliant pinks and reds and purples glistened in mid-air. The sheer beauty of it temporarily drove away my fear.

"It looks like the whole damned universe." Ethan's words were so soft I barely heard them.

I nodded. "I think it's a clock. It measures the positions of the stars and moon and planets."

Henry stalked back and forth, seemingly frustrated. We watched as he adjusted the dials again. Another set of glowing orbs sprung up. He stood back, his chin in his hand, studying them.

A dark figure appeared directly behind him. A chill sped through me. The light of the universe and stars crept into the crevices of an aged, misshapen face—the man's eyes like chips of hard black stone.

He'd been burned almost to cinders, yet he was still alive. A cold malice emitted from him. Evil. That's what he was; there was no other way to say it.

I wanted to run. At the same time, I was frozen in place.

Henry, startled, spun around on his heel. "Monseigneur Balthazar . . . You sent for me?"

"Yes. What news have you, Henry?" said the man. His voice sounded like air moving through old, dry reeds.

Henry bent his head slightly, in a submissive gesture, his

knuckles pressed together. "He continues to elude us. But we believe he hid the book before he left. We're getting closer, we'll have it in our hands soon." He turned back to the machine, his eyes large and glazed. "And then we'll have the instructions to operate this cursed thing."

Balthazar made a guttural, almost snarling, sound in his throat. "You are the only one of my useless descendants with a grand vision that befits my name. Do you remember, our destiny is written in blood? We, who will walk among the stars of a thousand thousand worlds." His lipless mouth curled upward in a grimace. "You will not disappoint me."

His accent was hard to decipher—it was thick, possibly French.

"I will not disappoint," said Henry reverently.

Balthazar strode around the astronomical clock, staring up at the galaxies, then snapped his head around to Henry. "This girl you spoke of—Cassandra—she can see through the wall, like the other one?"

Ethan's fingers tightened on my shoulder.

Henry hesitated for a moment, straightening his collar. "Yes, Monseigneur. But the other girl could only see through the wall in visions. This one can pass through. But I don't know how."

"Then she does pose a risk, however small. We have no measure, Henry, to know which of them has learned to pass through. They all must die, the ones on the other side of the wall."

My heart hammered in my throat—loud in my ears. Aisha sucked in a quick breath of disbelief. Balthazar's voice sounded in my head over and over. *They must all die. They must all die.*

Henry's face dropped. "We can't. They are Jessamine's playthings, her Toys. If Jessamine has nothing to occupy her, she might leave. We need her here. Her grandfather will surely return for her, sooner or later—and then we'll have him in our grasp."

The butler looked on coldly.

"You will find him in whichever world he has ventured," Balthazar said harshly. "You do not need Jessamine."

"But the girls, Monseigneur, they are promised to the serpent. We cannot travel between worlds without the power of her shadow. When I summoned the serpent to this earth, I made a bargain. Surely we cannot—"

"Listen to me!" Balthazar shook his disfigured head. "You have been on this earth but the blink of an eye. You cannot see as far as can I. A mosquito that lands on a man's limb will take but a drop of blood, yet its poison can take the life of that man. Might this girl be a drop of poisonous blood?"

"Cassie." Ethan's face was next to mine in the dark. He was pulling me backward. "We have to get the hell out of here."

I followed him woodenly, hardly knowing I moved. What did any of it mean? We were promised to a serpent—a snake? I was poisoned blood?

We returned down the corridor the way we had come. When we got to the door that should have led back through the bookcase, Ethan placed his hands around the long, ornate handles and pulled. At first, the doors refused to budge. Shouldering the wood, he pressed forward.

Too late. We heard the whispering voices.

The doors flung open.

Into darkness.

Unable to speak, Aisha pointed at a lamp—a lamp hanging from the arm of a stone statue.

We were back in the Toy Box.

Aisha whimpered. Ethan cursed. I was shaking so hard, I thought I might stumble. The tunnels had vanished. The wall had once again reappeared.

We fumbled our way toward the light. Jessamine stood at the entrance to the Toy Box, her arms rigid beside her body, her small fists clenched. "You hideous creatures! You destroyed my Raggedy and then went to hide."

Ethan stepped forward. "I did that. So you can punish me—not them."

"Those people terrorized us," I said quickly. I couldn't bear to see Ethan locked up again. "The fat man was carrying Angeline away, and Evander leapt to her honor. But Raggedy held Evander back. He did what he could to get away, to save Angeline."

Jessamine's lip quivered. "Beaumont Baldcott was being improper with Angeline?"

"Yes," cried Aisha. "I was terrified of him."

Jessamine stared at each of us in turn. "And what were you doing in the passage?"

"Searching for Sophronia and Philly," said Missouri. "We can't find them anywhere. I need to know they're safe."

Jessamine gave her a nod. "I hid them both cleverly in a storage cupboard. They're both in the kitchen now having nice cups of tea."

She turned to Ethan, her chin tilting upward. "Acts of heroism cannot atone for the destruction of a well-loved Toy. You will spend a day in the Toy Box to ruminate on your transgressions."

My heart dropped. "You can't leave him in there!"

Missouri cast me a warning glance.

"You wouldn't think it now," said Jessamine, "but Missouri spent quite some time in the Toy Box when she first came to us. She survived it and became quite beautifully correct."

Panic sped through me. "But there's something *in* the Toy Box. We all heard it. And . . . saw it."

Aisha clung to Ethan's arm. "It wanted to hurt us. Please, don't leave him with that thing."

"I'll be okay," said Ethan, without conviction.

"Enough, now." Jessamine's pale eyes bored into us. "It is nothing but an imagining of the darkness itself. You must repel it with as much gusto as you must repel darkness within yourselves. If you are weak, it will consume you."

Aisha and I glanced at each other, our breath rapid, but said no more.

The scraping sound of Clown echoed through the corridor. This time, he was coming for Ethan.

16. CONFESSIONS

Children, do not enter this maze
For the shadow, she knows all the ways
The only sound is the ticking clock
And the drum of your heart, *knock, knock*
As you follow your feet
Down the paths one, two, and three
And I have seen where path four leads
Straight to her. Forever more.

—P.

I washed away the heavy makeup, scrubbing my face dry with the edge of a threadbare towel, and stared at myself in the bathroom mirror. I felt exposed without the makeup, raw. Hastily, I drew new red circles on my cheeks and colored my mouth in red and my eyelids in pink and lilac. Now I could hide again, pretend this was happening to someone else. A world where there were people—or beings—who wanted us dead.

After we returned from the Toy Box, Jessamine had given us tea and sent us straight to bed. It was now morning, and Ethan had stayed in the Toy Box all night. I could barely allow myself to think of him and whether he was still alive. All night long, Jessamine had stationed Clown at the exit of the bedroom. I didn't know whether she thought we would try to free Ethan or whether she feared Henry and his sick friends would return and harm us in our sleep.

Aisha slipped inside the bathroom. She surveyed my fresh makeup, then eyed her own painted and smeared face. Leaning over the sink, she scrubbed at the heavy greasepaint.

I bit into my lip. "I can't imagine spending a whole night in the Toy Box. Do you think . . .?" My voice closed to a whisper.

She stood silently for a moment, staring into the mirror as water dripped from her wan skin, her face a mask of horror.

I handed her a towel.

"Please. Don't think about it." She wiped her face dry. Small traces of paint were left on her skin. "I need you."

I stopped and stared at her. "How can any of this really be happening? These things, these people . . ."

"I don't know. God, I don't know." Her eyes almost glazed over in a silent panic, a panic trapped deep inside her.

"I feel like it's all my fault," I whispered. "Missouri blames me. I-I don't even know what's happening. I don't know how we got to the other side of the wall or why."

She eyed me fearfully. "And you really have no idea how you get into the tunnels?"

I shook my head.

She tugged a brush through her hair. "Do-do you think that Lacey was taken . . . as an offering? The Provider said we were promised to a *serpent* . . . ."

The eyes of those people burned through my mind. Bright, hungered eyes.

"I don't know." Nausea rushed from the pit of my stomach into my throat. "But we have to find a way to get out of here. Today. Before they kill us."

Swallowing, she nodded. I turned to go, but she grabbed my wrist.

"Cassie," she began in a whisper. "I meant what I said before. I'm sorry for what I did to you. I never thought you'd end up in the Toy Box. I wasn't thinking. I wasn't myself. I was just raging inside."

"It doesn't matter," I told her. "None of that matters now."

"No," she said staunchly. "It matters. If-if the tunnel people come, and they do to us what that Balthazar man told Henry to do, then I want a clear conscience. Please, allow me that."

I bent my head. "Can I tell you something? Nothing happened between Ethan and me. And he never kissed me. Out in the forest, I was so scared, for you, and for myself. I kissed *him*. But he didn't kiss me back. And that's all—nothing else."

A gasp caught at her throat. "God, I've been incredibly stupid. I just assumed…." She trailed off, squeezing her hands together. "I guess I was jealous because I know he's liked you from the start."

"Aish, that's not true."

She exhaled a low breath. "Yes, it's true. I found out at Lacey's party two months ago. I overheard him say so."

"At Lacey's party?" Things like parties and normal life seemed like a dream now, so out of reach we could never return.

"Yeah. Dominic was bragging that he could hook up with you by the end of the night." She half-smiled. "Dom always thought he was such a player."

I remembered Dominic, with the surfer hair and tan, though he'd apparently never set foot on a surfboard. He'd approached me at the party—half-drunk and spilling a beer on my shoe—expecting I'd jump at the chance to go out with him. His jaw had hung open when I turned him down.

"Ethan told Dominic to back off," she said. "Dom said he knew Ethan hadn't taken his eyes off you since the day you walked through the school gates, and he tried to bet Ethan that he'd get you first. Ethan said he liked you way too much to make it a game."

I inhaled sharply, seeing a rush of images: Ethan at the party, how hot he'd looked in his white T-shirt and jeans, wavy hair messed and falling over one eye.

She watched my reaction carefully, pulling her bottom lip through her teeth. "Look, I'm not proud of what I did later that night, but after I heard what Ethan said, I was determined to get him before you did. I'd always liked him. The girls at school were crazy about him—they all wanted a chance to tame Ethan McAllister. But I always thought that when he did choose a girl, he'd choose *me*."

She pushed her thick, dark hair behind her ears, eyeing me with regret. "And so I made my move. I approached Ethan, crying that I had a really big problem and needed his help. I took him out to the yard, and up to Lacey's sisters' tree house. We sat there drinking a bottle of bourbon together. He was pretty drunk. We both were." She bent her head. "I . . . stripped to my underwear and told him I wanted to do it with him. He said he couldn't—that he was leaving. I knew it was because he wanted to be with you. So, I-I told him I'd seen you with Dominic in Lacey's bedroom. He stayed. And we *did it*. And afterward, he felt like he had to be with me, become my boyfriend. I knew he would. He's just like that. He's just *good*."

I expelled a lungful of air, slowly. "I wouldn't have guessed any of that." Aisha had always seemed so sure of herself back then. Like everything came to her so easily. "But it was his decision to sleep with you."

"I know. But it doesn't make what I did any better." Tears tracked lines through the fresh makeup on her cheeks.

A question crushed into me. "Do you love him?"

She squeezed her eyes shut. "Maybe I could have, if I hadn't had to live with the fact that he always wanted *you*. I knew it was only a matter of time before he'd decide to leave me behind." She sighed a low, sad breath. "You do have feelings for him, right?"

"I feel like . . . I don't even know who he is." It was true. Ethan was like the dark light of the forest at dusk—so *in between*. When we'd camped together, I'd come to know a side of him that was full of secrets. Even the notebook of his I'd found— with the ugly, twisted drawings of trees and the strange poem— still chilled me.

"Cassie," she said softly, "I've seen it on your face when you look at him. It used to hurt—so bad. But not anymore. It's already over between Ethan and me. But I want *you* to know it's over, okay? If this is our last day on this earth, I want you to know that. I want you to know how he really feels about you. How he's *always* felt."

I held her gaze for a moment, not knowing what to say. I'd wanted to hear those words for what seemed forever. Something burst inside me—something that had been held tight and compressed and hidden away. But I didn't know what it even meant now, for Ethan and Aisha to no longer be together. What *could* it mean, in a place as twisted as where we were?

We fell on each other in a hug. This was the Aisha I'd known before the Dollhouse, before she and Ethan had become girlfriend and boyfriend. I hadn't realized how much I missed her. It was like getting back a small piece of something from the real world.

Hearing footfall in the corridor outside, we broke away.

"It won't be our last day," I said, although the words sounded hollow, even to me. "I promise you that."

She shook her head sadly. "No one ever escapes."

Suddenly, I remembered Prudence's book, which I'd hidden away under the mattress. Between the Feast of Fools and the heavy tea, I hadn't been able to look at it again.

"Aish!" I held her arms. "In the Toy Box, when Jessamine put me there, I found a book—a book belonging to a girl named Prudence. She was the first one to be brought in here. And she wrote poems about this place all through the book. If *she* got away, maybe she knows a way out!"

Aisha sucked in a large gasp of air, her eyes wide. "Where is it?"

Before I could answer, Jessamine pushed open the door. "You will join the others in the ballroom. There is no breakfast this morning." She hesitated. "I checked on Evander earlier. He is doing well, and is pleasingly contrite, you will be happy to learn."

Aisha and I followed Jessamine to the ballroom. My mind was racing. I had to get back to the bedroom.

In the ballroom, Missouri knelt at the fireplace, poking at the flames. Sophronia sat with her needlepoint. Philomena was curled up on a chair with her headless teddy bear, sucking her thumb. Jessamine stood near the bookshelves, her expression anxious in a way I'd never seen it before. For once, the fire was roaring, and it was warm.

Missouri jabbed a poker at a thick rectangular object in the fire. An edge of gold leaf stuck out from the embers.

And suddenly, I knew.

I raced to the fireplace, knocking Missouri aside as I reached to grab it. But it was already half ash. Enraged, I didn't even feel the burn of the fire on my flesh.

"You," I screamed. "How dare you? You don't *want* us to get out, do you?"

Her gaze turned distant. "You don't understand."

"You're right—I don't understand you. Not for a second."

Aisha stood open-mouthed, staring in anguish at the burned book: our last hope.

"Calliope!" Jessamine glared at me. "I do not stand for fighting amongst you. It is intolerable."

Too furious to care about Jessamine, or her punishments, I stormed across the room. At the carousel, I clutched a pole, steadying myself, trying to calm my breathing. The book was gone.

Then again . . . the book had been so old that pages were coming free from their binding. Missouri might have snatched the book quickly and not noticed any pages falling loose.

Jessamine scowled and me. "Calliope, you will sit down at once, or suffer the consequences."

Immediately, Bear and Clara moved toward me.

Thinking quickly, I clutched at my stomach. "Forgive my behavior, Jessamine. My belly is sore. I need to run to the bathroom."

"You were just there," she said sternly.

"It must have been all the rich food yesterday. My stomach is upside down."

Sophronia stole a curious glance at me, her eyebrows knitting together.

"Then go." Jessamine gave a quick wave of her hand. "But do not stay away for long. I want you all together." She looked about her as if a demon might charge out at us from the shadows. Or something worse.

She knew. She knew exactly what was going to happen to us.

I rushed up the corridor, opening and slamming the bathroom

door to make it sound as though I'd gone in there. Then I raced into the bedroom. I lifted my mattress, looking through the dark gloom for any sign of loose pages. There was nothing.

I let the mattress drop heavily.

A bundle of discarded clothing was lying just under the foot of my bed. Once a week, the laundry was put into the dumbwaiter to be taken up to be washed—by Donovan. The pinafore I'd worn was still there. Snatching it up, I plunged a hand into the skirt pocket.

A single piece of paper.

All that was left of Prudence's book.

With shaking fingers, I pulled it free. It was too dark to read any of the words. I needed some light. Stuffing it down the bodice of my dress, I returned to the ballroom, noticing Jessamine's satisfied nod when I entered.

Heading straight for the library, I pulled out a book, checking to see if Jessamine was watching. She was busy reading Philomena a story. Missouri and Sophronia were facing away from me.

Aisha left her chair and came to stand alongside me. She pushed the book she'd been reading back into the shelf, and pretended to browse for another. "What are we going to do?"

I kept my gaze straight ahead, on the book I held open in my hand. "I found a page from Prudence's book in the pocket of the dress I was wearing that day."

Aisha inhaled softly as I carefully took out the paper and laid it out on the open book. The page bore an illustration of a half-human woman kneeling before Poseidon—with long fiery hair and a reptilian tail. Underneath, it said:

Granddaughter of Poseidon: Lamia. Lamia had an affair with Zeus, bearing him children. When Zeus's wife—Hera—found out, she killed Lamia's children in a rage. In inconsolable grief and hatred, Lamia roamed the lands abducting and devouring children. In Jewish tradition, Lamia is also known as Lilith.

Aisha's eyes were wide as she stole a glance at me. *Abducted and devoured children,* she mouthed.

My heartbeat grew scattered. Aisha's gaze shifted to a poem scribbled below it. I looked over at Jessamine again. She was still absorbed in Philomena. So much the better.

I squeezed my eyes closed for a moment, trying to calm myself. Silently, I read Prudence's poem together with Aisha:

A Lily Fair and dripping roses
In the dark fairground
Aeolian harps yearn as the merry-go-round turns
with bells and chimes and nursery rhymes
and silver eyes and lullabies
But one of them comes and goes, comes and goes
Like the pendulum to and fro
Follow her down past the mirrored tree
Pool of Mnemosyne, terror of memory
The fourth path leads to darkest reverie.

She sighed. "Wish she'd just spelled it out in plain English."

I glanced over my shoulder, half-expecting to see Jessamine standing behind us. "Okay, so she's talking about one person who comes and goes, while the others stay going around in circles, on a carousel. The others must be us. We go around in circles. Right?"

"The one who comes and goes has to be Jessamine," said Aisha darkly. "Who else can come and go at will? So she must be Lily Fair."

"I guess so." But I wasn't sure. I'd never seen Jessamine leave the Dollhouse.

"It says there's a fourth path—does that means there's a fourth tunnel?" Aisha's eyes widened. "Weren't there only three?"

We fell silent for a moment, jagged thoughts piercing my mind. I closed the book, keeping Prudence's page safe within it.

I looked at Jessamine again. She was having difficulty staying awake. Her eyes kept drifting shut. Why did Jessamine sleep so much? She never even drank the tea that she forced on the rest of us.

She rose heavily, looking around at each of us in turn. "You all mean a great deal to me. You have brought me joy, in your own fashion." She seemed to struggle for words. "It might be best if you all have a lovely cup of tea and recover properly from the excitement of yesterday."

My fingers tightened on the book's spine—tea meant sleep. We couldn't steal back to the Toy Box then.

An expression of panic crossed Missouri's face. "But we've just woken . . ."

Jessamine stood. "You will drink the tea. Sophronia, please do get the tea cart ready."

Sophronia did Jessamine's bidding without hesitation. She kept her eyes cast down as she brought back the cart of hot tea, her knuckles white on the handles.

"Now I will watch as you drink. Down to the last drop." Jessamine stood and paced around the room, stopping before each of the girls as they gulped it. "No child wants to take their medicine. And when they are better, none of them remember it was the medicine that made them so."

Aisha stared over at me with dread in her eyes. Jessamine watched Aisha drink the tea down to the last mouthful.

I couldn't let Jessamine make me drink that stuff. I needed a chance to get to the Toy Box. Ethan was in there . . . and somewhere, maybe, was the fourth tunnel.

I took a cup of tea from the cart as Jessamine watched Missouri drink her *medicine*. Reaching behind the seat of my chair, I poured the tea into the plush upholstery.

I made a pretense of drinking down the whole cup when Jessamine came to stand in front of me, wincing as though it burned my tongue.

Sophronia collected the cups and returned the cart to the kitchen.

Everyone's eyes grew heavy as the minutes ticked on.

Philomena curled up and slept on a rug on the floor. Missouri wilted against the back of her chair. Aisha's head rested on her arm, her eyes closed and her hand still holding the book.

Jessamine slipped into a deep sleep. Immediately, Clara tumbled to the ground—and stayed there. Clown slumped against the puppet theatre. I'd never seen the Toys fall down before. Was it Jessamine who controlled them? And if so, how did she operate them all those other times when she'd seemed to be fast asleep?

Only Sophronia and myself remained awake. I knew then that despite Sophronia's obedience to Jessamine, she'd somehow been able to conceal the fact she hadn't had the tea. So, she wasn't as dutiful to Jessamine as she pretended to be.

Like me, she stared curiously at the fallen Toys. I wished I knew what she was thinking. She never gave anything away. I hoped the fact that she had hidden from the party-goers yesterday with Philly meant she was on our side. I had the uncomfortable feeling that she observed everything that went on in the Dollhouse, silently calculating things known only to herself.

Clown rolled from the theatre onto the floor with a clatter.

No one woke.

There were no other Toys in the room.

Sophronia's cool gaze followed me as I rose from my chair and slipped into the corridor.

The mouth of the Toy Box opened ahead. I hadn't intended on returning alone. Fear raked through my chest with icy fingers, clawing me with every nightmare I'd ever had.

But Ethan was in there, *alone*. I stepped inside.

My feet stumbled, and I fell hard, stifling a scream.

Bear was lying slumped on the rock floor.

Had Jessamine had been so tired she'd somehow neglected to give them instructions, or do whatever she did to ensure they stayed awake to guard us? Somehow, Jessamine and the Toys were linked.

At least with all the Toys down—or destroyed in the case of Raggedy—none of them could pursue me.

I steadied the rapid breaths that rattled in my throat. Pitch-blackness enveloped me as I crept inside. My fingers found the secret lever that controlled the cave door and, with a grinding motion, it slid open.

A light glowed faintly on the arm of the saint statue on the far side of the cave. But there was no Ethan. Had he found a way to the tunnels?

Hands grasped my shoulders.

I whipped around.

17. INVENTION OF THE DARKNESS

I will be gone from here and sing my songs
In the forest wilderness where the wild beasts are,
And carve in letters on the little trees
The story of my love, and as the trees
Will grow the letters too will grow, to cry
In a louder voice the story of my love.

—Virgil, *Eclogues*

E than's face was before me, his eyes dark in the dim light. "Did you come alone?"

I nodded, catching my breath. "What were you doing?"

"Trying to find the goddamned way out."

I told him about Jessamine insisting we all have tea to sleep and how I'd tipped my tea into the back of my chair.

A grin made his eyes crease. "Go Girl Wonder."

A small bubble of joy rose inside of me. Ethan was okay. He was alive. "Were you scared . . . in here?"

He blew out a long breath. "Yeah."

"I hated you being in the Toy Box."

"It's okay. I'm okay." He grinned as though to assure me of that fact.

"Did that . . . *thing* come back?"

"Yeah." His face turned solemn. "Cassie, *it knows us*. At first I heard all these weird vibrations, and then I started to make out words. It *spoke* to me. It told me that my granddad is dying, and that I never should have left him alone."

A gasp caught in my lungs. "It actually said those things to you?"

His eyes glazed. "And it said . . . it said it knows the way out."

I took a step back. "No. Missouri said never to listen to it."

"Well she hasn't exactly been on our side. What if the *shadow* is trying to help us? It was there on the cave wall just before we got through. Think about it."

"I don't care if it wants to help us or not. Ethan, the first time I saw that thing was right when Lacey disappeared. I thought I was imagining things. But I know now that I wasn't. It took her away."

He frowned deeply, eyeing me as though shaken from a dream. "Then maybe she got out."

I glanced toward the wall, willing it to vanish, to crumble away. But it remained. "She would have brought help if she'd gotten out."

"I'm sorry." he told me, rubbing his forehead. "I think I'm going a bit crazy. I tried to find out for myself what operates the wall. I've walked all the way around this cave, checking the walls for a switch or a lever. But I found zero."

He leaned against the rock. "Cassie . . . I keep thinking . . . I know it sounds crazy, but maybe the people here *aren't* people? I mean, they're not *real*, not like how you and I are real."

I crossed my arms to keep from shivering. "I don't understand."

"I can't explain it any better than that."

"Nothing down here makes sense. But there's a fourth tunnel somewhere, and we have to find it."

"How do you know?"

"Missouri told me about The First One. She said The First One knew the secrets of this place. Well, I found something of hers—a book, full of her writings." I sighed in bitter frustration. "But Missouri burned the book, leaving me with just one page, just one poem. The poem speaks of a fourth path, and someone called Lily Fair who we're supposed to follow."

"Do you think she was using you to find the book so she could destroy it?"

"I don't know what to think," I said tightly.

He moved beside me, a triangle of lamplight forming on his cheekbone. My breath caught fast at the closeness of him.

It was so surreal to be here with him, like this. If I could go back—back to that first day of school, seeing him standing there with that trademark grin—and people had told me I'd end up in a place like this with him, trying to make a solid wall disappear, I would have thought they were insane.

His brown eyes stared into mine. "Cassie . . . what I wanted to tell you before, when I was in the cell, is that . . . when you kissed me that night, I didn't want it to stop."

I shook my head slightly, not trusting myself enough to answer.

His fingers brushed mine, sending a rush of warmth into my skin, then entwining my hand. "I didn't kiss you back that night because I didn't want you getting mixed up with me. I wanted you off the mountains."

"I didn't have the right to do what I did."

"Don't be sorry. Aish and I aren't together anymore—we never really were." He gazed at me intently. "I don't know what the hell I thought I was doing. And when she went missing, I tried to keep you out of my head. But then you came after me, up to Devils Hole. You almost sent me crazy. I've been burning up inside. I want *you*, Cassie. I always will."

I could hardly breathe, afraid that if I did, the moment would shatter. Was this real? I'd convinced myself for so long that he'd never want me. I had hardly allowed myself to trust what Aisha had told me. Besides, what did it matter? Ethan and how badly I wanted him? That belonged to something, and someone, from another life.

Oceans of black depths moved in his eyes, with an intensity that almost scared me. *The shadow is an invention of the darkness*, Jessamine had said. Right now, Ethan seemed like another of its inventions.

His breath warmed my cheek as his hand cradled the back of my head. "I want to go back to that night, and do what I wanted to do then."

He drew me close. The heavy scents of musk and cold sweat enveloped me. He no longer smelled of the forest. He was a creature of the dark, of the caves just like me. Blood pulsed through my veins as his mouth found mine. He kissed me hungrily. I could feel the muscles beneath his shirt as his body moved against me.

Blood pumped through my heart in a crazy rhythm. I'd never wanted anything more than him in that instant. I reached up with nervous fingers to hold his face, and I kissed him back, an all-consuming undercurrent moving through me. A sense of belonging that I'd never felt before warmed my skin.

He exhaled heavily as he pulled away. "Come on. Before Jessamine wakes up and finds you here."

"I don't care what she does to me. I want to stay here with you."

He shook his head, his mouth twisting into a small smile. "Don't make me pick you up and take you out of here myself."

"Just another minute." A raw need choked my words. I wasn't ready to let go just yet.

His arms enclosed me. I dropped my head against his chest.

A moment of complete stillness enveloped me—a moment when I could crawl inside and feel at peace for the first time in weeks.

But something else began to push into my mind. A dream. A nightmare.

The sound of tearing metal screeched through my ears. My bones were jolted by a tremendous force. It came to me as a memory, yet it was so vivid it was as though it were happening to me right then. I tried to fight it back, but it pushed into every space of my mind.

My father's face bends over mine, rain running in rivulets from his hair and collar, his mouth open and his eyes staring at me in horror. A hard, stony surface lies under me—the side of the road. He picks me up and runs with me to the car. My body feels small—I'm no older than two or three. My mother slumps at the wheel with her eyes closed, blood seeping from her temple into her hair. The high shrill of ambulances winds through my head. I hear screaming. The screaming is mine.

Grabbing both of my shoulders, Ethan held me at arms' length. "Cassie! What's wrong? Tell me!"

Every nerve in my body fired. A sense of dread enveloped me. I couldn't speak. Yet here with Ethan, in his arms, I was forced to confront the scenes that had rammed through my head. I couldn't run away, or pretend it was a dream.

It was real. *The accident had happened.*

Why hadn't my parents told me? What was so terrible they had to keep it from me?

"Nothing. It was nothing," I said quickly. "A nightmare."

He inhaled a sharp breath. "You scared me. You were standing there like you were in a trance...." Ethan trailed off, his body tensing. "Oh my god."

I looked up. We were on the other side again—at the tunnels.

Shuddering breaths rattled my body. Each time I'd entered the Toy Box tunnels, scenes of the accident had been replaying in my head.

But how? What did an accident that my family was in all those years ago have to do with these tunnels? It didn't make sense. Yet, I knew now with all certainty it was that memory that had brought me to the other side of this wall.

"Come on." I took his hand and we were running without another word. We took the third tunnel: the only one we hadn't yet explored.

Ethan held out a hand, touching the wall.

"This tunnel arcs around, just like the others."

We ran along a passage that grew progressively darker as the crystalline seams grew thinner and disappeared, plunging us into almost pitch-blackness. I could just make out an arched opening ahead. Ethan tightened his hand around mine, silently telling me we'd be okay. But neither of us knew what was through that doorway.

We stepped through it into a deathly cold black space.

A bluish light sprang almost immediately to life. A gathering of people encircled it. I stopped dead as a group of women in gowns stepped so close to my arm they almost brushed it. By some miracle, though, they hadn't seen us. Ethan took my hand and drew me back, close to the wall. Droplets of stale water splashed on my face from a ceiling I couldn't see.

I recognized the faces of the guests from the Feast of Fools. Only they weren't wearing the same clothes—or the masks. But still, they wore the clothing of a past era. Did they always dress in costume?

The muscles along my spine clenched as Audette and Henry stepped into the circle together. Audette's face glowing with excitement. Cold blue flames flickered mid-air in the middle of the circle, and the circle began a chant—low at first and then building, building, a crescendo of sound. I wanted to get away. But I was afraid to move. Afraid these people would notice us.

At some unknown signal, the assembled people produced small knives. Each of them made a cut across the palm of one hand. Red blood dripped to the rock floor. *Blood*. They *were* human, then. Or something like it.

An oily shadow rose from the flames. I felt Ethan's breathing in rapid intervals across my cheek. The shadow twisted as though it had been confined and was trying to free itself. It uncoiled to a soaring height—its jaw opening, large enough to swallow all the people.

The Provider held up his arms. "You, the entity we have brought to this world, may not touch those who have summoned you. This will hold true even though thousands of years may pass."

A rush of vibrating sounds filled the air. The sounds of the shadow.

A struggling man bound in ropes was brought into the circle. He was dressed differently than the others—his clothing was that of a working man, a laborer. His blond hair was damp with sweat and clinging to his forehead.

"I don't know anything!" His voice echoed around the dark spaces of the cave. He sounded young. He couldn't have been more than a few years older than us.

The Provider smiled narrowly. "Well, that's unfortunate, Thomas, seeing as you spent all that time trying to find out about us. And now, tonight, you'll know more than you ever wanted to."

"Please, allow me to go." His voice was raw, cracking in terror. "I'll forget I ever worked here. I'll move far away. For the love of God, I have a wife and baby. They *need* me."

A smile curved on Audette's heavily made-up face. She seemed to enjoy the man's pleas for mercy. "Quiet, or we'll bring your little family down here, too."

The Provider bid the shadow to slither closer to the working class man.

He stumbled, trying to get away. "What *are* you people? The old man should never have left Jessamine with you. You're all insane."

The skin around Henry's smile was taut. "He knows we won't hurt her. And we wouldn't have hurt you either, if you'd minded your own business and stuck to tending the garden, instead of poking around playing detective."

Sweat soaked through Thomas's shirt. "Jessamine's nurse . . . She didn't leave. You killed her." He pulled against his ropes.

Henry shrugged stiffly. "She was just another one who couldn't mind her own business." He paused. "I'm sorry, Thomas, but your time is at an end. Say whatever prayers you see fit."

The snake shadow reared up.

My heartbeat broke into a gallop.

Ethan's arms closed around me as the snake shadow plunged down on the poor, bound man, coiled around him, and consumed him.

Vomit rose in my throat.

The shadow retreated, merging with the darkness.

Lamps sprung to life in places around the cave as people lit them. My mouth went dry as an object at the far end of the cave was illuminated. The saint statue. We were in the Toy Box.

How was it possible we were back in the Toy Box?

As I shrank back into the shadows, I almost stumbled over something hard and metal. Bending down, Ethan scooped up the object—a toolbox of some kind. I guessed it had belonged to the gardener, Thomas. Ethan weighed it in his hands—ready, I knew, to use it as a weapon against anyone who came our way. Nonetheless, there was no way we could defeat these people if they attacked. There were too many of them, and they had the terrifying shadow at their call.

All we had was the cover of darkness.

I flinched as I noticed a blonde girl standing just a few feet from us. Was she the girl I'd seen at the carnival? She trembled as she laced her fingers together, as though saying a silent prayer. She didn't see us.

I took a step toward her, but Ethan pulled me back.

"That's Jessamine," he whispered.

Slowly, we edged toward the doorway and slipped back into the passage. Thin veins of crystal in the walls became wide seams. We needed to search for the fourth tunnel—if there was one.

But we didn't seem to reach the mouth of the tunnel. We were again plunged into deep, wide darkness.

A sudden terror shot through me. I couldn't see Ethan—I couldn't see anything. A cry escaped my throat.

"I'm here." His arms came hard around me, his heartbeat wild against my chest. He reached out in front of us. "The statue is in front of us, and the wall. We're back in the Toy Box."

"That's not possible—we just ran from there."

"I know. I don't get it either. It's some kind of crazy loop."

"But the people—"

"They've gone. I don't know how, but they have." He cupped my face in his hands. "We're okay."

"That thing that they summoned—"

"Cassie, we got away. Just hang onto that . . . please?"

We clung to each other as seconds ticked away. I was aware of each passing moment. Aware of each fleeting moment together with Ethan. I'd been sure, since the day I was first trapped in the Dollhouse, that I'd get away. But not anymore.

This was a waking nightmare. There was no escape.

Ethan pressed his lips to my forehead. "Cassie, I need to ask you something. It's crazy, but I'm going to ask anyway. Just before we got through to the other side, to the tunnels, you went into some weird trance. What was going through your head? Can you remember?"

"Yes." I said softly. I hesitated, but realized there was no point in concealing the truth. "I saw a car accident. My mother was driving—it was night and raining—and she steered off the road into a tree."

"When did that happen?"

"That's the crazy part. I don't know. I mean, it's like a memory, but my parents never mentioned any accident. But the memory is so real, I know it must have happened."

With a rush of fear, I felt myself as a small child again—thrown out of the car onto the road, seeing my unconscious mother through the wrenched-open car door. I felt the fear of the dark through the eyes of a small child.

I held tight to him, as another truth hit me. "Someone died in the crash."

"Who?" Ethan shook his head. "Your parents are still alive, aren't they?"

I nodded. "I-I don't know who it was. But I can feel it . . . feel the loss. I remember a feeling of desperation, like my whole world had fallen in."

And just like that, the fear that I had always carried with me, that blind terror of darkness, began to bleed away. There were worse things—things thousands of times worse—than darkness. There was being a small child on a dark road, in the grip of a terrifying accident. There was the loss of someone I had loved—a loss so total, I couldn't even remember it.

"So what do you think?" Ethan said slowly. "Could that accident possibly have to do with the wall?"

"I don't know." I blew out a frustrated breath. "I go into the memory, and that memory takes me to the other side. But . . . it's like, like I've been here before. I dreamed of the Fiveash house before I ever saw it."

He exhaled a low, sad breath. "Me too. Makes sense now . . . ."

"What makes sense?"

"I knew there was something about you—something different. I dreamed of you, over and over. For years. I almost drove myself to the point of insanity. I wrote endless poems about you, about a girl. I thought writing it down would get you out of my head. But I could just never picture you. Something was always blocking that."

Shock rattled me. "Those poems you wrote in your notebook . . . they were about me?"

"You sneaked a look at my poems?"

"Sorry." I was glad it was dark so he couldn't see me blush.

He rested his chin on my forehead. "There's some connection to this place. There's some connection between *us*. We need to find out what it is. Before we run out of time."

"Ethan?"

"Yes?"

"Are we just crazy? Are we just imagining each other . . . and this place?"

"I'm not imagining you." He kissed the top of my head. "I'm taking you out of here now, like I said I would."

This time, I didn't argue.

We made our way through foot halls of black air and back to the Dollhouse through the secret door.

Ethan stopped. "Go, before Jessamine wakes."

I nodded. The dolls were still fallen, lifeless, slumped to the floor.

High notes tinkled in the air—notes that at first sounded like a childhood memory. Instantly, I recognized the tune.

I clutched his arm. "The exit carousel. Can you hear it?"

His eyes gleamed wide in the darkness as he turned to face me.

Together, we raced down the corridor.

Around the corner, the red and green lights twinkled along the center column of the carousel. The carousel we'd ridden to enter the Dollhouse—the carousel that had stayed still ever since.

Sophronia stood holding the pole of a unicorn. She eyed us as the carousel turned—and she disappeared around to the other side.

Desperation fired through every vein. I ran as fast as I could— Ethan running beside me.

A large figure appeared with the next revolution of the platform—Raggedy, now haphazardly repaired, stitched together and slumped in a chariot. Standing next to Raggedy was Sophronia.

And Donovan.

The music stopped dead. The carousel's platform whirred to a stop.

Donovan had just helped Sophronia down from the platform when Ethan reached him. Ethan swung as hard as he could, cracking Donovan directly in the face.

Donovan fell to his knees, blood trickling from his nose. "What the hell was that for? I'm just bringing the ragdoll back."

Ethan towered over him. "You make that thing turn again. Or I'll paint the floor with you."

Raggedy woke, raising her grinning face. Moving awkwardly on unevenly repaired legs from the chariot, she advanced toward Ethan.

Sensing figures behind me, I whirled around. Jessamine strode up the hallway, her face incensed. The other three dolls moved abreast far behind her.

"You . . . again." She bristled. "It's always you, Evander."

Ethan whirled around to face Jessamine. "Make the carousel turn."

She acted as if she hadn't heard. She flung a hand toward Sophronia and me. "Get back to the ballroom, both of you. Stay away from this beastly boy." She took two steps toward Ethan, narrowing her eyes. "You just don't learn, do you?"

Ethan stared at me, silently telling me to do as Jessamine asked.

I heard the screech of the cell door open as I made rigid steps down the hall.

18. AEOLIAN HARPS

It winds through my mind
Like vines of knives
Cutting and sharpening
Into my veins
This knowledge of evil so dark
No trace of light remains.

—P.

We assembled at the table for dinner, and I tried to contain the whirlwind of disconnected thoughts and feelings spiraling through me. I could barely sit still, my hands restless in my lap. Aisha eyed me with a questioning look.

Sophronia hobbled to the cupboards to fetch the food for the night's supper. My spine froze as Sophronia opened empty cupboard after empty cupboard.

Everything was gone—every box and packet of food—even the boxes of matches for the fire. The only thing that remained was the large canister of tea. Something primal charged within me. Panic burned in my chest. Without food, how long could we possibly survive?

Sophronia turned around to Jessamine with huge dark eyes.

"Whatever is the matter, Sophronia?" Jessamine marched over to the cupboards, peering inside and then staring back at us. "Which one of you nasty Dolls has stolen the provisions?"

I jumped to my feet. "Donovan took them all, didn't he? He took them when he came down here."

"Of course not. How could you *instigate* such a thing?"

"I'm not *insinuating* it, Jessamine. It's true. You let him into the kitchen to recover from his bleeding nose. He sent all our food up on the dumbwaiter, didn't he?"

Her lower lip trembled. "He wouldn't do that."

"Wouldn't he? Why don't you ask him?" Fear and pain stuck into me like a knife. I knew now how they were going to kill us, how we were going to die. They planned to starve us.

Missouri stared straight ahead, her eyes red-rimmed and her face blotchy as though she were ill. Philomena sat rigidly, her small mouth drawn and her eyes staring at Jessamine in a silent plea.

Unless Jessamine was putting on a very convincing act, she was as shocked as we were to see that the food was gone. She sent us all into the ballroom to play board games, as though that might fix things.

Missouri took ragged steps down the hall.

"Are you okay?" I asked her.

She glanced at me with hooded eyes. "I must have picked up a bug or something." Putting out a hand, she tried to steady herself against the wall, but instead she slumped, falling hard to the floor. Sweat beaded around her closed eyes and forehead.

"Missy!" Philomena came running.

I knelt beside Missouri. "We need to get a doctor."

Jessamine stared down at her. "She'll be all right. You'll see."

Anger tore at me. I wanted to hit her, the way that Ethan had gone after Donovan.

"Philly," I said, trying to keep the rage from my voice, "could you get Missouri a wet cloth for her forehead?"

She seemed a little uncertain, but she ran out and along the passageway.

I turned on Jessamine. "No, she will *not* be all right. None of us will be all right. The Provider and Donovan have abandoned us. You need to let us out of here."

"You are perfectly horrid, Calliope." Jessamine seemed truly upset. "You all must stay here, with me. That is what you must do."

Aisha's eyes flashed. "We can't stay here. You saw the cupboards."

Jessamine eyes darkened. "Flibberty-flabber. You're all plotting against me. I should send you all to the Toy Box. Nasty little Toys."

Philomena stepped up behind us—a cloth in one hand and her headless bear in the other. "We are not toys, Jessamine," she said reproachfully, in her bell-like voice. She looked at me, a wrinkle appearing between her brows. "Are we?"

"No," I said firmly. "We are not."

We were made to have tea and sent to bed. Aisha and I tipped as much of the tea as we could down the deep cracks on the tiled floor in the kitchen. Jessamine caught Aisha and made her drink another cup—scolding her for being so careless.

I would go on my own to the Toy Box tonight. The thought of that chilled me, even as the last dregs of the hot tea slid down my throat—the tiny drop I'd drunk to convince Jessamine that I'd had a full cup.

I *had* to follow Prudence's directions and see where it was that Jessamine went at night.

This might be our last chance to get out.

The gongs of the clock shattered the deathly silence. The grating noise of Clown echoed in the distance.

Out in the hall, the bitter chill ate through my thin clothing. I crept to the cells. Bear and Clara were seated at the kitchen table, as usual. They were facing away and didn't see me.

"You're going to follow Jessamine?" Ethan's tall, dark frame was barely visible in the murky light of the cell.

"Yes."

Reaching through the cell bars, he pulled me in toward him. His kiss was gentle this time. He brushed my hair back from my face with one hand. His breathing was loud and forceful in his chest.

"You're not breathing right." I held my hand over his.

"I had asthma as a kid. Think it's come back." A quick smile etched itself into his face. "S'ok. I'll beat it down."

His face was gaunt, his cheeks hollow. There were dark shadows under his eyes. Like a ruined, beautiful angel. He shivered, white condensed air drifting from between his lips. "When we get out of here, I'm going to take you to all my favorite places. In summer, we'll go swimming at Ladies Well and go jumping off the rocks together. And I'll take you to see that new Ryan Gosling movie that's coming out in August. That's if your mum will let me." He gave me a faint smile.

I kissed his cold cheek. "My mom will love you."

"You be careful. Promise."

Nodding, I turned and ran down and along the halls, and let the darkness of the Toy Box reach up and wrap itself around me.

The glow of Jessamine's lamp flared along the wall, lighting the slick, wet surfaces. She, Clown and Raggedy vanished behind the far cave wall. Tonight I'd find out what compelled her to take these walks each midnight.

Complete darkness descended on me as I raced across the floor and touched my fingers to the wall behind the statue. A moment of stillness wrapped around me. I allowed visions of the accident, the feelings of loss and terror, to seep into my mind. I knew exactly how to *step through* now.

The tunnels were in front of me, opening to me, even before I opened my eyes and saw them.

The scraping of the wooden clown echoed in the first passage. I followed carefully, keeping close to the wall, blood pulsing in my head.

Peering slightly around a wide rock column, I saw Jessamine standing before Prudence's desk, flanked by Raggedy and Clown. She bent to collect the plate—the cake now nothing but slime with pink candles. "I must take this away now, Prudence. You are very naughty not to have the slice. I do worry about you." She sighed. "I worry about all my Dolls. They don't seem to know what's best for them."

Glancing up, she stared at a place high in the cave wall. "Will they stay with me when they cross over? No, they won't. And I'll be alone. It's not fair, Prudence. This isn't what I wanted at all. I despise Henry and all of those terrible people."

A mournful despair etched itself into Jessamine's eyes—a look I'd never seen before. I followed her gaze upward. An outcrop of crystal jutted from the opposite wall, water dripping from its shelf.

Wetness and decay saturated my nostrils.

Above the outcrop, an arch-shaped cavity had been cut deep into the rock. Half-concealed in darkness, I had never noticed it before.

I held a scream deep within my chest.

A skeleton.

Dark bones.

Stained yellow dress.

Skull.

Hat.

Hot tears wet my face. Strength deserted me—I crouched on the ground like an animal.

I forced myself to look again. The skeleton was propped upright and standing in the cavity.

The bones were aged. The skeleton had to have been there for a long time.

Jessamine inclined her head. "They're all plotting to leave me. Just like you, Prudence. I'm going to be alone here soon."

The skeleton was The First One. Prudence.

Jessamine and the Toys left the tunnel. I forced my body to rise. I needed to get out of there, even though my body was weighty with despair. We'd been wrong about everything. Prudence had never escaped the underground. She had died—just like we would die.

I wanted to get away from her remains, wanted to get away from the sight of what all the Dollhouse Dolls were to become. I turned to leave.

Air wafted around me—sharpening with an ashy, burnt odor.

The Provider was leaning against a crystal pillar, his arms crossed casually.

"Hello, Cassandra." He raised an eyebrow. "I thought you might come back. So. Are you with me?"

His question echoed in the dark spaces of the tunnel. I turned my back on his piercing, slate-blue eyes. "How can I be with you?" My voice swept from me like dry leaves in the wind.

"You are here, in my domain." He moved up close to me, circling me, his breath on my neck. "I knew you couldn't stay away. I knew you'd return. Even though you deny who you are."

Heartbeats scudded through my chest. "Who am I?"

"That I'm not sure of yet. You are a puzzle. I know one thing.

There are no accidents in this life. There is just denial. You came to this place by your own desire."

That wasn't true. I could *never* have chosen to come to this place. "You're a monster. How could you let us all die?"

He gave a sad sigh. "Don't think it didn't pain me to give Donovan the Monseigneur's order to clean out your cupboards. I have provided for you Dolls of the Dollhouse since the beginning. But you pose a risk that the Monseigneur finds unacceptable. And if you should figure out the extent of your power, you might cause harm to us in some way."

Me, cause harm to *them*?

"You are just like the one up there." He reached a hand beneath my chin, forcing me to look upward at Prudence.

I closed my eyes. "Why did you bring her here?"

He exhaled breathily. "I thought a girl with her special abilities would prove useful . . . ."

"But she could see too far, couldn't she? She could see everything you were doing behind the wall." My throat was tight.

"Ah, what happened to that delicate little bud you were when last we danced? You've grown harsh."

"You people killed her—you killed Prudence."

"No one killed her. She chose her own path." He waved a hand dismissively. "Believe me, it wasn't my choice to keep her here like this. A little morbid for my taste. But Jessamine is a sentimental little thing and wanted to keep her. So there she is. For all time."

It made sense now—Jessamine bringing the cake here, Jessamine disappearing every midnight. She must be coming here to *talk* to Prudence.

He smiled, watching me. "You are just like me."

"I am nothing like you," I spat out.

He brought something up to my face. A rosebud. Deep and red

in color. My fingers laced around the stem. The rose bloomed before my face. A single petal fell from the rose. It drifted to the floor, melting into a tiny pool that looked like blood. I remembered then that Henry was a magician. Did he think his horrible little trick would impress me?

"Cassandra," he said with surprising gentleness, taking my shoulders. "I care for you." Pale hair brushed his high, angular cheekbones. There was something almost vulnerable in his face, in the straight line of his mouth—yet also dangerous. My shoulders burned beneath the hold of his hands.

"I care a great deal," he said. "You are incredibly beautiful, and will only grow more so with each passing year."

I'd never thought of myself as beautiful. I could barely look away from his intense blue eyes. Could barely breathe. It was as if he were putting a spell on me.

"I will ask you again," he murmured. "Are you with me? If you choose, I will take you from this place and into worlds you cannot imagine. Everything . . . everything will be at your feet. Anything you desire will be yours. All you need to do is help me."

Electric pulses charged through me. I wasn't sure if it was panic, or desperation, or something deeper, something like desire—I could get away from this place. My mind screamed at me to accept, to flee this second-by-second terror, to escape the same fate as Prudence. "How? How will you take me with you if the Monseigneur wants me dead?"

"Ah, if you are under my watchful eye, and you agree to help us, I could persuade him to allow you your life. Now, Cassandra, what will you answer?"

I didn't think. In that moment of sheer panic and terror, I whispered, "Yes."

"Then you are mine." He dropped his head to kiss me—a hard kiss, a kiss that seared me.

I flinched, my mind tearing into pieces. His kiss was nothing like Ethan's. His kiss was alien and dark, as if he wanted to consume me. "If I go with you, the others can come—can't they?"

He shook his head. "Just you. I would save you all, if I could. But the Monseigneur has given his command."

"You tell him to take us all."

A strange look of regret entered his eyes. "No one tells Monseigneur Balthazar anything. Besides, you are the only one who can possibly be of use to me."

I edged backward. "Then I can't go with you."

He smirked. "You have given your word."

"I take it back." My words were hollow, tinny like carousel music. "I'm leaving now."

"Go where you will. There is no way out." His voice hardened. "You will die like the rest of them."

Bowing, he turned and paced away, as though the tunnel was just an everyday street and not a dark place filled with horrors.

Numbly, I turned and made my way back to the mouth of the tunnels. My gaze fell to the metal corner of a box—the gardener's toolbox Ethan had secreted behind a pillar. The gardener was just one more innocent person who had died in this place. Sheets of death hung in the air, suffocating me.

I lifted the toolbox. I thought it best not to leave it. And besides, it might come in handy. If I were going to die, it would not be without a fight.

Back in the Dollhouse, sharp footsteps and whispers traveled down the corridor. Had Jessamine discovered I was missing and sent everyone out looking for me?

I rounded the corner to find Sophronia and Aisha helping

Missouri from the bathroom to the bedroom. Bright splatters of blood trailed in a path on the floor.

I ran up to them. "What happened?"

Aisha looked over her shoulder at me. "Missouri woke up coughing blood. Jessamine took Philly down to the ballroom—she couldn't stand the sight of it."

"Cassie." Ethan stood with one hand on a bar of his cell, indicating the toolbox in my hand. Despite its weight, I'd forgotten I was still carrying it. Quickly, I slid it into Ethan's cell.

Sophronia went to fetch a mop from the bathroom while Aisha got Missouri settled in bed. Her rattling breaths dusted the air white. Aisha sat beside her.

"We'll get you out to the ballroom. The air's too wet and cold in here." I stood stiffly, my mind recoiling at the sight of her blood, at the memory of Prudence in the tunnel.

A strained sigh came from deep within her chest. "This is where I want to be. I don't want Philly to see me . . . like this." She eyed me strangely. "What did you see, Calliope?"

So she knew I had gone into the Toy Box after Jessamine. "I found her. I found Prudence."

Missouri's eyes watered, her features losing composure.

Aisha strode up to me, her hand gripping my arm. "You *found* Prudence?"

"She's dead. She never left here." The words fell from my lips like heavy stones.

Aisha turned slowly around to Missouri. "Tell me that's not true."

Missouri was silent for a time, then slowly nodded—her cheeks wet, shining.

Aisha's grip slackened and fell away from my arm.

Closing her eyes for a moment, Missouri took in a labored

breath. "How did you get past the wall, Calliope?"

There was no point in concealing the truth. She was sick—possibly dying. "I'm like Prudence—but different, because I can physically get through where she could only see." I took a deep breath, avoiding Aisha's look of confusion. "I-I've had dreams all my life. Dreams of the Fiveash house and of dark things. I can go to the other side of the wall through a vision. Or a memory. I'm still not sure which."

She nodded, as though she'd suspected as much. "I'm sorry. I'm sorry for everything. I've tried to care for Philly and Sophronia. I took it upon myself to make sure nothing—and no one—ever hurt them." She sighed. "I'll tell you what happened to Prudence now, if you want to know it."

"Yes." My voice was harsh in my ears. "I want to know everything."

Her chest rose. Her breath rattled in her lungs. "Prudence was brought in two months or so after I was. It was terrible of me, but I was glad to have someone else to share my days with, to share the horror with. I told Prudence everything I knew about Jessamine and the Dollhouse. Prudence took the news badly. She began writing madly every day, reams and reams of paper. There was one book in particular . . . she wrote on every page—yes, the book I burned. She was manic—writing poems in it until her fingers bled. I couldn't reach her. Couldn't stop her."

She squeezed her eyes shut. "And then one morning . . . one morning I woke to find her in a pool of blood. There in her bed. She'd cut her wrists. The shadow wrapped itself around her. Jessamine commanded the shadow to leave . . . but it was too late."

Aisha gasped. Horror charged through my entire body, turning my limbs to stone.

"Knowing the truth is what killed Prudence," said Missouri

softly. "She'd been here less than a month. That's why I knew if there was ever another girl brought down here—I'd never tell what I knew. I burned the book because I didn't want the others who were brought in to know about Prudence and find out that she died. I never wanted them to lose hope." Her eyes burned with a strange energy, even as her voice dropped to a whisper. "You see, I knew the truth. I knew there was no way out."

I knew there was no way out. I felt sick, imagining poor Prudence, imagining her terror and despair. And there was something else, something needling me beneath the horror.

"But she can't be The First One . . . ." I said slowly. "Not if she was brought in after you."

Missouri stared at me. "Why did you think Prudence was The First One?"

I realized then that Missouri had never said she was. I'd jumped to that conclusion. It had been me, racing ahead—barely listening or watching. I exhaled a long breath. "Then who is she? The First One?"

"I don't know," Missouri said. "I've seen her perhaps three times in all. I only ever catch a fleeting glimpse before she's gone. Years ago, when I first came here, was the first time I saw her. I knew she'd been here before, because Jessamine greeted her like an old friend. I've always felt that if we could discover the mystery of who she is, we could understand how to escape. But I haven't seen her for a long time. I don't know what happened to her. I hoped you could find out." Sorrow darkened Missouri's eyes. "There have been times down here when I wondered where this would all end. And I thought, if ever Donovan stopped sending down food, if it wouldn't be kinder for us to make our tea so strong that we would never wake . . . ."

A lost, bare silence drifted between us.

Aisha bit hard into her lip. "Is there enough tea?"

"Yes, I think so." She stared up at us. "Philly can't suffer. Please. If I can't leave this bed, please, do what you can."

We nodded. The enormity of what she was asking cast a long shadow between us.

"Missouri," I said slowly, "you said something about telling Prudence who Jessamine really was. What did you mean by that? Who *is* she? And the serpent that Henry spoke of—what does it want from us? Why doesn't it kill us? Please." I took her hands, which were ice cold. "I want to know everything you know."

Her eyelids drifted downward. "Are you sure, Calliope?" Her breath misted in white shrouds above her. "I'm afraid for you."

"I'm sure," I whispered. Aisha nodded, too.

"I will tell you both—but you must do something for me first."

"Yes?" I said.

"You remember the box of photographs on the desk, in that strange castle we found after escaping the fairground? Please bring them to me. And Jessamine's locket."

I frowned. "Where's the locket?"

"I'm not sure." Missouri coughed. "She keeps it hidden. Somewhere special. Somewhere no one else is allowed."

"Molly," I said, using her real name, "why do you need the locket and photos?"

"When you bring them, I'll tell you."

I tried to swallow a sigh of frustration. More riddles. More games. "There's something else. . . Prudence mentioned a fourth path. Do you know of any fourth path or tunnel?"

She frowned deeply. "No. I remember Prudence speaking of paths, but she was half-insane by that point. She wouldn't even respond to her name."

Her breathing slowed, her eyes remaining closed. She slid into a deep sleep.

Aisha stared at me with huge eyes.

I backed away from the bed. When I felt the wall behind me, I slid down to the floor, hugging my knees close to my chest. Part of me had torn away—screaming down the passage like a mad thing, yelling and fighting. Aisha still sat on the bed, stony-eyed and unseeing.

Philomena stepped quietly into the room. She stood on tiptoes to reach Missouri's arm, shaking it. "Wake up, Missy. Wake up! You can't be sick."

Sophronia and Jessamine walked in behind her—Sophronia reaching to check on Missouri. Sophronia's eyes widened in fear.

Philomena climbed up on the bed and shouted at Missouri. "Wake up! Wake up!" Tears streamed down her face as she shook her arm.

Missouri remained still and unresponsive.

Aisha stood rigidly. "Is she unconscious?" she whispered to me. "Is it some kind of a coma?"

Jessamine stood behind us, her mouth pulled to one side. "She'll just have a nice long rest and be better for it."

Aisha shook her head and glared at Jessamine. "No. She's sick. She won't just *wake up*."

Jessamine tilted her blonde head. "I had a long sleep like that once. I'd been ill and I slept forever. I woke in a dreadfully strange place. But I was quite all right. You *do* wake."

Aisha and I exchanged long glances.

"Jessamine," I said—a last, desperate attempt to get Missouri help. "Don't you want her to wake up now? We could take her to a hospital, and then we could all come back here—and have tea together."

Her eyes clouded. "We must be patient. You're safe, here. Perhaps we can make our own sanatorium. I don't have any nurses' outfits, unfortunately, but we can make do."

I stared at Missouri's wax-like face. *Don't die, Molly Parkes. Don't die.*

19. THE FIRST ONE

Lily Fair, Oh Lily Fair
How does your graveyard grow?
With silver'd eyes and whispered lies
And dripping roses all in a row

—P.

Jessamine commanded everyone to return to the ballroom, while she stayed with Missouri. Aisha dropped into a chair near the carousel, staring into nothingness. "There's no point in finding the locket now." She drew her mouth in. "She's not going to wake again."

I stared at her numbly. I knew she was right.

Time was a sick thing, diseased and decaying—the essence of it crumbling. I tried to hold on to what Ethan had told me about the Aboriginals' beliefs, that time was just a human construct, and people could travel backward and forward at will. I wanted to believe in that. And I wanted to believe that my time on earth—and the time of everyone else here in the underground—wasn't winding down like a clock.

Henry had given me a chance to escape, but I understood now there was no real escape. Whatever he was offering would only be some imitation of real life—and I would have been helping *them*, the tunnel people.

Sophronia stole glances at us from behind her book. I wanted to scream at her. *We are going to die with you, Sophronia, as complete strangers! We don't know any more about you than we did when we first came in here. And yet you sit here and read your life away. Why are you helping them? You get nothing from them.*

Philomena tugged at my sleeve. I took her onto my lap.

"Is my Missy going to be okay?" She looked at me with small, dulled eyes—not the eyes of a child.

"I don't know," I said, and immediately felt bad. She was still a child, no matter what she had seen. I had to protect her, as Missouri always had. "Of course she will," I added, squeezing her.

"Calliope," she said, "Is the sun ever going to come back?"

"What do you mean?"

"I remember it used to be day, and then dark. But now it's always dark."

She'd just been three when she'd come to the Dollhouse. Maybe she had forgotten there had ever been a world out there. A real world.

"Yes, Philly, there's a yellow sun. And trees. And flowers. And you'll see them again."

She was silent for a moment, as though she couldn't quite imagine what I was telling her. "Will you sing to me?" she said finally.

I tried to think of a nursery song. I remembered Missouri singing "Hush Little Baby" to her. My voice faltered as I began the song, making up words for all the ones I didn't know.

Philly didn't seem to mind and she fell asleep quickly. I laid her gently on the day bed to sleep.

My head swam. My body was growing weak and my thinking scattered. I needed to start looking for the locket. Even if Missouri didn't wake, if the locket was so important, it might contain a clue—perhaps, even, a clue to the identity of The First One.

I began looking through the trinket and toy boxes on the shelves. After a moment, Aisha stepped up beside me wordlessly and started helping. She cast me a wry, bitter look. Had Missouri sent us on a wild goose chase to take our minds off Prudence? Off our hunger?

Off death?

Wherever the truth lay, it was better to do *something* than just sit and wait to die.

Clown and Raggedy, who were in the room with us, didn't try and stop us. I wondered if that was because Jessamine was busy caring for Missouri.

Most of the trinket boxes held baubles and costume jewelry, hairpins and ribbons. Next we inspected every single toy—perhaps one of them had a chain around its neck. We opened every board game and looked inside. I'd already looked behind and under almost every book, so there weren't many bookshelves left to check.

After an hour, we'd exhausted every possibility in the ballroom.

Where else might a locket be hiding? I'd already searched every crevice and nook of the kitchen and bathroom when looking for a clue to Lacey's disappearance. Could the locket be in the Toy Box? Possibly. But Missouri had said Jessamine would put it somewhere special, somewhere no one else was allowed, and I trusted her on that. And we were allowed, even *forced*, to go to the Toy Box.

Philomena stirred in her sleep, murmuring something that

sounded like "Missouri." My heart ached for her. Missouri had made me promise to take care of Philomena. But how could I? How could I keep her from realizing what was truly happening to us?

Maybe when she woke up, I would take her on the carousel, and we could pretend we were riding away.

My spine stiffened. The carousel.

I crossed the ballroom and stepped onto the platform. Instantly, the carousel began to revolve. I threaded carefully through the animals until I reached Jessamine's favorite horse: the horse none of us were allowed to ride or even touch. The locket—could it be hidden somewhere in the fancy headgear or jeweled saddle?

Superficially, there didn't appear to be any secret hiding places. I looked underneath. A repair panel was fixed into place with four rusted screws. Was there any point in trying to get those screws out? Was I just crazy? Desperate?

Maybe. And we had the tools for it—Ethan had Thomas's toolbox hidden in his cell.

Aisha had followed me, curious. "Do you think it could be in there?"

"I don't know."

Aisha and I constructed a quick—and flimsy—plan. We'd open up the horse in the midnight hour, and then go and fetch the photographs that Missouri had asked for, while Jessamine was on her midnight walk.

Aisha stepped away quietly into the corridor. Neither Clown nor Raggedy stopped her. And Bear and Clara were still in the kitchen. Returning a few minutes later, she showed me a screwdriver she'd hidden under the long sleeve of her dress. That meant she'd been to Ethan's cell. I was desperate to ask whether he was okay, whether they'd spoken, what they'd said. But I kept my mouth shut.

Aisha and I were friends again, and that, in a place like the Dollhouse, was far more than I could have hoped for.

The gongs of the clock echoed along the corridor outside the bedchamber. Jessamine, Clown, and Raggedy were gone from their beds. Aisha and I rose to a sitting position at the same time. Jessamine hadn't been watching us very carefully as she'd given us our tea hours before, and once again, we'd managed to dispose of it after taking barely a sip. Jessamine was growing more and more distracted and distant. She, too, knew something was coming.

Thin threads of wind whistled down from the soaring ceiling, chilling me to the bone. Every sound was somehow magnified in the dead stillness of the hour, so loud in my ears I was sure even my breath would give me away.

Missouri had still not woken, her arms remaining in the same crisscrossed position Jessamine had arranged them in—as if she were already a corpse. I shivered as I passed her. Philomena was fast asleep, and Sophronia, too—as far as I could tell.

Aisha turned to me with a nod, her dark hair tumbling around the prominent bones of her face.

We padded down to the ballroom. The ballroom clock had the time at a minute past midnight.

Aisha handed me the screwdriver as we stepped onto the carousel platform. Resting on an elbow, I fiddled the screwdriver into one of the screws beneath Jessamine's horse. It was awkward to reach it and the screw had rusted badly, so I tried another. It turned. I undid three of the screws, catching them in my hand. I couldn't manage to turn the rusty one at all. In frustration, I tried to pull the panel down. Something slid across from the other side of the panel, tipping out onto the floor.

Aisha gasped.

A blackened locket bounced across the floor of the carousel. She snatched it up and concealed it in her clothing while I screwed the

225

panel back into place, my heart drumming.

There was no time to examine it now, even though a desperate curiosity fired through me. I knew we didn't have much time before Jessamine returned from her nightly visit with Prudence. Together, we ran down the hall and into the Toy Box, descending into the dark and fumbling toward the statue.

Closing my eyes, I imagined the tunnels. It was becoming easier each time to see them, to pass through.

Aisha touched my arm. "Cassie, we're here." She turned to me with a look of amazement on her face as I opened my eyes. Checking first for sight or sound of Jessamine and the Toys, we raced down the middle passage. Once again, the tunnel opened up into the wide castle grounds. The carnival stood dark and empty, with no gaudy lights illuminating the rides.

We crept around the trees and shrubbery to the cellar. It was silent. Only a few dim lights in the narrow castle windows told us that *someone* was there. Cautiously, we climbed in through the cellar door and through Henry's den. I thought again of how he'd touched me—how he'd kissed me—and felt suddenly sick. What would Aisha think if she knew?

The fireplace stood dark and cold. But a lamp was burning on the desk.

I stepped to the desk and began shuffling through the photographs haphazardly piled in a small metal box, as Aisha drew out the locket and held it up to the lamplight.

"What could be so important that Missouri wants it?" she whispered. "And why does Jessamine hide it?"

I shook my head. The metal of the locket was dark, tarnished. Carved into the surface was a miniature carousel horse—one that exactly matched Jessamine's blue horse.

Gently, Aisha opened the tiny latch.

"Look," she breathed.

A gold border framed a sepia photo of a man and child—the man around seventy and the child not more than ten. An inscription opposite said, *Tobias James Fiveash, 1916*: the owner of the circus, and the original owner of the Fiveash mansion.

The child stared out blankly from the photo. I recognized the eyes and the firm set of the mouth.

"God," Aisha breathed. "That girl has to be a relative of Jessamine's—maybe a great-grandmother."

That had to be why Missouri had said Jessamine wasn't The First One. She *wasn't* abducted and brought here like the rest of them. Her family had already been living here for generations. But why would her family have put her down here? And how did she become so strange and cruel?

I flipped over a photograph and recoiled. It was a picture of a magician and his assistant. They looked exactly like Henry and Audette, down to the smirk playing on Henry's lips. I grabbed another photo—this one of a young girl of about fourteen on a trapeze, her features too blurry to make out clearly. My fingers were numb as I shuffled though the images of big tops and clowns, trying to find another photo of the girl. My heart stilled as I picked up a portrait of a young circus performer standing beside an aged, white-bearded man. I recognized the man—Tobias. The performer wore a feathered headband, her pale eyes staring from the photo with a quiet directness. Jessamine's eyes.

I showed the picture to Aisha.

Inhaling sharply, she traced a finger over the girl's face. "She . . . she looks exactly like Jessamine."

Aisha took another photo from the desk. I heard her sharp intake of breath beside me, and I didn't want to look, but I turned my head rigidly. The picture was of the same girl. She was standing in front of a circus trailer, five dolls in her arms. The dolls were miniature versions of Clown, Raggedy, Clara, and Bear—with, additionally, a boy version of the Raggedy doll.

I kept looking at the photos, even as the voice at the back of my head was telling me things I refused to believe.

Newspaper clippings sat below the photographs. I picked up the first—a torn shred of paper with a picture of a young girl of about fourteen with soulful, haunting eyes and dark hair.

. . . and vanished from her bedroom in the middle of the night, Prudence, 14, is still missing. Known for her uncanny psychic abilities, Prudence predicted the untimely death of a senator and his family back in June of this year. Her parents remain desperate for any information in relation to their daughter . . .

Below the article was a news item about a hurricane that had happened around five years ago, in America. I guessed the article was from an American newspaper. The story about Prudence was just a few years old, matching what Missouri had said. She was real, a real person. She hadn't exactly seemed that until now. She'd been a mysterious figure of the underground world.

Another newspaper clipping was lying on the bottom of the box, this one yellowed and fragile. I lifted it out carefully. Aisha put down the photos she was looking at, and bent her head over the newspaper article.

The clipping detailed a train derailment of 1920, in a set of mountains in Mexico named Copper Canyon. An entire circus train had fallen down a steep embankment, killing most of the family and crew of the Fiveash Circus. Accompanying the article was a picture of a girl lying in a hospital bed with a bandage wrapped around her neck and left shoulder, blonde hair fanned out on the pillow.

My spine chilled as I read:

Jessamine Fiveash, aged 14, heir to the Fiveash fortune and one of the few survivors of the derailment, sustained multiple injuries, including serious cuts above the collarbone. Jessamine's twenty-year-old cousin, Henry Fiveash, and his fiancée, Audette Blair, and Jessamine's grandfather and owner of the Fiveash circus—Tobias Fiveash—also survived. Jessamine's mother, at the time wheelchair-bound, did not survive the derailment. Jessamine's father died in a tragic circus accident just five years earlier in 1915.

Aisha cried out, bringing her trembling hand to her mouth. I stood rigidly, unable to process what I had just read. The description of the girl's wounds matched the scars on Jessamine's neck exactly. But this Jessamine was fourteen in *1920*. It wasn't possible that this was the Jessamine of the Dollhouse. And it wasn't possible that Henry and Audette were the people this article.

Not possible.

Not possible.

Not possible.

Quickly, I bundled up the photos in a ribbon, as though the touch of them would burn me.

"Let's get out of here." Aisha's voice was as tight as a violin string.

We slipped out of the room—and froze.

Someone was standing in the dark corridor. There was a sad stoop to her thin shoulders. The girl in the striped stockings, the girl I'd first seen at the fairground. She flinched, turning slightly, and I guessed she'd heard us. I couldn't see her clearly in the gloom.

"Hello," I called quietly.

She didn't answer. She just ran.

Aisha's fingers tightened on my arm as I started to go after her. "Don't," she said fearfully.

"It's all right," I reassured her. "I've seen her before. I don't think she's one of them. She seems different."

We followed the girl deeper into the castle, into rooms we hadn't seen before. I caught sight of her as she disappeared into what looked like a library on the other side of an enormous room, a ballroom. It was empty of people. Eight massive fireplaces stood on either side. A strange sculpture stood in the center of the room—made of some kind of black stone, it was a twisting tree that reached from floor to soaring ceiling, the roots and bare branches looking almost identical to each other.

"*Follow her down past the mirrored tree,*" gasped Aisha, quoting the line from Prudence's poem. "The top of the tree looks like a mirror image of the bottom."

A chill sped through me. We went on, past the sculpture and into the library. A bookcase had been shifted aside, revealing a hidden staircase. There was nothing to do now but keep going.

The spiraling, stone steps were old and worn beneath our feet. The stairs ended at a landing. Yet another corridor, and yet more doors, branched off of it.

Aisha looked around, panting. Which way had she gone?

At the end of the corridor, a light shone dimly from under a door. Drawing a deep breath, I pointed, and together we advanced slowly.

The door was unlocked. I eased it open a crack. The room was bare but for two pieces of furniture—a bed and a low dressing table that was covered in ornate trinket boxes.

A girl lay curled up on the bed, cradling her knees close to her chest.

Her hair spilled out on the patchwork bed cover—a whitest shade of blonde.

Her shoulders tensed as she heard us step into the room.

She turned and sat up, her eyes huge.

Shock traveled through me.

Lacey.

20. SERVANT OF THE SERPENT

Lily Fair with palest hair
In the forest dark
Leads the children so far in
They never will come out

—P.

I threw myself on her, hugging her, laughing with joy and relief. "Oh god, I can't believe it's really you." Drawing back, I gazed at her in astonishment. "Have they kept you here all along? Are you okay?"

Biting her lip, she nodded. "It's a terrible place. They starve me and beat me and make me do everything for them."

Aisha hadn't moved from the doorway. She stood by the dressing table, staring fixedly at the trinket boxes there. She grabbed one of them, studying it and turning it over.

"Aisha!" I cried. "It's *Lacey*. We found her!"

But Aisha's expression was cold as she raised her eyes to Lacey.

"So tell us again how they beat you, *servant of the serpent?*"

I gaped at Aisha.

Lacey paled. "What?"

"These jewelry boxes," said Aisha, "I *knew* I recognized them. They're the same as the ones you have in your collection at home, in your bedroom. They came from here, didn't they? Were they gifts from the castle? From The Provider?"

"Aisha," I said. But suddenly I felt cold. A rush of images darkened my mind. I saw Lacey in the forest, hiding her bracelet from my view. I saw Lacey and her fear of dolls. I saw Lacey pulling me into the school hall, trying to find out where Ethan had gone. Blood ran through my veins in icy rivulets.

"You're—you're wrong," breathed Lacey. "You're mixed up."

"Why'd you run from us?" said Aisha, taking a step toward Lacey. "You saw us, but you ran away . . . ."

"I didn't know who you were." Lacey's blue eyes grew round in that innocent, blank stare I knew so well.

Woodenly, I reached for her arm. The bracelet looked much older than something given to her by her grandmother, as she'd claimed. The dark metal seemed medieval, tiny trees carved around it—trees that mimicked the black, mirrored tree sculpture in the ballroom. "Who gave you this?" I said. My voice was shaking.

"My grandmother. I told you."

"No, she didn't," Aisha spat.

Lacey lifted her chin. "You're sick. Both of you. Starvation does that. You're imagining things."

A sick feeling roiled in my stomach. "How did you know they were starving us?"

Lacey opened her mouth, then closed it. Fear flashed in her eyes. "I don't know what you're talking about. You both have to go. If they find you here, they'll hurt you."

"Hurt us more than starving us to death?" Aisha arched an eyebrow, tossing the trinket box onto the bed next to Lacey.

Lacey flinched.

"God . . ." My voice came from a faraway place, in a strained whisper. "You're Lily Fair. You're the one who comes and goes while the rest of us go 'round and 'round. You're The First One."

Aisha jabbed a finger at her. "*You*—live out in the sun—while the Dolls are left to rot and die—never to see sun again."

Lacey wrenched her wrist away from me. "Let go of me." Her body shook all over.

My legs weakened. "Why did you do it, Lacey?"

"You have no right to judge me." Her mouth was a thin line. "I was just a little kid. Nine years old. I was on a school camping trip in the forests. The Provider and the Dolls stole me from my sleeping bag. I was knocked unconscious with chloroform and taken down to the underground. I woke with my face painted, and dressed like a doll. Jessamine said I was hers . . . forever."

I gasped. The monsters that Ben Paisley had seen in the forest all those years ago had been *real*. They abducted Lacey.

Lacey closed her eyes. "I made a deal with The Provider. I said I'd bring more girls if he'd let me go. Well, what would you have done? I was a child—alone with monster toys and ghosts. The Provider had me back in my sleeping bag before dawn."

Blood drained from my head. "What did you say? *Ghosts*?"

Her blue eyes dulled. "The Provider and Jessamine."

"They're ghosts . . ." Aisha mouthed, her lower lip trembling.

Words choked in my throat. It made a horrible kind of sense. The faded photograph of Tobias and the somber little girl in the locket etched itself into my mind, until I could almost see it before me. The eyes of the girl were not *like* Jessamine's—they *were* Jessamine's.

The photograph was nearly a hundred years old.

Jessamine, both in her life and her afterlife, was over a hundred years old. The Provider, too.

My body numbed. But my mind was wild. My mind was a pulsing, raging animal, battering itself against its cage.

Lacey stared down at the bracelet like it was a snake wound tight around her arm. "So I'd know it wasn't just a nightmare—he fixed the bracelet to me."

Aisha, her eyes filled with fear and confusion, advanced toward her. "Why me, Lacey? Why did you choose your best friend?"

"I didn't choose you." A low, pained sigh emitted from her chest. "When . . . when I brought little Frances—Philomena—down here, a photo fell from my wallet. Jessamine saw it—an old photo of me and you, from when we were thirteen. She insisted on having you from that moment on. Nothing could change her mind."

Aisha clenched her fists. "The hike was your idea in the first place. And when we were out in the forest, you kept telling me I needed better photographs, pushing me to go farther, and whispering in my ear that Cassie was trying to take Ethan away from me."

Lacey looked away.

"Lacey," I cried. "Why didn't you just tell someone? The police? Your father?"

"The Provider said if I didn't do what Jessamine wanted, if I didn't keep the Dollhouse secret, he'd bring my little sisters to the underground," she said, her voice cracking. "He told me that he'd give Amy and Jacinta to the serpent. And he would—I know he would."

"So you took the sisters and daughters from other families for sacrifice," spat Aisha. "I'll never let you forget what you did." Hatred was etched on her face. "I know why Prudence called you Lilith in her poem—she named you after the monster who abducted

234

and ate children. It's a good name for you. *Prudence died here*. How does that feel, Lily Fair?"

Lacey turned back to us, her eyes growing anguished. "I don't know where Prudence came from—I didn't bring her here or find her in the forest. But I know she hated me." Her hands balled into small fists. "You don't know what it's been like for me. All the lies I've had to tell, all the people I've had to hurt. From the day The Provider brought me back to the school camp I've barely eaten, I've barely slept. I've had to live with this every single day . . . ."

There were so many words I wanted to say to Lacey right now. But none of them would change things. There was only one thing I needed to know. "Lacey," I said, leaning forward to grab her shoulders. "Tell us how to get out of here. You've come and gone from this place for years. Do one thing right. Tell us how to get out."

Her gaze became distant. "They force me to come back here every month, so that I never forget. So that I never tell. I take a bus to the forest and wait for night to fall. Then the serpent shadow takes me. At the end of my time, the shadow takes me back. I just tell my parents I'm staying at a friend's house—they never check."

Her eyes clicked to mine. "There is no way out. None at all. Once they have you, you can never, ever get away."

A strange darkness crept into her eyes—like black, rolling mist—until I couldn't see the blue of her eyes at all. "I've become the darkness, just like them . . . ."

I released her, stepping backward, horrified.

Lacey couldn't help us. She wouldn't.

She was one of them.

21. SOPHRONIA'S SIGHT

Cassandra, I see you, I have always seen
The darkness that seeks you, in your dreams.
Don't follow me, to the gray in between.
When nothing remains and no light is left
Remember some things are worse than death

—P.

Aisha and I made our way through the pitch dark Toy Box. My mind spun with thoughts of Lacey and all she'd done to us. All this time—for years—she'd known exactly where Molly Parkes and little Frances Allanzi were. And all the while she'd searched for Aisha, she'd been the one to blame. I dreaded having to tell Ethan what we'd discovered. In some ways, it would have been better if we'd found Lacey dead.

A scraping noise sounded in the darkness.

"Clown," breathed Aisha. "He's here."

The grating noise of Clown followed behind us in his usual slow scrape at first, but then growing louder, faster. Jessamine and the Toys must have spotted us on their way back from the shrine.

"Run!" Aisha cried beside me.

We sprinted through the darkness. Breathlessly, we rushed from the Toy Box and along the passage to the corridor.

Clown came toward us at a sickening pace.

"Only bad Toys play at night." Jessamine appeared before us in the corridor outside the ballroom, her arms rigid by her side. Putting her arms in the air, she stopped Clown and Raggedy as they closed in on us. For a second, my eyes blurred. Jessamine's fingers seemed to stay still at the same time as they moved. No, they moved ever so slightly even when they were still—flickering like an old movie. Jessamine herself was like a darkness—a darkness over which images were superimposed.

Why hadn't I noticed that before?

She reminded me of something. My physics teacher had slowed down a movie once and amazed the class with the black void in between every frame. The frames ran so fast that our brain perceived the movie as fluid movement. At twenty-four frames per second, our brains filled in the blanks. The frames formed the illusion of movement, but underneath, it was just a black screen. In the old movies before film had sound, you could clearly see the flicker.

That was Jessamine.

An icy chill sped along my spine. Missouri, Sophronia, and Philomena had been sleeping in a room with a century-old ghost for years—*and they knew*. Because I knew now, with all certainty, why Missouri had wanted us to fetch the locket and the photographs. We'd asked to know everything that she knew, and this was her way of telling us.

Inside me, a point of light died. Something like white noise rose in my mind. If ghosts were real, that changed everything about the world.

Aisha advanced toward Jessamine, her bony shoulders trembling. "There was never any chance of convincing you to let us out of here. Never any hope for us. Because you're not even human. *You're not human!*"

Jessamine stared straight at Aisha, and then turned and simply vanished. Bile churned in my stomach. One moment she was there. The next—gone.

Aisha's face was distorted with fear and hopelessness. Her white nightdress streamed behind her as she raced down the corridor. "Jessamine! Hey, Jessamine!"

"Aisha!" I screamed, rushing after her. Sophronia and Philomena stepped out of the bedroom, obviously awoken by my scream, and followed me.

Aisha grabbed a large knife from the kitchen and held it in her quaking hands.

"No!" In his cell, Ethan jumped to his feet.

Clown moved as fast in Aisha's direction as he had in the Toy Box. Bear, Raggedy, and Clara advanced on her together.

"Jessamine!" Aisha shouted—to the air, to the ceiling. "Soon, all you'll have to play with here is skeletons. *Just skeletons!*" She held the knife to her chest. "What's the point? What's the point of living another hour here?"

"Stop it!" I raced toward her, but Clara pinned me hard against the wall.

Jessamine appeared, her hair flying around her as though it had an energy of its own, her silence more terrifying than any of her words had been.

"No, please," I begged Aisha.

Aisha lifted the knife, as if to plunge it straight into her heart. But

Raggedy and Bear closed in on her. The knife fell from her hands as they picked her up, pinning her to the wall. She cried out in terror.

"Let her go!" I yelled at Jessamine, who stood perfectly still, gazing rigidly at the dolls. Controlling them. *Moving* them.

Sophronia limped along the passageway, standing in between Aisha and Jessamine. She leveled her gaze at Jessamine. "No."

My mouth dropped open.

Jessamine's gaze snapped to Sophronia. Her concentration broke. Raggedy and Bear set Aisha down. Aisha spun away from them, whimpering, clutching her throat.

"You spoke," Jessamine said flatly.

"I always could." Sophronia's voice was clear and firm, with a strong Indian accent.

"Lies! Lies and trickery!" Jessamine pointed a finger at her.

"*They* are the ones who lied to you, Jessamine," Sophronia told her. "They told you that you could keep us forever. But they are taking us away from you."

Jessamine eyes became dark pits. "I did my best for you. For all of you. I gave you refuge from the world above. But you give me no gratitude, and no comfort. You are spiteful and cruel, like the world whence you came. Take them." Jessamine waved a hand in our direction, then turned to Philomena. She was huddled against the wall, thumb in mouth, eyes rounded.

"Come, Philomena. We will leave these wretches to their own devices." Jessamine gestured to her.

Philomena backed away from Jessamine.

"They have poisoned you against me!" Jessamine's voice rose thinly.

Philomena ran shrieking down the passage toward the ballroom.

"Philly!" I cried.

I started to go after her but it was too late. The four Toys moved in on us—even Sophronia—dragging and pushing us with a crushing force into the cell next to Ethan's. It was so small we were practically immobile. There was no room to lie down or even sit.

The bars slid shut, enclosing us. I didn't know whether it was better that Philly hadn't been locked up too, or worse because she was now out there alone with Jessamine. From the day I'd first entered the Dollhouse, it had been obvious that Philly was Jessamine's favorite. I prayed that she wouldn't hurt her.

Sophronia stood wraithlike in the dark light of the cell, her black hair a shroud around her face and shoulders, watching me.

"Who do you serve?" she asked. Her eyes and voice were direct, nothing like the guarded, secretive girl who'd stayed in the background, never drawing attention to herself.

Ethan closed his hands around the bars that separated his cell from ours, veins in his neck straining. "What on earth does that mean, *who do we serve?*"

Her expression was resolute. "Were you sent here?"

"No." Ethan eyed her strangely. "How could any of us have been sent?"

Her shoulders relaxed. "I've been watching you, and you do not behave like seekers, but I needed to be sure."

Aisha was shivering, her arms wrapped tight around her shoulders, staring at Sophronia in shock.

"Seekers?" I shook my head. "I don't understand. Why haven't you spoken? Who *are* you?"

Sophronia bent her head. Her long black lashes rested on her cheek. "I decided to become the eyes and ears of the underground. I could not do that if Jessamine did not trust me. Without words, I was a doll. I was a plaything who never contradicted the odd thoughts in Jessamine's head. It calmed her." She paused, meeting our gazes. "And I have been trained, from when I was very small, to remain silent."

"*Trained*? How did you get here?" Ethan demanded.

"It was foolish of me to come here." She sighed regretfully. "But I was thirteen and desperate to prove myself."

Ethan's brow drew down over intense eyes. "Okay, I think you need to tell us your story."

"I will tell you it. My family came to this country from India, attempting to trace the book—the first part of the books of the *Speculum Nemus,* otherwise known as the books of the Mirrored Tree. I wanted to show how I could help."

"What's so special about the book that made your family come so far to find it?" I asked.

"The books of the Mirrored Tree are unlike any other that exist upon the earth," she answered. "They have the knowledge to allow us to travel anywhere between the stars. Other planets. Universes."

"You can't expect us to believe that. And anyway, there's only one universe," Ethan said warily.

She expelled a tight breath. "I cannot speak more of this. You can choose to accept what I am telling you—or not. My family and ancestors had kept the first of these books safe, in a sacred temple in India for centuries. Jessamine's grandfather—Tobias—stole it from us. And now The Provider and the others seek the second book, the book that will tell them how to work their astronomical clock, and travel where only humans with this knowledge have ever ventured before."

"We saw the clock," I gasped. "And we heard someone named Balthazar talk about the book. He spoke very strangely, like an actor."

Sophronia nodded. "Monseigneur Balthazar is a spirit who speaks in the only way he knows, in the tongue of someone who lived in the fourteenth century, and who has spent the centuries speaking both with ghosts and the living. His speech is an odd mix, that is true. He is a vile man."

The stone-cold eyes of the Monseigneur penetrated my mind.

Aisha laced her hands together, bringing them up to her mouth. "How did Lacey lure you here?"

Ethan shot her a strange look. "Lacey?"

Aisha nodded slowly, anger once again flashing in her pale eyes. "Cassie and I found Lacey tonight. She betrayed us. She's been helping The Provider bring girls here ever since she was nine years old. She was the first one to be kidnapped, from that school camping trip we all went on in the mountains."

Ethan stared at her, stunned into speechlessness.

Sophronia inhaled deeply. "This is how it happened. I told you my family came from India seeking the book. While I was helping my family do research, I found an old article about the Fiveash mansion and its connections to Tobias, and I caught a train and bus here from Sydney to find out what I could by myself. My family was engaged in other important investigations. I met a blonde girl in the forest." Sophronia's eyes darkened. "I asked her if she knew of an old house in the woods. She said that she did and she would show it to me. I shouldn't have trusted her. It was a discredit to my training. I was captured and brought down here. The most important thing for me to do then was not give away who I was because my family also has knowledge of the contents of the second book, the book that Balthazar and The Provider so desperately want. If they had discovered my true identity, they would have used me to try to draw out my parents and capture them. I vowed I would die before I spoke and revealed the truth. And that is my story. And here I have been for three years. I am now sixteen."

"Why didn't you at least speak to us, or to Missouri, if not to Jessamine?" I asked her. "You could have helped us. We could have helped you."

"Remaining silent is a practiced discipline. You cannot simply turn it on and off. And when the last two of you came in, I did not know whether you were enemy or ally. After all, you came in with the girl who brought me here—the girl you call Lacey."

Ethan doubled over, a hacking cough erupting from his chest.

"You're getting worse." I stared at his hunched shoulder blades, fear striking deep within me. People could die from asthma if they didn't get help.

He glanced back up at me, his eyes softening. "It's nothing. Just a cough."

"It's not nothing. You need medicine." I wished I could touch him. But the bars separated us.

Sophronia gazed at him with worried eyes. "It must have been a shock for you, Evander, seeing Jessamine as you just did. I can tell that Calliope and Angeline have just discovered what she is."

He shook his head. "I already knew."

Stooping down, he collected the toolbox from the floor and lifted it to the shelf. He pulled out an assortment of small digging tools, clamps, boxes of matches, and a half-burned candle, then peeled back what seemed like a secret bottom. A tattered leather diary lay beneath it.

Holding out the diary, he twisted his mouth. "The man the shadow killed in the Toy Box was my great-grandfather, Thomas McAllister."

I gasped. "*Your* great-grandfather?"

"Yeah." He let the diary fall open. "I found his diary and it told me everything. He was a gardener on the Fiveash estate, back in 1920. I never knew that he worked there. All I knew was that he disappeared when he was nineteen, leaving behind a wife and baby. The baby is my granddad."

"But we watched Thomas die. We saw him taken by the shadow," I said quietly. Images of his death struck at me like a deadly snake. "That was two days ago."

"I can't explain it," said Ethan. "But the third tunnel must take you back to the past. Somehow, we witnessed what happened back in 1920. I've been trying to plot out the secret tunnels behind the wall in my head. The tunnels all lead back here at one end. It's all like one big circle of secret tunnels around the Dollhouse. Which means none of those places are really there. The tunnels have to be a portal to other places and times."

He stared at me. "Did you notice that not one of those people in the other Toy Box noticed us? Not even Jessamine and she's got eyes like a hawk normally. I think they were all human and not ghosts when they killed Thomas."

"Yes." I'd thought we were just lucky. But what Ethan said made sense. Crazy sense.

Ethan ran an agitated hand through his hair. "Thomas knew Jessamine. In the diary he said he was worried about her. Thomas wrote in his diary that he didn't like the strange things happening down here in the underground. His last entry says that he was going to try to find out what was happening."

Sophronia bowed her head. "I am sorry for your ancestor."

Ethan gave her a tight smile.

Silence plunged between us.

"So what now?" Aisha's words skittered away like small, hard stones.

"Do we somehow convince Jessamine to let us out, then make a run for the tunnels?" Ethan suggested.

"There might be food in the castle, where we found Lacey," I said. "Getting some food would buy us some time. I mean, they're all spirits, but Lacey's not. They have to be feeding her somehow."

Sophronia's eyes deadened. "I suspect they will kill you as soon as they see you. I think that The Provider has chosen to take away our food so that he will not feel directly responsible for our deaths.

He is a strange mix. I do not think he is interested in cruelty for cruelty's sake." She sighed. "I wish that I knew more about the books and the serpent. But I was told little by my parents."

"What *is* that thing?" Ethan spoke between his teeth. "The serpent? We heard The Provider make some kind of bargain with it, some bargain that involves us."

"I do not know what she wants with us. But I sense her. I see her silver eyes in my dreams. And we have all seen her shadow roaming the underground." Sophronia leaned against the cell bars, shifting weight from her bad leg.

"Were you born that way?" asked Aisha sympathetically, glancing down at Sophronia's leg.

"No. I was an unwise child when I first came here. Escape was the only thing on my mind. I did not stand back and observe, as I had been taught." Slowly, she lifted the hem of her dress above her left knee. The knee joint jutted out at an odd angle, her leg twisted.

We gasped at the bent leg.

"That's a break that didn't heal properly." Ethan's brow furrowed.

"Yes. I climbed up inside the fireplace on the first night I came here. But there is no way through. Hot ash fell down and into my eyes. I lost my footing and fell. I tried to set my leg myself, though as you can see, I failed to get the bones straight again."

"We saw the grate at the top of the underground chimney. Donovan has it bolted down." Ethan pulled his mouth tight. "I can't imagine suffering through a broken leg down here."

"I used much meditation to cope with the pain." She smiled, flashing straight, white teeth. "You know, you three coming into the underground has been very good luck. For the first time, I see a way where there was none before."

"What do you see?" I asked anxiously.

"For some time, I have wondered if it is Jessamine's energy that gives life to the Dolls. But she kept it all so carefully controlled, so regimented, it was difficult to know with any certainty. You three appear to have taken away some of her energy, and so I could observe things that I couldn't before. I witnessed the Toys falling asleep when Jessamine did. And not only that—*the carousel turned.* As though there was no longer any control over it."

Ethan's jaw tensed. "I didn't know what to think when I saw you on that carousel. I thought you went to warn Donovan that the Dollhouse was unguarded."

"Quite the opposite. At the time, I was looking for an exit, trying to see whether anything else was different now that the Toys were asleep. I saw the carousel turning. Had I been capable of running, I might have reached it before Donovan came down to the underground. But as soon as I made it onto the platform and around to the other side, Donovan was already there, bringing Raggedy back."

My stomach clenched. Had Ethan and I heard the carousel sooner, we also could have reached it in time. "Sophronia, how can we make that happen again? How can we make the carousel turn?"

Her dark eyes surveyed me intently. "Jessamine controls everything in the underground. The carousels, the lights, the Toys—and us. But it drains her. It drains her energy. I suspect that the pretense of being human is a constant drain, too. And now, with the extra Toys to control—you three—she sleeps far more than she used to. Your energies, Evander and Calliope, are especially taxing on her. You never stop. Ever since you both arrived, you've been constantly rattling the bars of this prison, trying to find escape. She can barely manage to contain you."

"If she loses control again," I whispered, "then the carousel will turn . . . ."

"Yes, I think it might," said Sophronia.

Aisha stared at us with pale round eyes. "But we're trapped in the cells. Jessamine can leave us in here for as long as she wants. She might leave us here until we die. She hates us."

Sophronia wrinkled her smooth brown forehead. "Do you not understand? She also controls the cells. She is the lock. If the carousel turns, the cell doors open . . . ."

Ethan's eyes blazed. "But how? How do we make her lose control while we're all locked away?"

"That I do not know." Sophronia bowed her head. "I've spent many hours pondering that. The only thing I am sure of is that she hates any reminder that she is a spirit. That day in the kitchen when you came at her with a knife, I'm quite certain her main fear was that everyone would see that she didn't bleed if you stabbed her. If we had something that would remind her . . . ."

Aisha's face lit up. She uncurled her fist and showed Sophronia the object she held in her palm: Jessamine's locket, open and displaying the photo of Tobias and Jessamine.

Sophronia's eyes widened in wonder. With trembling fingers she picked up the locket with her thumb and forefinger. "I have never seen this before."

Reaching inside the bodice of my dress, I pulled out the bundle of old photographs I'd taken from Henry's den—the picture of Jessamine holding miniature versions of the oversized Dollhouse Dolls on top.

Sophronia's lips parted in shock as she took the bundle and pulled open the ribbon. She fell silent as she examined the pictures, but I could sense thoughts eddying swiftly through her mind. I had barely seen a flicker of emotion from her since I had been there, and now I understood how much she was holding back. "If she sees these things—this proof of her past existence—she will be forced to stop pretending." She looked up at us. "This is perfect."

Turning sharply, Ethan lifted the toolbox from the Toy shelf. "And why don't we give the locket and photos to Jessamine together with a big fat reminder of 1920?" He held out a stamped timesheet with the name Thomas McAllister written clearly across the top of it. "She knew Thomas, and from what he says about her in his diary, he was the only person she trusted aside from her grandfather."

"Yes," cried Sophronia, her face alive with hope. "This could be our chance."

A *shushing* sound echoed from somewhere above. We stared out into the corridor.

A massive blackness eddied across the ceiling, clinging and dripping like blood along the rock surface.

The shadow.

It slithered along the ceiling—up the passage and into the bedroom.

"No!" I screamed. Desperately, I whipped around to face Sophronia. "Will it hurt Missouri?"

She pressed her lips into a bloodless line. "In our sleep, it cannot hurt us. But in a coma, I am not sure. If she can hear it, it can harm her."

A small figure raced down the corridor toward the bedroom, hair across her quivering face—Philomena. "Don't you hurt my Missy," she screamed at the shadow. "Do you hear me! Don't you hurt her!"

I rushed to the bars. "Philly, we need you to do something for us." Taking the locket and photographs from Sophronia, and the timesheet from Ethan, I held them out to her. "Please, take these to Jessamine. And tell her the shadow's here. Can you do that? It's important if we want to help Missouri."

She nodded numbly, clutching the items in her tiny hands.

I gripped the bars. "When you give them to her, say, 'this is who you are.' Then you must run back to us as fast as you can. Do you understand? Hurry!"

Her body shook beneath her nightdress. But she took off down the passage without another word.

We watched her disappear around the corner.

"We must prepare ourselves," said Sophronia. "We must act swiftly and surely. I cannot run and I will rely on you three to get Missouri and Philomena to safety."

Ethan gazed at her intently, sweat beading on his forehead. "Countdown."

22. WITHER THE ROSE PETALS

Evil stalks the hallways of my dreams
Balthazar in the bedchamber, watching me
Dead of breath, and burnt and charred
Wither on the vine, roses of the graveyard
Molly, forgive me; unlike you I'm not strong
Torment mocks me, leaves me strung
So tightly, wound around and 'round

—P.

A flurry of papers shot into the end of the hall.

Crashing sounds echoed from the ballroom. A high thin scream shattered the air—Jessamine's scream—as Philomena ran toward us with her arms covering her head. Books flung themselves into the walls and ceilings behind her.

Terrified, she turned and watched, standing stunned and fixed to the spot.

"Run!" Aisha screamed at her.

Abruptly, the doors of the cells slammed open.

We were free.

Ethan rushed into the corridor.

"You get Missouri. We'll get Philly," I told him, desperation sharp in my voice.

Aisha and I raced down the passage.

Raising her arms, Aisha desperately shoved a desk away as it flew toward Philly. I scooped the little girl up in my arms.

"Go!" Aisha roared.

We charged forward as a maelstrom of splintered desks and shelf toys rounded the bend behind us. Clown, Raggedy, Bear, and Clara lurched erratically toward us. They fell with heavy thuds. Only Raggedy continued on, crawling along the floor in jerky movements.

"She's trying to kill us!" I dodged the gramophone as it slammed into the wall.

"Hurry!" Ethan's hair fell across his face in ropy lengths as he brought Missouri's limp body out from the bedchamber. The serpent-shadow retreated across the hallway ceiling, writhing, denied its prey.

Above the clamor, a tinny sound rose.

The carousel. The way out. It was starting up.

We rushed to it, jumping onto the platform. Philly clung fast to me.

Ethan laid Missouri in a chariot. Aisha reached an arm out to Sophronia, helping her on board.

A buzzing, electrical sound shot through the air as the lights dimmed. A spinning chandelier moved erratically toward us. It was the chandelier from the ballroom. It whirled crazily in the air, then swooped in and dropped, crunching heavily against Aisha's thigh. She screamed. Ethan leapt across to heave the thing from the carousel.

A grinding started beneath our feet. A tiny red light lit up on the center column. Then more lights, green and red—twinkling. My breath quickened in my chest.

The carousel lumbered clockwise. Darkness closed over me as the carousel turned.

We were on the other side.

I jumped from the platform with Philly—Sophronia following more cautiously. Ethan helped Aisha down from the platform.

The carousel stopped dead.

We fled along the pitch-dark passage.

Philly whimpered into my shoulder. "Are we in the Toy Box?"

"No, Philly. We're on our way to the sun and the flowers. Not long to go."

We made our way along the passage as it wound upward—we had to be close to the exit.

The weight of Philomena pulled on my leg and back muscles. Sweat formed on my scalp. Carefully, I lifted her down onto her feet and clutched her hand. "We have to keep running, okay?"

The black air filled with Ethan's strained gasps as he ran with Missouri in his arms and Aisha's muffled cries of pain. The chandelier had hit Aisha hard.

Abruptly, I came up against a flat, cold object. "Watch out," I called to the others. "There's something here."

Desperately, I felt along its surface with my free hand.

"What the hell?" said Ethan as he stepped up alongside me. A metal noise resounded as he banged on the thing in front of us. "That wasn't there before."

A glow sprang to life. Sophronia's face lit up above a candle. "I brought the candle and matches that were in the toolbox."

My heart fell into a pit. It was a wall—plates of metal bolted together to form a solid wall. The surface of the metal entirely blocked the passageway—floor to ceiling.

"Donovan walled us in," said Aisha thinly.

"No . . . ." I breathed. All the air was sucked from my lungs.

Philomena stared up at me, whimpering. But I had no words of comfort to give her. Not even a word of hope. Letting go of her hand, I slammed my fists all over the plate metal like a mad thing.

Ethan laid Missouri on the floor. Then, with a yell of fury, he charged at the wall, kicking it over and over again. Exhausted, he knelt, breathing hard into the floor, bending his head down to his hands.

Sophronia limped over to sit on the floor. She pulled Missouri's head onto her lap. Aisha struggled to sit beside Sophronia, gripping her injured thigh. Her dress was damp with blood.

Minutes bled away.

There had been no way out—right from the first day we'd come down to the underground. I understood that now. Before, there had at least been hope—hope that the world stood on the other side of the carousel.

Behind us, away in the distance, the tinny music of the carousel rang in the dark air.

"She wants us to come back." Philomena's voice was small, afraid.

"We got this far," said Aisha in a dead tone. "I'm not going back. I can't go back." Her fingers moved awkwardly to pull away her shredded dress from her thigh. A cut gashed her leg from thigh bone to knee.

"Oh god." I clamped my hand over my mouth.

Ethan pulled his jacket and shirt from his back, moving to wrap the shirt around Aisha's leg. Blood seeped into the white material. I lifted my dress over my head. Ethan and I ripped it into lengths— Ethan winding the fabric over the bandage he'd already made.

Sitting beside Aisha, I pulled Philly onto my lap.

We sat in heavy silence—a silence that thickened and suffocated the air.

A grittiness entered my head, like my mind was filling with sand. Cold gripped me. I shivered in my thin slip.

Could we go back?

There was no food left in the Dollhouse. No warmth except for damp, mildewed blankets. Nothing worth going back for.

Except the tea.

If we went back—Jessamine might well kill us.

But to stay here and slowly starve to death, in the darkness after the candle gave out, seemed infinitely worse. It would be unbearable to have Philly suffer it all—and Missouri had made us promise that Philly wouldn't suffer.

I stood up.

Sophronia stared up at me with an intense gaze—a gaze that melted away, pulled inward. She settled Philomena's head against her chest, and made a slow, single nod at me—a nod that told me, *this is our time to die.*

"We forgot to have a nice sleep before our journey," she told Philly. Philomena stared round-eyed at Sophronia.

I bent to take Philly from her. The little girl clung to me so fiercely it hurt my ribs.

Aisha's eyes closed for a moment, her face deathly pale. "It's too dangerous," she said finally.

Her eyes opened dully then—as aware as I was that the word *dangerous* had lost all meaning. She struggled to her feet.

Without a word, Ethan moved to gather up Missouri.

Sophronia held the candle and Philly's hand as we walked the long path back. I helped Aisha walk as best I could, slinging her arms across my shoulders, while Ethan carried Missouri in his arms.

My legs shook as I lifted Philly onto the unicorn. Aisha and Sophronia limped to a chariot. The carousel spun slowly counter-clockwise.

Debris lay scattered and broken through the passageway. We picked our way through it. Aisha moaned softly at the sight of the chandelier that had cut her leg—it lolled upturned against the wall. The Dolls were lying still on the floor ahead.

The narrow crevice that led to the bedroom was an ugly eye in the wall—even more terrifying than it had been the first time I had seen it. In there, everything was about to end.

I took Philly inside the room, and led her back to bed. She held me tight around the neck, her eyes bright and watery. "I want to go to the flowers."

"You will," I whispered. "I promise."

Ethan laid Missouri down on her bed—she looked like the inanimate doll she'd seemed the first time I'd seen her.

Aisha swung her bandaged leg onto the bed, and leaned back, breathing hard.

"I'll make the tea," Sophronia said softly.

23. REQUIEM

She nourishes the poison in her veins
and is consumed by a secret fire.

—Virgil, *The Aeneid*

Wind shrieked down the corridor, swirling into the room.

"What is that *wind*?" Ethan turned to stare at me. "Where is it coming from?"

I shrugged. It didn't matter anymore. Nothing did. "You heard Sophronia. We can't wait. If we linger, Jessamine might take the tea away from us."

Ethan shook his head. "I'm going to look." Ethan strode away determinedly.

I gave Sophronia, who had returned with the tea trolley, a pleading look. "Please, give us a moment."

Aisha's mouth pulled into a tight line as she gazed at me. "Promise me you'll both come back." Her jaw clenched. "Promise me."

"We promise," Ethan told her.

Sophronia stood in the corridor watching silently as Ethan and I ran to the storage chamber to get our flashlights, then rushed away down the corridor.

Cautiously, we edged toward the ballroom. Nothing was left untouched. Every book and toy was gone from its place on the shelves. In a shadowed corner, the rocking chair creaked slowly back and forth.

"We should go back," I whispered, my voice as dry as autumn leaves. Jessamine was in that chair, I was sure—watching us.

He shook his head. "*You* can."

Wind whistled around the corner, coming from the Toy Box. Teeth clenched, I followed Ethan as he continued down the corridor.

Turning our flashlights on, we stepped into the clawing darkness. Wind howled in from an unseen source. The serpent shadow was *here*. I could sense her all around us. Ethan gripped my hand and drew me close. He held me in his arms, his mouth pressing against my temple.

"I'm sorry," he said, "but I can't give up. It's not over."

A shudder passed though me. "I made a promise to Missouri. About Philly. I can't let her starve to death. If Jessamine takes the tea away, then our last chance is gone."

"I know," he said. "You should go back. Drink the tea with the others if I don't return."

"I'm staying with you."

The decisions we faced were too big.

We kissed. I saw him, that morning we trekked in the forest, sun slanting across his back, his lopsided grin as he turned to me—with that wistful look on his face that I'd convinced myself wasn't really there. You could make up stuff in your head and focus on it so much that it became real.

I took his hand. "Let's go."

Together, we continued on.

I shone the flashlight upward around the ceiling and down again. The red velvet curtains had been torn away. The stone statue of the saint lay smashed to pieces on the ground. Slowly, I raised my eyes to the space where the statue had been. A hole gaped in the wall—a small cave. The cave had been behind the statue all this time. Bits of cement were scattered across the floor—the statue must have been cemented to the wall.

The cave was crammed with large canvas bags, piled on top of each other. I looked back at Ethan. Terrible thoughts crowded my head. *Were the bags filled with the dead? Had more people died here, just like Prudence?*

Ethan stepped up to the bags, feeling their contents through the fabric. "Feels like rocks."

He cut into one bag fiercely with a sharp razor he must have found in the toolbox. Dirt plumed into the air. Shining clear objects spilled to the ground, clattering on the rock.

Gasping, I looked down at the transparent stones—Diamonds.

He cut open another bag. Dark pebbles of gold fell free.

He crouched to the floor, scooping handfuls of gold and diamonds into his hands and looking closely at them. "God, look at all this."

A rustling sound came from farther in the cave. Something teetered—and fell. Ethan gave a shout and scrambled backward.

A bundle of bones now lay on top of the scattered nuggets and diamonds—tattered bits of dark material sticking to the limbs and ribcage.

A skeleton. Around the neck was a blackened chain that might have once been gold—a broken clasp where something had broken off. The clasp was missing its locket.

Jessamine.

Did she die in there—in that terrible place? All alone in a cave? She had said she woke up in a strange place.

Ethan pulled himself to his feet. "C'mon. Let's see if we can make some explosives from the lamp oil." His eyes were desperate above the glow of his flashlight.

"No explosive we can make is going to get through that wall, Ethan," I said, as gently as I could.

Suddenly, Ethan stiffened. His eyes went wide with terror.

Something blacker than the air inched around me, layering itself on my skin like plastic. Suffocating me. It whispered to me, but the words were underneath everything—words spoken at the bottom of a deep pool.

The shadow.

I heard Ethan's shout, felt his hands on my shoulders—trying to wrestle the shadow. But his voice sounded so far away.

The shadow's words echoed a deep, biting longing. She hooked tiny barbs into me, everywhere. She told me I wouldn't feel it for long—told me it wouldn't hurt for much longer. She told me that if I just gave into it, it would be over soon. I just needed to give myself to it. That was all. Forget the others. Go with her. Take my pain away . . . .

No. No. I turned, staggering, barely able to stay on my feet, as if she were a physical thing, as if I could shake off the serpent.

Jessamine stood behind me, head lowered.

"Get that thing off her!" Ethan shouted.

Jessamine lifted her arms in the air, trembling.

The shadow fled my body.

I collapsed onto my hands and knees. Dropping to the ground, Ethan cupped my face in his hands. "Are you okay? Cassie, are you okay?"

Gasping, I let him help me to my feet. I couldn't speak. The darkness of the shadow filled every space of my mind.

"Look what you've done to us," Ethan raged at Jessamine. "We're all going to die—and that thing almost killed Cassie." He directed a glance down at the skeleton. "You want us all to end up like you?"

She was still shaking as she stared at the bones. "The Provider says there are different planes of existence."

"Did he put you in that cave to die?" Ethan demanded to know.

"Of course not." She looked troubled. "I was playing," she said, "just playing an awfully fun game of hide and seek. And I got stuck."

I shivered as icy wind blowing from the cave bit at my face. *Wind.* If there was wind, could there be a passage beyond the canvas bags? "Where does it lead?"

Her expression darkened. "It's quite nasty. You mustn't go through to the end—you must never do that. It goes to the terror."

"What is the terror?"

"I told you before, Calliope, about the pool of memory. That's why you mustn't go. Memories can only bring you pain. And the pool is guarded by the serpent with the silver eyes. You cannot get past her. You see? You *must* stay here with me."

"Please, tell me—what's beyond the pool?" I asked desperately.

She stared at me blankly. "The world, and every bad thing you can imagine. Everything I tried to protect you from."

Ethan straightened. "Then we're going that way." He climbed over the bags and crawled inside the cave, shining his flashlight about the interior.

I hesitated. We'd sworn to Aisha we would come back. But Jessamine had said the world was at the end of that tunnel. *The world.*

Jessamine clutched at my arm. "Why couldn't you two be obedient like the others?" she said pleadingly. "They're in their beds now, having a beautiful sleep."

Ice ran through my veins. They had sworn to wait. "They're sleeping?"

"Oh yes. I gave them the tea they'd made for themselves. A sleep is always better with a cup of hot tea."

A low pained sound escaped from deep within me. "You made them drink it," I whispered.

She nodded. "They were being quite naughty and refused to take the tea, until I told them you and Evander were dead. Now come with me, Calliope. There's enough tea left for you."

"Did you know, Jessamine,"—my words rasping and weak—"that the tea was made so strong they will sleep forever?"

Her eyes widened. "That is a nasty untruth, Calliope!" she spat.

"Is it? *Is it*?" My voice rose to a scream. "Go check the kitchen. There's *no tea* left."

Her face grew as white as chalk, and she knotted her fingers together. "Then—then we must make do. The three of us. The ballroom is a mess but together—"

"No." I was shaking so hard my knees almost gave out. We won't go with you to the ballroom. It's over, Jessamine."

"You don't understand. We must have patience. Patience is required to—"

"No!" I shrieked at her. "I know why you're always talking about having patience. All this time, you've been here waiting for your grandfather Tobias to come and find you. Well, he's never coming to get you. He died a long time ago. And so did *you*. You're a ghost. A *ghost*."

Her face visibly faded, becoming almost bluish, her eyes dark pits. I remembered I'd once seen Philomena draw a girl with black holes for eyes. Jessamine. "You do not understand," she said tightly.

"You're right. I don't understand anything here. You. This place. The crazy huge furniture. The Dolls." I pointed at her. "Your grandfather was trying to keep you a little girl!

"You are quite wrong. Grandfather built this to protect me."

"Protect you from what?"

"That is not your concern."

Ethan reemerged from the cave, his face flushed and covered in a fine sweat. "The tunnel there is just a long vertical drop. And I can't even fit my shoulders into it."

"Ethan," I cried, "they've all taken the tea." I stared accusingly at Jessamine "She told them we were dead."

His face crumpled in anguish. "No . . . ."

She tilted her head, watching us for a minute.

"I tried to give you everything you needed. But you willfully disobeyed, at every step. Perhaps it is better if you are gone from here. Follow me. Since you insist, you may leave the way in which you came in."

The muscles in my back tensed, pulling tight against my ribs. I could hardly believe what she was saying. "Donovan built a metal wall there. We can't get through."

"I can make that wall disappear," she told me, with a vague shrug.

Ethan's eyes widened. "You'd—you'd let us go? Just like that?"

"I've grown tired of your company," she said, and, inclining her head, retreating toward the Dollhouse.

Ethan and I exchanged tense glances. We had nothing to lose.

We stepped after her through the Toy Box and the eerily quiet corridor.

I stopped at the entrance to the bedroom, my heart glitching in my chest. Every one of the girls slept, arms crossed over their chests.

Not one of them had escaped the Dollhouse. Would they lie there forever like that?

Two full cups of tea waited for Ethan and me. The other three cups were empty.

Ethan's arms came tightly around me. I turned to him, watching his eyes fill with pain.

The sound of the carousel echoed in the empty air.

The red and green bulbs of the carousel's center column lit up as we walked toward it with Jessamine and stepped onto the platform.

Ethan pressed his hand over mine as I clutched a pole, giving me a half-smile. "Don't be scared," he whispered. "I'll always be with you."

Complete darkness descended on us as the carousel turned and then stopped on the other side. Ethan jumped from the platform, holding out his hand to me. I touched my fingers to his.

Something—a force—threw me backward. The carousel began turning—fast this time.

"Cassie!" Ethan's voice rang out sharply.

Desperately, I rushed to my feet.

Light shone dimly in my eyes.

I was back. In the Dollhouse.

Jessamine stood beside me, her expression smug.

"What did you do?" You can't leave him out there. Make it move!" I rattled the pole manically. "*Make it move!*"

"He was a beastly boy. You will see you're much better off without him. Now, come and join me in the ballroom. We will continue your instruction and education."

My lower lip quivered. "Please . . . please. If you won't let us leave, bring him back. We'll do as you say."

"I'm afraid he can't ever come back in." She pursed her lips. "You will join me, when you are ready." She paused. "Things always seem worse, just before they turn for the better."

Her voice seemed far away, floating between layers of air and rock. Blood roared in my head.

With her hands behind her back, she skipped away down the corridor, singing a nursery rhyme to herself.

I backed away until I hit the wall, not realizing I was screaming until I finally heard the sound echo back to me from the corridor.

The Dollhouse was deathly cold, deathly quiet.

I was alone.

It wasn't supposed to be like this. I wasn't supposed to be here, alone with a ghost.

Remembering the tea, I stumbled for the bedroom. Now, I craved sleep. Ethan—I would never see Ethan again. Never see my mother, or the sunlight, never feel the touch of wind on my face.

In the bedroom, four girls had been, at last, transformed into dolls. They lay in their beds, with waxen faces and still limbs. Four dolls who would never again open their eyes.

Dark liquid spread across the floor, forking into paths.

The tea.

Jessamine had poured the last of it out.

All breath left my chest.

A small object lay under a bed. Philly's headless bear—the only thing she'd brought in from the outside world. Numbly, I picked it up and laid it in the crook of Philomena's arm.

Up the empty corridor outside, only the wind sounded.

I climbed into my own bed and pulled the covers over. My arms folded across my chest automatically.

Would I be the last one here to die? Molly Parkes hadn't taken the tea. She hadn't needed to. If I lay here long enough, I would soon grow sick, I would soon find sleep. And Ethan would sleep, alone, in the darkness on the other side of the carousel.

But no sleep came. Instead, I kept seeing the cave we'd discovered—in the Toy Box wall—an ugly wound in the wall, with wind like blood flowing out. I pictured Jessamine crawling through the tunnel, almost one hundred years ago.

I sat bolt upright. Could this tunnel be Prudence's fourth path?

Ethan had said he couldn't fit into it. But that didn't mean I couldn't. I was far smaller than he.

I could travel through the wall between the Dollhouse and the castle, while Prudence could *see through* the wall. I didn't have control over where I ended up, and I'd never passed through the wall to the fourth tunnel. It had remained hidden from me. But Prudence, she could see everything. She'd seen Lacey, and the mirrored tree sculpture, and four paths. If the cave were the entrance to the fourth path, could she have seen through to the end of it?

Prudence had spoken of a pool. And Jessamine had said there was a pool at the end of the tunnel—and the world.

I had to try.

In the storage room, I pulled on my jeans, T-shirt, jumper, and jacket. Then my ski cap. It was going to be even colder than the Dollhouse in the tunnel.

I put two pairs of socks on each foot, then my boots. I took leather gloves from the drawers and wriggled my fingers into them. I didn't know to whom they had belonged, but they were an American brand and I guessed they had been Prudence's. My stomach sank as I thought of her again.

Shoving the big flashlight down my jacket front, I was as ready as I was ever going to be.

I picked my way around the fallen Toys and smashed furniture and torn books. Hesitating as I reached the ballroom, I peered inside. Jessamine sat in her rocking chair, waiting for me, her hair tangled across her pale, exhausted face. She was sleeping—for the moment. I had to be quick.

The Toy Box was empty and still as I made my way through it. The shadow's whispers vibrated through my ears. Missouri had said that if we didn't let the shadow into our minds, it couldn't harm us. Before, in the Toy Box, at my weakest hour, it had tried to claim me, and I'd allowed it in.

Shadow, you cannot claim me.

Shadow, I will not let you in.

My feet slipped on the scattered diamonds as I struggled to climb up to the cave's opening. I clambered over the canvas bags, dirt and dust thickening in my nostrils. But almost immediately the tunnel dropped away, descending steeply downward, just as Ethan had described, at almost a ninety-degree angle. If I started down this passage, there was almost certainly no way of getting back up again. And there was no telling how far it went down—it could go for miles like this.

Ice-laden wind breathed over me as I began the downward climb. My foot skidded. Something moved below me.

A large animal?

I knew it wasn't.

With nausea rising in my heart and stomach, I braced myself against the tunnel walls and shone the flashlight downward again. Something climbed—fast—with jerky movements that belonged to no animal.

Much bulkier than a human.

I backed up—straightening each leg against the rock as I pushed myself up. My legs burned with the effort. The thing crawled toward me erratically. I trained the flashlight's beam directly on it—

the thing that was surely about to devour me from the legs up.

Dead eyes glared at me above a wide grin. It moved a large lace-up boot near its head at an impossible angle, and pushed itself forward. *What was it?*

Struggling upward, I bumped my head—hard. The thing pushed at me—pushed me up—at a crazy speed.

Both of us tumbled from the opening.

It crawled forward grotesquely. I scrambled to get to my feet, my layers of clothing impeding me. Whipping my flashlight out, I shone it downward. The thing was slickly wet, covered in black mold and rotting clothing. But almost as soon as it broke free of the cave, it collapsed.

I should have known that thing would be in the Dollhouse somewhere. Every child knew that a Raggedy Ann doll came as a pigeon pair with a Raggedy Andy doll. And a small version of it had been in Jessamine's photograph with her collection of dolls. The hair had been eaten away and the clothes were stained and dark—but it was unmistakable.

I could only guess why he was in there. Perhaps Jessamine had put him there for protection. Judging by the condition of him, that time was many decades ago. I doubted he was much protection, anymore. Perhaps a tiny part of Jessamine's energy had been stored in the Andy doll and then long forgotten.

I exhaled, waiting until my heart stopped pounding. If I'd been farther in when the doll rushed at me, I'd have been crushed to death against the rock.

Carefully, I stepped around the hideous doll and crawled back into the cave.

Wind blew around me, biting into the skin around my eyes. I welcomed it—despite the pain, the odor of slime and dank was overpowering. My arms and back scraped and slid along rock. I made the backward descent down into the vertical tunnel.

My legs burned as I struggled to keep myself from falling—positioning them hard against the rock. There was nothing to grip onto—just small, slippery ledges.

I kept moving. I didn't know how long I'd been in complete darkness. Probably less than ten minutes. My heart dilated and constricted—a caged animal in my chest. I tried to disengage my brain, stop all thought—stop everything except the relentless climb downward.

The tunnel changed course and flattened out. I wriggled my body around under a protrusion of rock so that I now faced upward. Crawling was easier now—my body almost horizontal. I inched along like a worm on my back. I wished I could face forward, but there was not enough space to turn around in.

Icy water drizzled on my face and ran underneath me.

The tunnel sloped steeply upward ahead, ending in a high ledge. I had to go uphill over this ledge, feet first, on my back. There wasn't enough space above or around me to do anything else. I grunted with each small effort.

A sharp rock edge scraped along my side, ripping through my jacket to my skin. Trickles of water ran along my ribs.

Almost immediately, my body began to shake. The cold chewed into my bones like a rabid dog.

I couldn't last like this. I didn't know how long I had before my body refused to move, before it shut itself down to conserve energy.

I tried to find a foothold on the upper ledge—but my body kept slipping down, now on a sharp uphill angle. My legs flailing, I tried again. And again. And again. Climbing backward, on my back, with barely any room to move, was impossible.

Exhausted, I leaned my head back in a small crevice of icy water. My head froze, hurt. Even if I made it—I couldn't manage miles more of this.

And in the end, was it all just to deliver myself to the serpent? I sensed her, waiting for me.

Shadows slipped and slithered on the rock wall. She was here with me.

I felt the barbs pierce me. It wasn't so gentle this time. The shadow was anxious, tired of waiting. Its darkness tightened around me.

I will not let you in.

A whisper drifted through my mind, but not the shadow's whisper. It was Ethan. *Don't be scared—I'll always be with you*, he'd said.

I hung on to his voice, to the arms that had held me in the dark, to the eyes in which I'd found home.

The shadow wrenched itself from me—leaving me breathless.

I was cold, so cold.

Water gurgled around me. If it rained in the outside world now—the tunnel might fill with water. And I'd drown, drift, forever.

But if rain and wind from the outside could reach in here, perhaps there really was a way out.

I threw my body forward again. My legs found purchase on the rock ledge. I used elbows, hands, head, shoulders—everything to get the rest of me up there. I pushed my legs out—forcing my body to follow.

I made it. I was moving again. The tunnel opened out, until I was able to turn around, and a few minutes later—walk. I walked on for what seemed hours.

The shriek of wind intensified. A deeper sound boomed in my ears. An underground river?

Extending an arm out, I shone the flashlight around. A cathedral-sized cave stretched before me, pillars of transparent crystal rising from a wide milky-blue pool. A waterfall rushed from the soaring ceiling of rock into the pool.

The pool.

The pool of Mnemosyne.

No. That was a myth, a tale.

There was nowhere to go but straight down.

Fifteen feet or so straight down.

I crawled to the edge and let myself drop. I caught a dim reflection of myself on the water's opaque surface just before I hit it. My body splashed into ice water. As the freezing water closed over me, shock charged through me. Terrified, I struck out, struggling to the surface. Taking a lungful of air, I swam to the slippery, crystalline walls. My feet found purchase on an underwater rock shelf.

My limbs ached to the bone.

I sensed the shadow. But it didn't come to me, it didn't seek me. With a sickening in my stomach, I knew it no longer had to seek me. Because I'd come to it. The shadow and the serpent were one. I was here, in the bowels of the serpent. I felt it begin to digest me, disassemble my mind.

She was coming.

The serpent was coming.

Snatches of sound echoed in the cave. I strained to hear.

I remembered being so sick once that my mother had to take me to the hospital. I was only three. My temperature rose so high, I imagined things, hallucinated. Family came to visit—but they sounded so far away, so garbled. Like a radio transmission fading in and out.

That's what the sounds reminded me of now.

Then I heard it clearly. Girls singing. An old nursery rhyme I couldn't place.

A light wavered near the middle of the water. Not light exactly—more like a reflection of light.

In the middle of the soft glow, a ghostly, almost transparent figure—a girl—stood on the water. Her hair fell in long, dark waves. She turned to me. She wore a yellow dress—a dark stain of blood on the bodice. Her eyes were haunting, filled with pain and sorrow so intense I could scarcely bear to look at her.

"Prudence." The name slipped from my tongue.

She gave a single nod, then tilted her chin and pointed upward, to a spot beside the waterfall. My gaze traveled up the rock wall. Thick lines formed a strange, crisscrossed pattern in the rock. They were tree roots, aged and gnarled, that had grown the way roots grow when there's no soil and only rock—along every crevice.

She stared at me, her small face tense, anxious—as though she wanted me to do something.

Then I understood. My stomach tightened, knotting inside me.

Above the roots was a tree. In the world.

In the light and sunshine and rain.

The way out.

24. POOL OF MEMORY

I've seen her since before I was born
Her long dark hair and eyes like pools
Of memory
Cassandra, Cassandra I sensed you torn
Between innocence and remembrance
Don't seek the shadowed night
Of Mnemosyne
Don't follow me
For I am long gone.

      —P.

The barest glimmer of light shone far above. Daylight—a thing I hadn't seen since I took my first step into the underground beneath the old Fiveash house. I could see that the crisscrossing tree roots grew thicker and stronger toward the higher reaches of the cave wall until they disappeared beneath the rushing waterfall.

Rush! Move!

Something stopped me.

Why should I be the only one to leave?

Far away, through the long, narrow channel I'd just crawled through, four dolls were lying there still in their beds, four dolls who might never wake. I imagined the ghost of Jessamine rocking in her chair, listening to the empty echoes in her now-lonely rooms and corridors. No more waltzing practice, no more nursery rhymes, no more whispers in dark corners.

Ethan remained in the pitch dark on the other side of the carousel. His last words to me seemed a rustle of leaves left behind on a winter tree: *I'll always be with you . . . .*

I turned quickly, desperate to see Prudence's face again—wanting her to take away my guilt, tell me it was okay for me to be the only one to escape. It was Prudence who had shown me the way all along. Her poetry, scribbled in the depth of her despair and madness, spoke of everything she'd seen.

She still stood on the milky-blue surface of the cave's pool, but already her light was fading. I reached to her. She'd been the girl who was haunted by the visions she'd seen beyond the Dollhouse walls. She had seen further than anyone else, and she'd paid the price with her life. Bowing her head, she became completely translucent. And then she was gone.

I immediately felt the loss of her.

Strange thoughts crowded my mind. I had been here before, standing at the edge of this pool. Murky, long-forgotten memories were like trains rattling through thick fog, bearing down on me. If I stayed here long enough, soon I would remember everything—I could feel it. I willed the memories to come. I wanted to know everything. I gazed into the pool, trying to see deep into it.

This was what Jessamine had warned me about. But I was compelled.

The temperature plunged. My lungs began to burn with cold, my breaths whitening.

Where the waterfall hit the pool below, icy, jagged shapes formed. A thin film of ice spread across the pool's surface. If the cave grew any colder, the water would freeze. I stared up at the flowing waterfall in horror—if that froze, it would seal the opening above.

A dark shadow swam below the surface of the pool.

Adrenaline fired in my veins.

I needed to go.

Edging around the walls of the cave, I stayed as far as possible from the water. Spray from the waterfall splashed my face as I reached the tree roots that clung to the cave wall.

Grasping an overhead root, I tried to pull myself up. My legs were heavy as I stepped upward. My feet slipped along the wet edges of the roots.

Something rose behind me.

I turned to face her.

Silvery scales caught the light of crystalline pillars in the recesses of the cave. Large, unblinking eyes watched me. She watched me with eyes like glass, *eyes that knew me.*

My mind bent inward—turned on itself. I could not be seeing this creature. A creature like this should not exist.

Her shadow moved through the air, dropping and wrapping itself around my body. *"Why do you seek me?"*

The voice chilled me to my core. She was using her shadow to speak to me.

"I didn't seek you." My words rushed out.

"Look inside," she hissed. "See the centuries pass through my eyes."

Her gaze was like knives piercing my soul, hypnotizing me.

She pulled her shadow back to her body and slipped away into the water. I sensed her icy satisfaction at my fear. Trembling uncontrollably, I scanned the cave. *Where was she?*

With a crash, she reared up in front of me. I threw my back against the wall, a scream fleeing my throat.

She opened her monstrous jaw and smashed it against the wall, narrowly missing me. Her teeth meshed in the roots of the tree. The roots ripped away from the wall as the serpent dove down into the water.

My body shot into the air. With a frantic grab, I managed to catch hold of a rock ledge beneath the waterfall. An earsplitting crash sounded from above. A wall of wood steam-trained past me. The entire tree that stood above the cave was coming down. *Straight down.*

Branches whipped past my face. I felt the leaves and tremendous whoosh of air. Any second, a branch would hit me and I'd be torn downward with the tree.

25. BREATHE

The only hope for the doomed, is no hope at all..."
—Virgil, *The Aeneid*

I clung to the ledge as the entire tree was wrenched down through the pool below—the tree taking the serpent with it. The top branches disappeared below the water's surface. The pool had to be endlessly deep.

Again, the pool's surface iced over. Above, beams of light shone from the gashes in the earth from which the tree had been ripped. Thin sounds cracked through the air. A splash of water from the waterfall turned to ice before it hit the palm of my hand.

Get out! Fast!

If the water all turned to ice, the way out would be blocked.

I'd be sealed in with a ceiling of ice.

I climbed upward on the jutting ledges, the rocky surfaces growing frosted and slippery.

The serpent was rising up through the depths of the pool. I could sense her. A presence—palpable, ancient. I tried to close her out of my mind. I was a seed pushing through the earth to find the light. I would not give in. I was so close now.

The quickest way up was straight through the surging water. Taking a deep lungful of air, I climbed up into the stream, letting the freezing water drown me. My heavy clothing dragged me backward. Clinging on with one hand, I tugged at the zipper of my jacket. The stream tore the garment away.

My lungs hurt, my brain screamed for oxygen. There was no air left in my lungs. I clawed and pushed myself through the top of the waterfall, through the surface of the river above.

I squinted in the sudden world of light, breathed in pale-colored air—stunned at the sight of forest and sky.

I was *out*.

Blowing out a lungful of stale air, my eyes adjusted to the vast landscape surrounding me, to the incredible *bright*. My lungs filled with oxygen.

Water swirled around my chest. Thrashing through the water, I reached the bank and pulled myself up. From above the river, there was no hint of the serpent cave that was lying beneath.

But I could hear her.

A blood-curdling screech.

The trees around me rattled.

Go!

I loped away, raw panic winding along my spine.

My body ached and pained as I ran.

I ran for miles and miles.

Until I was certain I was out of her reach.

Stopping to draw a breath, I kicked my soaked socks and shoes into the forest. Next I tore the wet knit caps, gloves, and clothing from my body. They slid from my body like cold fish skin.

Sun fell on me, soft but intense and beautiful. I consumed the gentle warmth like a starving person, gazing upward at the green leaves and snatches of pale blue sky through the branches.

I yelled. Yelled into the trees. Fear, horror, grief, sorrow, relief—every emotion cut through me.

Now, I had to bring help to the Dollhouse. If there was any hope at all, that hope was fast ticking away to its last second.

My wet slip stuck to me as I blundered forward.

At the back of my mind, thoughts struck at me with viper's fangs. The hatred and bitterness of the serpent had been palpable. Why did she hate me so intensely?

Twigs needled the underside of my bare feet. I could run and run out here and get lost and never find my way. I had to concentrate on where I was headed.

Cassie, you know some things about these mountains. Remember what Ethan told you about the different types of forest here, back when we doing that school project.

I stared at my surrounds. It wasn't alpine forest. So I had to be lower on the mountains than that. It wasn't subtropical. Just fairly ordinary-looking trees and shrubs. I turned to see mountain peaks rising in the distance. I was no longer on Devils Hole. I was close to the bottom of the mountains. But I had to reach the very bottom—where there would be roads and, hopefully, people.

Ethan had once told me: if lost in a forest, look for a river and follow it down. I hadn't run very far away from the path of the river. I could still hear it gurgling. I followed the sound until I located the river, then stepped along the smooth rocks on its bank. My feet were sore and scratched. I wanted to rest, but I couldn't stop. Not now.

Pushing myself onward, I looked for signs of campers or hikers, but saw nothing.

The river flattened and widened out, running thinly over grayish pebbles. A high rock ledge spanned the water ahead—the river streaming underground. I stopped still. I'd have to climb around and onto that ledge. I had little strength left.

A small head appeared over the edge of the platform. A child— a girl—wriggled down onto her stomach and threw a fistful of leaves down. The leaves swirled down to the water.

She was dressed in normal little-girl clothes—a green jumper and pink track pants. No ball gown. No strange, vintage dress. A cry caught in my throat. Catching sight of me, she stared at me with curious eyes for a moment—then waved.

I waved back.

A smiling woman appeared on the rock ledge, a camcorder in her hand as she filmed the girl. The woman's smile dropped from her face as she noticed me through her camera viewfinder. Her hand reached to her mouth.

I tried to speak, but no voice would come.

Two more figures appeared on the ledge—a man and a pudgy boy.

They stared open-mouthed at me.

I gazed down at myself. The side of my slip was tattered—blood soaking wetly into the material. The scrape on the rock in the tunnel had cut deeper than I'd realized. My limbs were bruised green and purple. The boy stared in horror at my face, shielding himself from the sight of me with his hand. I remembered then—the doll makeup. It would be smeared all over my face.

Stepping forward, I wrapped my arms around myself, shivering.

The man held up two hands, indicating for me not to come any closer. "We'll get you help." He turned back to the woman. "Kate, get the kids in the car."

The woman reached for the little girl's hand, confusion in her eyes. "But—"

"Just get them out of here—could be dangerous. We don't have to get mixed up in it. We'll get the police."

He stared past me to the woods. He didn't give me another glance as he pulled the boy away. The woman and girl left—the girl looking back over her shoulder at me.

I heard a car roar away and knew there must be a road just beyond the rock platform. A road meant I was close to help.

But some of the roads around here could be empty of cars all day.

I forced myself to head through the shallow river and up over the boulders to the ledge. A child's toy had been left behind on the rock—a small purple teddy bear—and a cane picnic basket. There was nothing to do but walk along the road until I could flag down a car.

Strength left my legs and my body. I could no longer feel anything.

My body collapsed on the hard rock.

Stipples of light flickered over my eyelids. Something pressed at my chest—a heavy weight.

One of the Dolls?

Raggedy?

I wasn't out of the underground, after all. Getting out of there had been a dream. The glassy eyes of the serpent bored into the back of my skull, mocking me.

"She's alive." A voice—human. Deep.

"Vital signs are okay," said another. A woman.

Sunlight dashed into my eyes as I opened them. People in blue-and-white clothing swarmed around me. A silver blanket covered me. My mind felt sluggish, as if thick fog swirled inside my head.

Sets of hands lifted me, carrying me through the air.

A face moved in front of mine. Mom's dark eyes.

Mom. It was Mom.

I wanted to touch her, to make sure it was really her. She brushed hair back from my face.

"Move back, please." A strident male voice.

I stared about me. Police and ambulance officers stood in a loose circle. I was on a stretcher, being taken toward an ambulance.

Wait! Wait! My words came out in a throaty whisper.

Mom squeezed my arm beneath the blanket. "Cassie, baby. I can't believe it's you. I thought I'd never—" Her eyes were bright with tears. "You have to go now. They need to get you to the hospital. It's okay—I'm here. All the way."

"No, I need . . . ," I rasped. My voice refused to work. Holding up my hands, I tried to mimic writing on a piece of paper.

The paramedics pulled a bed halfway out of the back of the ambulance and moved me onto it. One of them took my left hand and inserted a needle. He fitted a thin tube into my hand, and someone else hung a bag of fluid on a frame above my head.

"Just one more needle. Stay calm," a woman with a blond ponytail told me.

Cold liquid was squirted on my arm and side, and a needle jabbed me. Things were being inserted on the side of me that I'd gashed—clips? Then bandages were wrapped around my arm and torso. I was naked underneath the blanket—my wet slip and underwear gone—*when did that happen?*

"Almost ready to go," the blond woman said.

I tried to get up. I couldn't let myself be taken to the hospital—I needed to bring help to the underground. A crushing weakness claimed my body.

"It's okay. You're safe now," she said soothingly. "You've been given painkillers. They'll kick in soon and help you relax."

Shaking my head as hard as I could, I jabbed a finger at the palm of my hand again, making a writing gesture. I looked pleadingly at my mother.

Mom bent her head back to the ambulance crew. "She wants pen and paper."

"Time for that later," a paramedic told her. "She's hypothermic. She's lost her voice because she's been wet and cold for too long. We need to get her off for treatment."

Digging in her bag, Mom shook her head. "It's been nineteen days since I've heard my daughter's voice. I'm not going to silence her now."

Nineteen days. I had no idea how long I'd been underground until now. It seemed I'd been gone forever.

Mom handed me a pen and held up a notepad to write on. My fingers felt numb and strange. I curled a fist around the pen.

5 still underground. Rescue!!! I pressed the pen so hard it tore the page.

Mom's eyes were huge as she took the notepad and read it. Wordlessly, she handed it to a police officer who was standing to the right side of me.

The officer's face paled. "Are they in immediate danger?"

I nodded frantically.

The officer turned and shouted a jumble of words.

A plain-clothed man strode up, staring down at me. "Cassandra, do you remember me? Detective Martin Kalassi. Who are the others? Can you write their names?" He returned the notepad to me.

I started writing before he finished speaking:

Ethan

Aisha

Molly

Frances

Sophronia

Lacey was maybe down there too. But she didn't need rescue—*not her*.

The detective's eyes widened. "All alive?"

Nodding, I started scrawling again: *Yes. Poisoned. Dying. Under Fiveash house!*

My mother gasped.

"Poisoned? Hell." He clutched his forehead. "They're all at the Fiveash house? Underneath it? So, Donovan has another basement we didn't find before?"

I nodded. How could I explain what really lurked beneath the Fiveash mansion?

"We looked thoroughly—we found nothing," he told me dubiously.

I shot him an insistent look. My mind felt heavy and sluggish as I tried to remember the order in which we'd accidentally pressed the knobs on the boiler. I scrawled on the note pad: *Push knobs on basement boiler. Sequence 4, 2, 3, 1. Floor is elevator.*

Detective Kalassi raised his thick eyebrows at me, an intense look springing into his eyes. He turned and called to the blond paramedic. "Can she be stabilized enough to be transported? We may need her someplace else."

"Where to?" asked the paramedic.

"The top of Devils Hole."

She crossed her arms. "If you get us a chopper all set up with full gear."

"We're going to need a few of those, by the sound of it," he said grimly.

The detective stepped over to confer with police.

I felt myself graying out again—my head growing fuzzy. I was desperate to stay awake, but I couldn't. It was like they'd given me Jessamine's tea and my mind was slowly stepping downward.

26. FROM DARKNESS TO NIGHT

We are such stuff as dreams are made on;
and our little life is rounded with a sleep.

—Shakespeare, *The Tempest*

Loud, whirring noises reverberated through my head. Waking with a start, I stared around me. I was still on the stretcher, still hooked up to the IV line, but I was no longer an ambulance. I lifted my head and stared out the window. Helicopter blades jutted out above—I was in a helicopter, on the ground. Out in the darkening sky, other helicopters were coming down to land.

Why was the sky getting dark? How long had I slept? I struggled to sit up. Everything ached. The night air breezed around my face and a cool mildness saturated the air.

The ponytailed paramedic I'd seen before slid the door across and stepped into the helicopter. She checked my heart rate and then took the IV line from my arm. She bent her pinched, concerned face down to mine. "Hi, I'm Sarah. How do you feel?"

"Where am I?" My voice came out in a hoarse half whisper.

"At the top of Devils Hole. You've been asleep for a little while. But that's good—your body needed rest. You're doing well."

I nodded, flinching as I caught a glimpse of myself in a shiny, stainless-steel panel to the side of me. I looked like someone in shock, my eyes wide and glazed. A digital clock on the panel displayed the time: 4:45. My back chilled. Earlier, when I was first rescued, the time had only been around three in the afternoon. "Did they find them? Are the police—?"

"I'm afraid all I know is that they're searching the house. It's taken quite a while to organize the equipment and rescue squads. Great to see you get your voice back, but try not to use it too much, okay? You might lose it for days if it's strained any further."

My lungs tightened until I could hardly breathe. It had been almost two hours since I'd been rescued. Two hours while the girls remained in their beds. Two hours while Ethan was trapped in total darkness between the carousel and a steel wall. Even if rescuers managed to get down there, would Jessamine allow them inside? I had no doubt she could tear the rescuers apart limb from limb if she wanted. And I'd seen and felt what the shadow could do. A cold sweat prickled my skin. How could I warn the rescuers about what lay in wait down there? How could I even begin to tell them? There were no words that could prepare anyone for the horrors of the Dollhouse.

Sarah stared at me in alarm. "You're hyperventilating. Cassie, I want you to concentrate on slowing your breathing."

I nodded. Struggling, I pulled myself to a sitting position. Someone had put clothes on me—dark blue pants and shirt, which had to be a spare set of clothing of one of the paramedics. Bending my head, I took long breaths.

"Good." Sarah handed me a small carton—a type of milky

energy drink. "Sip it slowly," she instructed. "Like one sip every few seconds. If you start to feel bad—stop."

I pretended to take a small sip, but instead drew the thick liquid down in gulps. I felt my body gearing up again, craving food. Through the open helicopter door I could see the Fiveash mansion—every light in every room blazed, with police and rescuers moving through it.

The paramedic smiled briefly at someone at the foot of my bed— and then left. I turned to see my mother sitting there. Mom crept down to my side and pressed her face to my shoulder, her face wet.

"I didn't want you to see me crying," she said. "But I can't stop." Her eyes held back pain as she gazed at me. "Each and every day you were gone were the longest days of my life."

I hugged her. "They were long . . . for me too. I missed you."

"Are you okay?" She squeezed her eyes closed. "You don't have to tell me what happened. Not yet. You're here and you're alive, and for now, that's enough."

"I'm okay," I told her, even though I didn't know if I'd be *okay* ever again.

A large-framed man strode across the grounds and stuck his head inside the helicopter—Detective Kalassi. "Cassandra, good to see you awake."

"Did you get underneath the basement floor?" I asked him.

Deep lines indented the skin between his eyebrows. "Yes. Unbelievable. Donovan has a treasure trove of old circus gear down there. We found a tunnel, but there's a problem. There's this thick metal wall. That can't be the way you got out. We need you to tell us where and how."

"No," I told him. "You *have* to get through that wall. Past the wall, there's a carousel. You'll need to cut through the carousel too. Please hurry!"

He listened carefully. "But how did you get out?"

"I came through the mountains. Through a tunnel only big enough for one person to crawl through. Only big enough for someone my size. You can't go that way."

"You mean from here all the way down to where you were found?"

The detective and Mom stared at me incredulously, horrified.

I nodded.

He cursed under his breath. "Okay, with all the injuries you sustained, I agree we can't go that way. Don't worry—we've got specialist equipment being flown in. We'll get those kids out of there."

I stared up at the house. "Donovan Fiveash built the wall, after we got trapped down there. Make him show you whatever tools he used."

Detective Kalassi twisted his mouth to one side. "Donovan's gone. But we'll see what we can find."

"Wait—let me come with you."

"Cassie, no," said Mom quickly, "you need to rest."

He shook his head. "Sorry. You're still recovering. We need to work fast." He marched away, yelling out orders to the rescue squads and police.

Sarah came to check me again. She handed me another of the milk drinks. I took it gratefully. Time moved in small, sluggish steps, like a slow-motion movie. Everything was going way too *slow.*

More helicopters came—news helicopters, the logos of their various stations emblazoned on their sides. Soon, reporters crashed through the bushes into the clearing, with cameras and lights. A female reporter had her hair tidied and face fixed before she spoke dramatically into the camera.

Men and women in heavy armored uniforms carried equipment from one of the police helicopters down to the shed. Above the noise came the high screeches of drills. I willed the last vestiges of daylight to stay. I wanted the children of the underground to come out into daylight—not the night. I needed to see Ethan's face the second he was brought up. But darkness pulled in—falling into every space.

"I want to stretch my legs." I glanced at Mom and Sarah.

Mom frowned. "I don't think you should be walking around just yet."

"I need to. I feel cramped."

Mom glanced at Sarah, and Sarah gave a cautious nod.

I breathed deeply as I stepped out into the night air. My legs felt wrong and sore—but I could stand. I had to get down into the Dollhouse and make sure that the rescuers knew where to go to find everyone, despite what the detective had told me.

Some kind of sixth sense made me turn sharply and look into the line of trees across the clearing. A light dimly flickered. Jessamine stood there, indistinct and pale in a knee-length dress. So forlorn and fearful. She gazed at me unwaveringly, as though the police and reporters streaming through the grounds between us were just imaginings.

Panic gripped me. Jessamine had decided to let her dolls go.

But without her there, who would hold back the shadow? Then I understood. The girls had been rescued. The shadow couldn't touch them now.

The image of her faded until she became darkness.

Mom stepped up behind me and put her arm around my shoulder.

I whirled around. "They've got them out. Let's go!"

"Cassie, we don't know that—"

I tugged at her arm. "Come on!"

As I ran across the grounds and weaved my way through the people, reporters looked my way in surprise, scrambling to get their cameras ready. Mom caught up to me as I reached the house.

A rescue officer burst from the house, carrying a small body in a blanket. Reporters went into a frenzy. Police held the reporters back as Philomena was placed on a stretcher. I cradled her as paramedics began setting up an IV line—whispering to her that she was okay now.

A doctor injected a liquid into Philly's thigh. She woke with a sharp intake of breath. She let out a high-pitched scream. "Monsters!"

"It's me, Philly—Calliope," I cried. "There's no monsters here. No monsters anymore. These are good people." A tear slid down my cheek. "You're safe. You're safe, baby. Tomorrow, you'll see sun and flowers. Just like I promised."

Her eyes wide, she clung to my arm. My mother stared at me.

Detective Kalassi raced over, thumbing his chin in confusion. "Her name is Philly? This one isn't Frances?"

I touched a finger to my mouth. "She's been Philly—Philomena—for the past year. It's what she knows. But, yes, you have her name right."

Nodding at me gratefully, he turned to speak into his phone. "Amy, Martin Kalassi here. We have Frances Allanzi. Repeat, we have Frances Allanzi. Yes, alive." His booming voice was jubilant. "Please inform the family and have them escorted and waiting at the Sydney Children's Hospital. Oh, and Amy, tell them she answers to the name Philomena."

I brushed damp hair from Philly's clammy skin. "Your family— everyone Missouri drew in the pictures for you, you'll see them very soon."

She shook her head. "They're all gone. Where's Missy? Where's my Missy?"

I looked over my shoulder, and my heart fell. Missouri was being brought out—her head lying back limply across the rescuer's arm.

"No, they were never gone," I told her. "You'll see them, Philly. Your brother and sister, Mommy and Daddy. I promise. You'll see Missy later."

I hugged her and nodded at the paramedics to take her. I didn't want her seeing Missouri now. Philly was placed inside a waiting helicopter, my mother holding her hand all the way.

I rushed to Missouri. Her face was alabaster, like a monument on a grave.

Gazing at the rescuer who held her, I could barely form the words, "Is she . . . alive?"

He stared back with grim eyes, his face rigid, giving the slightest shake of his head.

"No," I breathed. My knees found the dirt.

Rescue hadn't come quick enough.

I hadn't been quick enough.

Paramedics spirited her away—the helicopter taking off almost instantly. A reporter scrambled to stand in front of the helicopter as it was taking off, yelling to the news camera that one of the abductees was dead.

A large hand touched my shoulder. "I'm sorry."

I gazed upward at Detective Kalassi.

"I know that was Molly," he said gently. "Molly Parkes." He gazed regretfully at the helicopter as it disappeared into the night sky.

He turned at the sound of a commotion behind us. Paramedics carried a girl to a waiting helicopter. Detective Kalassi and I hurried across. Sophronia lolled on the stretcher as they gave her oxygen. A paramedic injected her with the same stuff they'd injected Philly with. I held her hand as the IV was inserted.

Her dark eyes fluttered open, but just barely, heavy with confusion. Sweat beaded on her forehead. She fixed her gaze on me. "I see it in your eyes . . ." Her words came out in the barest whisper. "You saw her . . . the other side of the shadow."

I bowed my head. Sophronia saw things no one else could. "Now *we're* on the other side," I told her.

Mom tugged the blanket up under Sophronia's chin. "You're safe. You're safe now. You'll be reunited with your family very soon. What's your name, honey?"

"It is Sophronia," she replied.

"I don't know this one," Detective Kalassi shot me a puzzled glance.

I wanted to tell Sophronia to give her real name to the police—so they could find her family. But I suspected she didn't want to. She was smart enough to know what she wanted. Her eyes drifted shut as they took her away.

Shouts came from the direction of the house. A rescuer carried a limp body, surrounded by police. *Aisha.*

Aisha's sleeping face was bloodless, her lips purplish.

Please let her wake.

Two paramedics laid her gently on a stretcher and then unwrapped the bloody bandage from her leg—the bandage that had been my dress.

"Amy, we've got Aisha Dumaj here." Detective Kalassi spoke into his cell phone. "Yes, she is . . . but barely. Please don't tell her family her condition. Just let them know we've got her." He placed the phone back in his pocket. "The father's in hospital having an op," he told my mom in a hushed tone. "Had a massive stroke this morning—the whole family's there with him."

Bags of blood were readied and hung as they prepared a transfusion. "Run in two units," someone called. Moonlight washed over Aisha's smooth features.

"Aish," I said, "Aisha. If you can hear me, it's Cassie. You're out of the Dollhouse. You're free. You're going to wake up back in the world. You're going to go back to school, and become a photographer and travel everywhere . . . ."

Mom held her hand, speaking in a low voice close to her ear about her parents, about Raif—reassuring her she was back in the world she'd known.

She didn't rouse. Two of the paramedics exchanged worried glances. "We need to get this one to hospital—fast," one of them said.

Aisha was spirited away in the same helicopter I'd been brought here in. The reporters who hung behind the line of police officers openly speculated on-camera whether Aisha Dumaj was going to *make it or not*. I wanted to scream at them.

The din of helicopters taking off crowded everything else out—camera crews running for cover. Then the voices began again all at once.

The crowd quietened as a body was brought out from the house—this one completely wrapped in a blanket.

Jessamine's skeleton. Mom gasped loudly beside me.

The reporters went into a frenzy, speculating into their news cameras about the identity of the body.

Detective Kalassi turned to me. "I've just been informed by the police that this person died a long time ago."

"Her name was Jessamine," I said softly.

"Jessamine. Okay, we'll find out about her later. I need to ask you this—do you know of any more . . . bodies . . . that we haven't yet found? The rescue team is saying it's a dark rabbit warren down there."

A name slipped out. "Prudence . . . ."

"Prudence? Was she alive when you—?"

"No. Molly was the only one to know her."

"Okay." He gave a worried nod. "Full name, age, and description if you can?"

I gazed at the ground. "Fourteen, long, dark hair, blue eyes, pale. About my height." I thought about the newspaper clipping we'd found in the castle. "As far as I know, she came out here from America. I don't know her last name."

"And where . . . ?"

"Behind a wall of the Toy Box . . . I mean, in the cave where you found the other body."

But rescuers wouldn't find her.

They couldn't get beyond that wall.

"My God, what you kids went through." He shook his head, sighing heavily. "We'll keep searching."

I grasped his arm. "Where's Ethan? Why isn't he out?" I was aware of blood pumping in my veins. "He should have been the first one you found."

"I'll go find out what's happening," he told me.

But I raced away to the steps of the Fiveash house. Police held me from going farther. "I have to get down there!" I struggled to get past them.

The crowd hushed as a silhouetted figure limped from the house, a rescuer on either side helping him along.

"Ethan!" I rushed over and wrapped my arms tightly around him.

His chest rose and fell sharply, his breaths shallow. Moving back slightly, he studied my face, his dark eyes haunted and shadowed. "How did you—?"

"I'll tell you everything when we're alone," I said quietly. "Right now, you need help. You need to get better."

Paramedics brought a stretcher and equipment over. Ethan sat heavily on the stretcher, leaning over onto his knees. A paramedic checked his lungs and clipped some kind of sensor on his finger, then slid an oxygen mask over his face. Ethan collapsed back on the stretcher.

I knelt beside him, watching color slowly come back to his grayish skin. Reaching out, I enclosed his fingers in mine.

His eyes flickered open. "I know how you got out. You went the way that I couldn't. But it should have been me, Cassie. Not you."

Tears wet my face. "You gave me the strength to do it."

He stroked my hair as I laid my head on his chest. "I was so damned stupid to believe Jessamine."

Mom and Detective Kalassi stepped over, Mom raising her eyebrows slightly in confusion at the exchange between Ethan and me. The last time she'd seen Ethan, he'd been Aisha's boyfriend.

"Could I please ask you to move back?" a paramedic asked me gently. "We need to administer some steroids."

Reluctantly, I rose and stepped away. Mom encircled me in her arms.

"Ethan McAllister," said Detective Kalassi, "we're all very glad to see you safe. We had enough kids disappearing in the forest without another one." He exhaled a long breath of air, his eyes sad and filled with regret. "Now we know. We know that the answer to those disappearances lay here at the Fiveash house."

Ethan nodded, taking a deep breath under the oxygen mask. "How's my granddad? Can someone tell him where I am?"

The detective rubbed the back of his neck, exchanging a quick glance with Mom.

Ethan pulled the mask from his face. "What's going on? He's okay, right?"

Detective Kalassi hesitated for a moment. "He's been a bit ill, but he'll be okay. He's being cared for. And I'll make the call now and have someone tell him about you."

"Wait." Ethan eyed him with a direct stare. "There's something you're not telling me. Who's taking care of him? Where is he?"

An uncomfortable silence followed.

A police officer moved purposefully through the crowd toward us—a slightly-built blond girl following him. I breathed in sharply when I saw who they were—Sergeant Dougherty and his daughter, Lacey.

"Tell me where Granddad is," Ethan insisted, his gaze still locked on Detective Kalassi.

Lacey put a hand over her mouth as she stepped in front of Ethan. She wore white—all white, looking like the most innocent person who'd ever lived, her pale hair back in clips. "Ethan, didn't anyone tell you? Your granddad is in jail!"

Ethan's eyes enlarged with fear and anger.

"I'm so sorry. It's just terrible," she told him. "But when they found the other stuff too, they had no choice but to put him away."

"What other stuff?" Ethan roared.

Lacey flinched. "I'm afraid he buried these girls' belongings in the ground outside his cottage—and it got found. The police have been digging all around his house trying to find the bodies of the girls. But goodness, he was hiding the girls *here*, all along."

Ethan struggled to his feet, his eyes blazing. "I'll kill you. I swear," he bellowed at Lacey.

A police woman grabbed Ethan. "You're unwell. You need to rest."

Sergeant Dougherty jabbed a finger at Ethan. "Don't go you dare go threatening my daughter!"

I moved away from Mom, into Lacey and Sergeant Dougherty's view, folding my arms tight against my ribs.

"Cassie!" Lacey cried, her voice high pitched and excited. "Oh God! There you are! You're alive!" Tears rolled down her flushed cheeks.

She rushed to hug me, but I held up both hands to stop her. "You tell them!"

Lacey opened her eyes wide. It was an expression she'd been practicing for years—an expression that had fooled all of us. "I don't understand."

I marched toward her. "Tell them the real story. Tell them it was *you* who's been helping Donovan all along. It was *you* who hid Aisha's camera in the McAllister's cottage. And if anything else was found, *you* put it there too."

She splayed a hand over her throat. "What?"

"Cassie!" Mom called anxiously.

Sergeant Dougherty's face paled then grew blotchy. "You'd better stop right there, Miss Claiborne. Making wild accusations isn't going to—"

I shook my head. "I won't stop until the truth is heard." Stepping back beside Ethan, I linked my hand with his and stared directly at Lacey. "No more lies. Let it end here. Tell them how you betrayed Aisha and then Ethan and me. Tell them how years ago you betrayed Molly and Frances too. Tell them about the bargain you made with their abductors . . . *Lily Fair!*" I heard my words end in an almost hysterical cry.

Her bottom lip quivered. "You must have been through a lot. You're imagining all kinds of terrible things."

"We need to calm things down." Detective Kalassi held up a hand. "I can't guess at what's going on here, but—"

"You know what you did," Ethan stormed at Lacey.

Lacey brought her arms in close to her thin body, her mouth drawing in defensively. "Why are you both against me? Maybe you're angry because you were captured and I wasn't."

Ethan's eyes filled with fury, hardening and becoming almost glassy. "My grandfather is going to die in jail. Because of you!"

She looked away. "He's old anyway. He was going to die soon." She snapped her head around to him, her expression growing cold. "And I can't help it if he's bad."

Ethan fingers stiffened on mine, then he let his hand fall away. He turned to Detective Kalassi. "I have a confession."

"No confessions," the detective was quick to say. "It's not the time."

Ethan fixed his gaze on the night sky. "No, I need to say it. When I was nine, Donovan Fiveash made me an offer I couldn't refuse. I started helping him abduct girls. It was me all along. Not Granddad. So you can get my Granddad out of jail—right now."

I clutched Ethan's arm. "What are you saying? You know that's not true!"

Reporters swarmed in, jostling to get their microphones in closer. Police instructed them to move back. They shuffled back, but barely.

Ethan turned his head away from me. "Donovan was paying me to help him. When I was a kid, he used to pay me with money. This time around, he said he'd give me gold and diamonds." He gave a short, hollow laugh. "Well, he double-crossed me and trapped me down in the underground with the others. He said he didn't trust me anymore. I punched him to the ground when he showed his face down there. But he got away."

"No . . . ." I didn't believe any of that. I could never believe it.

Detective Kalassi blew out an incredulous breath. "Son, I'd advise you not to say anything else. You've just had a huge dose of oxygen, and maybe it's affecting you."

"It's not the damned oxygen." Ethan's jaw clenched. "I found

Donovan's stash of treasure, and I took some. Then I kept looking for a way out."

Tears streamed down my face. "That's not true. You know it's not."

"Don't believe me? Check my pockets," he said in a dead tone.

Detective Kalassi stood still as a rock for a moment, then gave a stiff nod to the police officer who was still standing on the other side of Ethan. Crouching, she reached her hand inside the pockets of the vest and baggy trousers that Ethan wore. I stifled a gasp as she held out a handful of clear, shining diamonds and small gold nuggets.

Mom held her hand over her mouth, her eyes huge. Camera crews moved in closer, recording everything. Recording every second.

Ethan glanced at the stones, then up at Detective Kalassi., his face grown expressionless. He didn't look my way again.

Three more helicopters landed, the noise driving through my skull, leaves stirring up and whirling in the black air.

Lacey ran off sobbing—her father following after her.

Ethan doubled over, struggling to breathe. The paramedics forced him down onto the stretcher, placing the oxygen mask over his face. I ran alongside as they carried Ethan to a helicopter on the stretcher.

As the paramedics readied the helicopter, I bent down to Ethan, gently touching his arm. "I'm on your side. I'll always be on your side."

His eyes were empty as he opened them. He tore the mask from his face. "You shouldn't be."

"I know you're just worried about your grandfather, and you said those things because—"

He touched a finger to my lips. "You have to forget about me. They're going to put me away for a long time."

"That's not going to happen. I won't let it happen. Lacey is the one who did the wrong thing. You didn't do any of those things you said you did. You *didn't*. We're alone now. You don't have to keep pretending."

"Cassie, I just admitted to what I did. There's nothing you can tell the police to change that. Trust me when I tell you that no one is going to believe a single bad thing about Lacey. Look at her. But they'd believe any damned thing about me and my grandfather." A sighing breath came from deep within his chest.

"I know. But it's not going to help your grandfather if you go jail too. It's Lacey who should be locked up."

Police walked up to the helicopter, watching. Watching to check that Ethan didn't run away.

Ethan glanced at them, his jaw growing rigid. "Maybe she's not the only one to do bad things," he told me. "If Henry got her to do his bidding, why is so hard to believe he got hold of me too?"

I shook my head vehemently. "I don't believe what you told the police for a second."

He pulled his mouth into a hard line. "I care about you, but I'm not who you think I am."

"Who are you?" My voice trembled as I spoke the words.

"Someone who played everyone along. Including my grandfather. Including you. I'm not proud."

"No . . . ."

"Did my feelings for you seem real in the underground, Cassie?"

"Please, don't say any more . . . ."

His voice had become so, so cold. Like someone I didn't know. "I have to, or you're going to keep on hoping. When Donovan double-crossed me, I needed someone to get me out. I thought you could, through the walls of the Toy Box. But there was no way out, for any of us. Just . . . don't think about me anymore, okay?"

My legs weakened. I tried to speak, but nothing came. Everything inside me shattered like glass.

Paramedics slid Ethan onto the bed of the helicopter. I could barely see or hear or feel as the helicopter lifted.

A cold, slow panic traveled through every vein of my body.

I'm not who you think I am.

I'm not who you think I am.

I'm not who you think I am.

What was the truth?

Why *had* he put the diamonds and gold in his pockets?

Across the grounds, Lacey stood with her father's arm around her, looking like a little, lost girl. She stared up at the departing helicopter, recoiling when she caught my eye. As I locked gazes with her, a look of guilt stole into her face. She drew her hands up to her lips—the lips had just told terrible lies. Her fingers trembled.

She began screaming—high, anguished screams that cut through the night above the noise of the helicopter blades.

Reporters rushed over with their cameras and microphones, expecting to see something shocking but finding nothing.

Lacey raced away from her confused father, taking a microphone from a reporter.

"I can't do this anymore," she cried. "I can't. I won't." Her frantic voice rang out clearly—louder than I'd ever heard her speak before. My breath caught in my chest. Every camera turned to Lacey, filming every word she spoke.

"It was me helping Donovan," she said. "You don't know what's really down there. None of you do. Except for those who lived it. There's dark things. Far worse things than you've ever seen in your nightmares. Spirits. Shadows that eat you. Shadows that use you for terrible things. You think you're all safe up here in the real world. *Well, you're not.* They're coming for you. The lord of the castle underground will never rest in his grave. And the serpent will always want her revenge."

An earsplitting sound crashed through the forest. In the distance, the tree line thrashed wildly, as though caught in a violent wind.

But there was no wind on this night.

I saw what no one else could see—yet. The trees were being pulled directly down through the earth.

The serpent was coming.

The ground rumbled and shook. Shouts and screams rang out as people looked around in fear and panic.

Directly beneath my feet, a loud cracking sounded.

"The ground's unstable!" yelled one of the rescue crew.

Paramedics and police sprinted in all directions.

Reporters and everyone else scattered—fleeing for the forest as the entire front of the Fiveash house crashed to the ground.

The upstairs room with the toy dollhouse sat exposed to the night, the wall gone. In the dollhouse, a tiny window lit up yellow against the darkness, and I knew Jessamine was there.

The house fell in on itself, bricks tumbling and flying out.

The earth began crumbling away.

Lacey stood, immobile, her eyes closed. As if she could not hear the melee around her.

Someone pulled my arm, desperately calling my name—Mom. Rescuers quickly shuffled Mom and me into a helicopter.

The house and shed disappeared into the shifting earth—trees pulling down along with them. A vast hole appeared.

I gazed down as the helicopter lifted.

Everything was gone.

It was as though the earth had turned inside-out.

At the ragged edges of the hole, a shadow slithered out onto the ground. A shadow just a shade darker than the night. It moved like blood—thick, filmy.

The helicopter dipped for a moment, then rose into the clear sky, the whirr of the blades cutting across my mind.

THE DARK CAROUSEL SERIES

Sign up for news and free Anya Allyn stories here:
http://anyaallyn.com/newsletter/

Anya Allyn grew up in Sydney, Australia, and now lives by the beach on The Central Coast. She spends her days with her partner and four boys—all incredibly cool people. As a child, she could be found reading, sketching comic strips or fainting during choir practice in her school convent. She has worked in entertainment, web content, and most recently as a Features' Editor for Fairfax Media in Australia. Dollhouse is her first novel.
http://anyaallyn.com

Printed in Great Britain
by Amazon

42286129R00184